"A memoir disguised as a novel. And it works—beautifully. . . .

So does the Huffakers' marriage, though it begins inauspiciously. . . . What holds all this together through thick and quite a bit of thin is love. It pervades the garage in which the newlyweds first live. It warms the furnished rooms in Omaha, where Huffaker senior is a furniture salesman. And it lasts even through good times. An affecting memento."
—*The New York Times Book Review*

"Storytelling is novelist Huffaker's strong suit and it is as strong as ever in this affectionate memoir . . . an affecting story . . . simply and beautifully written." —*Publishers Weekly*

"Huffaker is a great storyteller."
—*Columbus Dispatch*

ONE TIME, I SAW MORNING COME HOME
was originally published by Simon and Schuster.

Books by Clair Huffaker

Badge for a Gunfighter*
Cowboy
The Cowboy and the Cossack*
Flaming Lance
Guns from Thunder Mountain*
Guns of Rio Conchos*
One Time, I Saw Morning Come Home*
Posse from Hell*
Seven Ways From Sundown*
The War Wagon

*Published by POCKET BOOKS

CLAIR HUFFAKER

One Time, I Saw Morning Come Home

A Remembrance

PUBLISHED BY POCKET BOOKS NEW YORK

ONE TIME, I SAW MORNING COME HOME

Simon and Schuster edition published 1975

POCKET BOOK edition published October, 1975

The author gratefully acknowledges permission to reprint the songs in this book. Any omission is inadvertent and will be corrected in future printings on notification to the publisher.

Lyrics from the song "Red Wing," words by Thurland Chattaway, music by Kerry Mills, used with permission of the publisher, Shawnee Press, Inc., Delaware Water Gap, Pa. 18327.

Other acknowledgments are made on pages where the songs appear.

Standard Book Number: 671-80106-6.
Library of Congress Catalog Card Number: 74-8342.
This POCKET BOOK edition is published by arrangement with Simon & Schuster, Inc. Copyright, ©, 1974, by Clair Huffaker. All rights reserved. This book, or portions thereof, may not be reproduced by any means without permission of the original publisher: Simon & Schuster, Inc., 630 Fifth Avenue, New York, N.Y. 10020.
Front cover illustration by Robert Schulz.

Printed in the U.S.A.

For the waltzing lady,—
she of the soft, and sun-swept hair,
and the grass green, dew-swept eyes.

Contents

1

Pony Boy

Pony boy, pony boy,
  Won't you be my pony boy?
Don't say no, here we go,
  Off across the plains,
Marry me, carry me,
  Off across the plains. . . .

"Pony Boy," written and arranged by Jimmy Carroll, recorded on Golden Records, © 1960 by Fairyland Music Corp.

In the beginning, there was the earth.

And then, there was music.

Orlean knew these two things in much the same easy way that she knew she was sixteen and that it was a hot September day. There are some things you just simply know, and don't have to bother your mind with.

At the moment, Orlean was quietly involved with both earth and music, sweeping the dusty kitchen floor and singing to herself in a low voice. "Pony boy, pony boy . . ."

Suddenly there was a shuffling sound and then a thumping from outside the kitchen door.

The neighbor's brown-and-white spotted cow again! Two days ago it had got loose and eaten two of the three geraniums Orlean had grown in a pot on the back step. It sounded like that cow was back for the third and last one! Luckily, Orlean was armed with her broom, and she started swiftly for the door. That final red geranium was probably the last living flower for a dozen miles around. In her little mining town in the Rocky Mountains, almost no delicate growing thing could survive. Tumbleweeds and sagebrush and stinging nettles and bitter milkweed managed to make it up through the hard earth to the music of the sun. But none of the pretty and gentle things, like a geranium, seemed to be able to hold onto life against the summer heat and the winter cold and the killing taint of arsenic, that was always and always in the air. The mine

3

and the billowing smelter on the hill made the arsenic, and it was as hard on people as it was on flowers.

The mining smoke made beautiful orange and red and yellow sunsets, and death.

But Orlean was not going to let her last geranium die without a battle. That cow was about to be clouted on the rump with all the ferocity an avenging broom could muster.

Orlean jerked the door open wide, her broom raised high.

But it wasn't a cow.

It was a young man loaded down with groceries, who was thumping the door with his foot.

He had two bulging brown bags under his arms, and a sack of eggs held between his teeth, and he was trying to smile within slight embarrassment.

"Oh!" she murmured in her own sudden and greater embarrassment, quickly lowering the broom and taking the package of eggs from his mouth. That was the first word she ever said to him.

And it was also the first and only instant that Orlean ever fell in love. That tiny, inner magic took less than the blink of a fleeting second, and yet the magic was so strong that it lasted always. How such a thing could happen so fast, and so forever, she never really understood, or even tried to figure out. It was like all those other things that you just simply know, and don't have to bother your mind with.

The young man was tall, and overwhelmingly handsome, with a jaunty leather cap angled rakishly down over incredibly bright, sparkling blue eyes that seemed filled with silent, mischievous laughter. Yet there was something else deeper in his eyes. Orlean could see that he would understand about earth and music, and about mean spotted cows, and the crucial importance of one last, red geranium.

"I'm from Swenson's Groceries?" He made a question of the words.

She nodded timidly, quickly backing out of his way with the eggs.

He stepped to the kitchen table just as one of the large sacks started to rip slightly, but he got there in time and put them down safely. Relieved, he turned and took off his cap, smiling. "You were holding that broom like a ball bat."

"—I thought you were a cow." As Orlean finished speaking in her shy voice, she wished she'd said it some other way, but the words were already out.

His smile deepened. "One time up in Wyoming a fella mistook me for a mountain lion and took a shot at me, but at least that was at night."

Orlean wanted to explain the whole thing about defending her geranium, and make him understand. But the words she needed just weren't coming to her, and he was already starting back toward the door.

Before going out he looked back once more with his sky-blue, penetrating eyes and said, "My name's Clair. Thank you, Miss Bird."

And then he was gone.

But he knew her name! Orlean quickly put the eggs down on the table with the other groceries and hurried to the window. He was pedaling down the dusty street on Swenson's delivery bike with the big, bent, wire basket on the back. Then she realized crushingly that he'd have to know her name, just to know where to make the delivery.

Ten thousand things she could have said and should have said, and she hadn't said one. Why couldn't she be quick and glib like all those other girls who always seemed to have something to say? Now he turned at the corner and went out of her sight on the bike, still looking handsome, somehow, even from the back. Orlean moved slowly from the window then and silently busied herself sorting the groceries and putting them in the cupboard and icebox.

While stacking the last cans of beans in the cupboard she finally broke her silence and muttered angrily to herself, "Boy, are you a dumbbell!" Then, in a higher, self-mocking voice, "Ohhh, kind sir, I thought you were a cow! Just what every man has always wanted to hear. Why couldn't I have told him he *did* look more like a mountain lion, or Rudolph Valentino or something?!"

Then she went out into the small back yard and split some kindling at the woodshed, so that she could get a fire started in the stove.

By the time Orlean heard the distant clanging of the bell on the Bamburger trolley coming slowly back from Salt Lake, the house was clean, the wash done, and supper was cooking on the glowing hot stove. Her two sisters, Melva and Margaret, had taken the Bamburger to town, and a few minutes later they arrived in the gathering dusk.

The twenty-mile trolley trip to Salt Lake cost ten cents per person each way, so a trip to town was something special. And Margaret, a red-headed pixie of a girl a little younger than Orlean, was still filled with the excitement of the big city. "We saw a Rin Tin Tin movie that, *honest*, you wouldn't believe!" she said. "Orlean, he jumped a *thousand*-foot cliff to save a little boy in a river!"

Melva, the oldest of the sisters, shook her head in amused agreement. "Like the man says, I swear that dog's just not human."

"Oh, Melva!" Margaret laughed.

There was time before supper, so Melva made some secret coffee and she and Margaret told Orlean all about their day's trip, and how the city was changing and growing right before your very eyes.

The stern-faced Elders in that Mormon town would have been outraged about the church-forbidden coffee. But the girls were agreed that what the Elders didn't know couldn't hurt them. And besides, in some mysterious way it made the coffee taste better.

Finally, Orlean mentioned as offhandedly as possible the thing she'd been waiting anxiously to bring up from the beginning. "—Swenson's,—has a new delivery man."

"He clerks there, too," Melva said. "We gave him our order this morning on the way to the Bamburger."

And then, looking at Orlean thoughtfully, she added, "He's a nice-looking boy."

"Boy?" Orlean frowned. "He's a young man."

"What I meant was," Melva said, "he's only about your age."

"And that's not all," Orlean went on, taking a sip of coffee. When she was alone with the sisters she'd grown up with, she could sometimes work wonders with words. "He may be kind of young, like you say, but he's been around a whole lot. Why, he was even in some kind of a shooting scrape up in Wyoming, but got out of it okay."

"That's awful!" Margaret's eyes were wide with delight. "Did he shoot somebody?!"

"Oh, no. —I guess he just sort of managed to smooth everything all over, finally. I can tell that he's just naturally that kind of a strong, quiet man."

"Boy, that's swell!" Margaret said. "I'd like to hear all about it!"

"No!" Orlean said quickly. "I know for sure he wouldn't want to talk about it any more. I was just saying he's a man, not a boy like Melva said."

Melva began pouring what was left of the coffee, splitting it three ways. "Must have took him most of the afternoon to bring in all those groceries."

"Oh, no. We just talked for a little while. His name's Clair."

"Clair?" Margaret said. "That's a funny name."

"It's not either funny, Margaret! It's just different."

"What's really funny," Melva said, "is that just about nobody's ever seen him around here before. He's one of old Frank Huffaker's sons, and that family's been here for years."

Margaret's eyes grew wide again. "That shooting up in Wyoming! Maybe he's been in jail!"

"Oh, I doubt it very much!" Orlean said quickly. "I don't think it was anything anywhere near all *that* serious, at all."

"Well, maybe not." Margaret was still enchanted by

her idea. "But where's a better place to learn to smoke at our age than in jail?!"

"He smokes?!" Though Orlean didn't like even the look of cigarettes, this was a telling point in terms of a young man being adventurous and mature beyond his years.

"How do you know?" Melva asked.

"When we left Swenson's I saw him go out and up and light one, right back there in the alley."

Melva looked down at the table. "Altogether, it looks—like he's pretty fast."

"Well," Orlean reminded her, "we're all three of us drinking coffee. We're fine ones, or that darn Church either, to blame a man for smoking a cigarette if he wants to."

"For heck's sake," Margaret said, "nobody's blaming him for it."

"For that matter," Orlean went on firmly, "one of these days I'm going to have a cup of coffee and try a cigarette *too*."

"When you do it," Margaret asked, "can I do it with you?"

"You two will get us all thrown out of town, or at least out of the Church." Melva stood up. "We'd better start setting table. Al will be home pretty quick."

"It's almost time," Margaret said in a sudden, excited panic. "I've got to run to meet Darrell at the Ward." She hugged and kissed them both and then hurried out.

Melva called after her, "Don't be too late after Ward meeting."

As the other two sisters began to put the plates out, Melva studied Orlean for a long moment. "—I forgot that we're a little low on salt."

"I thought we had plenty."

"No, I should have ordered another two-pound bag. —Would you mind going down to Swenson's for me,— tomorrow, and getting it?"

Orlean hesitated, then put the plate in her hands down on the table and said, "Oh,—no."

"It's time you started getting out once in a while, like Margaret does with Darrell. Otherwise, you'll just waste away around this house and work yourself to death, and wind up the only Old Maid in the family."

They were both starting to smile now, as they worked.

"Well, Melva, sixteen's hardly an Old Maid age."

"It's as good an age as any to start worrying."

A little later Al came home, walking heavily down the half-mile long, dark path from the huge mill looming high above, and showing deeper black in the sky than the black mountain it was built on.

It was always like this when a mine-shift went off. A seemingly unending, antlike stream of dimly seen, almost invisible men who all looked alike in the dark, each wearing Levi coveralls with suspenders that came up over the back and snapped onto the chest-high bib. And each man was carrying a black, now empty, lunchpail.

Al was big and stout, a jolly man who laughed and talked too much and too loudly. But he had a good heart, was a good provider, and a good husband to Melva.

When Orlean went to sleep in their small back room, Margaret still hadn't come home. She went to sleep with music within her playing gently in her mind.

The music was, "Pony Boy."

2

She Wore a Yellow Ribbon

In her hair,
She wore a yellow ribbon,
She wore it in the winter,
And in the month of May,
And when you asked her
Why she always wore it,
She wore it for her lover
Who was far, far away. . . .

THE NEXT day, after finishing her chores, Orlean heated the iron on the stove, which was still hot from cooking breakfast, and brought out her good dress, the blue polka-dot print with the white lace collar, to press it.

She was relieved that Al had already gone to work, and she was alone with Melva. Al would have roared and rocked with laughter and said something like, "All that fussin' just t' walk down t' Main Street? This is Magna, not fancied-up Salt Lake! Heck, a gal could walk downtown in a gunnysack, an' worst'd happen's they accidentally sell her f'r a bag a' grain!" This was one of his well-meant, repeated jokes, on the few times in the last months that Orlean had built up enough courage to leave the house. But today she was being even more careful, wanted so much more to please.

And Melva understood.

After brushing her hair a long time, and then tying it in her favorite yellow ribbon, Orlean finally came into the kitchen, ready to go.

Melva was drying dishes at the sink, and she turned and said quietly, "—You sure do look pretty."

Orlean smiled with shy pleasure. "Well, I guess I better go. —Anything else I should get downtown?"

"—Just the salt."

Orlean took a tin cup of water from the sink and went out the kitchen door to kneel on the step and water the last geranium.

"Honey," Melva called from the kitchen. "That flower might look real nice pinned on your dress."

Orlean hesitated with the cup of water, and Melva came to the door to look it over more closely. "You can see that copper mine air's got to it. It's still pretty now, but it'll be dead tomorrow. Might as well wear it."

After a silent moment, Orlean said, "No." She began to slowly pour the water onto the hard, barren earth in the pot. "It will live another day."

Melva took the empty cup from Orlean's hand and said, "You don't need a flower, anyhow." She smiled. "You're one all by yourself, little sister."

Their eyes met for a long, warm moment, and then they hugged each other.

It was only three short, dusty blocks down to Main Street, but in its own way, to Orlean, it seemed more like a thousand miles. She kept to the harder dirt of the sidewalk, thinking of the empty times she'd tried to make this walk in the last little while, and finally gone back home fighting down tears.

A model T chugged by, belching heavy smoke and dust from its rear end and wheels. After it was gone she passed some children playing kick-the-can in the street and shouting in high, thin voices as the battered can flew here and there. She paused to pat a friendly, panting dog who was sitting on the sidelines of the game. And then she went on to Main Street without seeing anyone else at all.

Turning left on Main Street, where the town's single line of business buildings began, Orlean had the hollow feeling that she could see her whole world, now and forever, and she didn't want to face it.

A couple of sections of the seven or eight block stretch had cement sidewalks, and those short, cemented walks, plus some tall, wooden, electric light poles, were the most up-to-date things in town. Running west, Main Street finally made an abrupt right turn, veering off and down toward the endless gray flats where an immense, low dyke contained the muddy slag from the mine. Otherwise the street would have run right into the steep, battle-scarred mountain with the smoking mine high up on it.

Close on her left, the Gem Theater was playing "Her Gilded Cage" with Gloria Swanson. And from there on, business buildings were packed pretty solidly along that side of the street clear to the mountain. But on the right hand side of the dusty street, buildings were older and more scarce, most of them with badly peeling paint and dirty, often cracked windows.

All in all, there were about fifteen saloons along the street, four grocery stores, two lumberyards, a combined fire station and sheriff's office, a boarded-up furniture store, two drugstores, the A.C. Automobile Sales and Service Shop, and a J.C. Penney.

Orlean was starting to get that same feeling again. Just turn around and go back home. But she forced herself to walk on toward Swenson's Groceries. Thank Heaven it was only half way, and it was on the left side so she didn't have to cross Main Street. She passed the Hi-Ho Bar & Grill, and heard the clicking of pool balls along with men's low voices and laughter. That wasn't too bad, because somehow they were friendly sounds.

A little farther on, Mrs. Gelbert, carrying a pink parasol and wearing a ruffled dress, went by her on the sidewalk. Mrs. Gelbert didn't slow down, but glanced at her briefly and said, "My, don't the townspeople look fine today."

Orlean had no answer, nor the time to make one anyway, for the old woman had already swept imperiously on by. Mrs. Gelbert lived up on the B & G Row, a double line of brick houses on the corner of the mountain near the mill. The Row was where the mining superintendents and high-up bosses lived.

Two more cars went grumbling by, one of them slowing for a gray mongrel scratching its ear in the road. The horn made two or three raspy, irritated noises before the dog got up, and he and the car went their separate ways.

And then, finally, Orlean was at Swenson's.

When she entered the store, Mr. Swenson saw her

from behind the counter and said, "My goodness, I haven't seen you in a coon's age."

She nodded and smiled shyly at him, then started looking through the store as though there were many purchases on her mind.

She found Clair at the far end of the cereal counter, where he was stacking round boxes of oatmeal. Even without his rakish cap he was as handsome as ever, his black, wavy hair falling down over one eye. He smiled happily and said, "Hey, there. Did I forget to bring you something?"

"Oh,—no," she managed. "I,—was looking for the salt."

"It's over this way." He led her a few steps to where it was and then said, "How much do you want?"

She was relieved to have this answer right at hand. "Two pounds."

"Anything else?"

"No," she hesitated, "—I don't think so."

"Well, sure is real nice seeing you again so soon."

She could feel herself blushing slightly, along with her small, timid smile.

"Listen," he continued. "It's too hot a day for you to carry this clear home. I could drop it by for you after work."

"It's,—too much trouble."

"No, it ain't. I can just wheel by on my new Indian. Do you like motorcycles?"

"—I suppose so."

"Then I'll show it to you when I come by. It's a honey."

"—All right."

Orlean took a hesitant step backward, then turned and hurried away.

A little later, Wayne came out from behind a nearby stack of shelves that he had been dusting. Wayne was Clair's younger brother, and the two of them resembled one another so much that they were sometimes mistaken for each other by people who didn't know the family too well. It was Wayne who had persuaded old man Swenson to hire on his big brother, despite the somewhat shady reputation that Clair was rumored to have built up in Wyoming and in Salt Lake.

Wayne started dusting the shelves next to where Clair was stacking the boxes of oatmeal. "Boy, you are really somethin'," Wayne said in a low voice, so that Swenson wouldn't hear and think they were loafing on the job. "—A real lady killer."

"Oh, come on, kid."

"Less'n a week in town, an' you're already breakin' all these poor gals' hearts." Wayne shook out his dust rag. "That one's name's Orlean Bird."

Clair said quietly, "I got a feelin' that she'd faint dead away if anybody said 'boo' to her."

Wayne nodded. "She's always been sort of tongue-tied, sort of a wallflower kinda gal. Even more that way now,—than before."

"Than before what?"

"Before what happened to her Ma and Pa. They both died this year. Pa in January, and Ma in May. One right after the other." Wayne hesitated, thoughtful as he worked. "Some say her Ma went because a' heartbreak. The other Bird kids got over it okay, an' more or less normal. But not her. She ain't hardly showed her face, or said a word t' nobody, ever since."

"I guess, maybe, she's kind a' easy t' hurt hard."

"Yeah." Wayne sneezed as he wiped an unexpected, heavy layer of dust from a high shelf. "But there're a whole ton a' cuties around town that've been givin' you the eye, and that're real high-livin' sports, Clair. — Beats me that ya'd see anything in a quiet, sorta backward little girl like Orlean."

"Well, for one thing, Wayne," Clair said, "I kinda like the way she wears that yellow ribbon in her hair."

3

The Daring Young Man

Oh, he flies through the air
With the greatest of ease,
The daring young man
On the flying trapeze.
All his movements are graceful,
And the girls he does please,
The daring young man
On the flying trapeze. . . .

THE SUN was almost going down when Clair roared into Orlean's yard on his big, scarlet Indian, gunning the engine just the right amount to make the rear wheel spin in a skidding, sharp turn that threw up a cloud of dust behind him. Turning into the sun, he noticed with a certain pleasure that large, scattered chunks of the vast, flaming yellow and red sunset over the western hills were almost exactly the same color as the brilliant scarlet of his cycle.

Wayne, the bag of salt in one hand, was sitting behind Clair on the seat, too independent to hold onto his older brother, but staying in place by leg grip and balance alone.

Clair parked in the yard, and as they got off Orlean came out of the door toward them, studying both Clair and the powerful machine with wide, slightly awestruck eyes. Melva came out behind her, drying her hands on a dish towel.

"Well, there she is," Clair grinned. "Ain't she a honey?"

Orlean nodded quietly. "Oh,—yes."

Clair wiped an imaginary spot off the gleaming red body. "Two-stroke cylinder, thirty horses. Only four years old and good as new. She'll do sixty on a straightaway, then turn on a dime and give ya change."

"It,—certainly is beautiful," Orlean said.

"Would ya like t' take a ride on 'er sometime?"

Forcing as much enthusiasm as she could manage, Orlean said, "Oh,—yes!"

Melva looked at it suspiciously. "My Al says them things are about the same as open, travelin' caskets."

"Oh, no, ma'am." Now facing the older girl, Clair took off his cap. "Not if ya know how t' handle them."

"One time," Wayne said proudly, "Clair drove a cycle right smack through a speakeasy in Salt Lake. In the front door and out the back at a real good clip, and he did it so fast and smooth that nobody even spilled a drink." Then, seeing Clair's frowning expression he added lamely, "—He just did it that one time—on a bet. Uhh,—here's your salt, ma'am."

"Thanks." Melva took the salt. "I'd rather get it out here than have you drive through the kitchen with it."

Wayne dropped his eyes slightly. "Yes, ma'am."

"Don't be too long, Orlean. —And *don't* go for a ride on that bike." Melva turned and went back into the house.

"Never mind about her," Orlean said. "Her bark's worse than her bite."

"Oh, shoot, anybody can see that." Clair grinned easily. "Well, I guess we better be goin'."

Wishing him to stay, even a few moments longer, Orlean said, "It's—such a beautiful motorcycle. Why don't you use this, instead of Swenson's beat-up old bike, to deliver groceries?"

"*What? Use this* to deliver groceries?" Clair was appalled. "Why heck, that'd be like,—usin' a racehorse to pull a plow. That'd be a terrible thing for a fella to do."

"—Oh." Orlean retreated inwardly, distressed at seeming to have somehow offended him. "—Of course, you're right."

In turn, Clair now sensed her inward retreat, and he smiled suddenly, warmly. "Hey, listen! Ya want me t' show you what this sonofagun can do?"

Orlean found herself returning the smile. "Yes, I'd like that."

"Okay." He got on the seat and kicked the resting

rod back up into place. "Nothin' too fancy. Just give ya
an idea how easy she handles." He now kicked the
engine to low, growling life and gunned it slightly a
couple of times. Then, making a graceful, arcing turn,
he drove slowly out of the yard, Orlean and Wayne
following him as far as the street.

On the long, empty, dusty road, Clair swiftly accel-
erated, going from almost a stop to a breakneck speed
within a hundred feet or so and churning up huge mists
of billowing dust. Then abruptly, at full speed, he hit
the brakes and swung the front wheel at the same time
so that he skidded completely around in a long, spinning turn and came to a sudden dead stop facing back
in the direction he'd come from.

Watching his spectacular turn breathlessly, Orlean
didn't know if she was more excited or more terrified.
But in either case there was an overwhelming and joy-
ous feeling within her of deliciously shared danger and
adventure.

As he roared back down the street toward where
they were standing, Orlean said in a small, thin voice,
"Does—he always stop that way?"

Wayne shook his head. "Not with me ridin' in back
of him he don't. I'd a' wound up sailin' about three
blocks farther on up the road." Then, as Clair began at
high speed to swerve widely from left to right on his
way back down the dusty street, he added, "I got a
hunch that, maybe, he's tendin' t' show off just a little
bit."

"He is?" This thought delighted Orlean more than
she could say. "But—he won't hurt himself?"

"Nah. He can do anything but backward somersaults
on them wheels."

Now Clair cut off into a big, empty field across the
street. He sped around the field in a wide circle once,
and then with perfect balance and precision he made
three or four swift, constantly narrowing figure eights
on the motorcycle, the last one so tight and fast that the
front wheel was almost turning around and into the
back wheel in a swirling blur of dust.

Still hardly breathing, Orlean said, "That's—just un-believable!"

Wayne glanced back at the house. "I hope your big sister ain't watchin'. She'd likely have a heart attack."

Clair saved his best trick for last. Finishing the figure eights, he started back across the field toward them with a tremendous burst of speed. And leaning back, at the same time pulling up on the handlebars, he raised the front wheel high off the ground into the air, so that he was traveling on the wildly spinning back wheel only.

"My *gosh!*" Orlean gasped. "He looks just like he's on a rearing stallion!" And then, in sudden terror, "He could go over *backwards!*"

But by then Clair was already near the edge of the field and he put the front wheel down, easing off on the gas so that as he crossed the street toward them he was moving slowly and in easy control, the engine idling quietly.

"My *goodness!*" Orlean stammered. "You could,— you could go to work for a *circus!*"

Clair's smile was broad and delightedly triumphant. "Sure is a grand cycle, ain't it? Hotter'n a firecracker!" With a deft flip of his wrist he gunned the idling engine into a loud roar.

But then his smile disappeared instantly as the gunned-up motorcycle stuck at full gas and came to sudden, furious life, snarling forward and thundering past Orlean and Wayne and on by them into the yard. By whirling around swiftly, they were able to see what happened in the next few, shattering seconds.

The cycle was hopelessly caught at full gas intake, and within twenty feet it was charging along like a maddened freight train. Clair almost ran into the house but somehow managed to pull off at the last moment, so that now he was headed like an unleashed bolt of lightning toward the neighbor's fence instead.

Just before the crudely built and sloppily white-washed wood fence, there was a small rise in the ground. And when the Indian hit that rise it took off like a low-flying airplane, so that Clair and the cycle hit the fence head-on about two feet off the ground, and went right through it in a huge explosion of flying lumber and deafening noise that didn't even slow them down.

Orlean realized numbly that Clair was now speeding into the domain of the mean spotted cow that had eaten her two geraniums.

The cow realized it at about the same time.

Most cows are not noted for their agility, but this particular situation seemed to be somehow inspiring to this particular cow. As the roaring monster that was half machine and half human lunged toward the stunned, spotted cow, it snorted in absolute horror and leaped high onto its hind legs like a startled gazelle.

Clair ducked as he and his motorcycle flashed beneath the upraised forehooves of the rearing cow, and an instant later he and his cycle crashed wildly on through the other side of the fence.

The cow, having performed what was without doubt the most fantastic athletic feat of its life, now became totally petrified and fell down on its side, where it lay without moving hardly at all for a long time.

Orlean, seeing all of this action in terms of split-second thoughts, was glad that the spotted cow, mean as it was, hadn't been hurt. But still, within that brief fraction of time, she remembered her two destroyed geraniums. And for a fleeting moment, in her imagination, it wasn't Clair on a motorcycle charging a mean spotted cow. It was St. George on a great stallion, charging an awful dragon. That cow might think twice before breaking out and coming over here again.

But these tiny, swift thoughts took place at almost the same instant that Clair went speeding out of sight through the second, far side of the fence, and the overpowering fear in her mind was that he might be seriously hurt, or even dead, by now.

She and Wayne broke into a run toward the demolished section of fence as Melva appeared in the door.

"He's okay!" Wayne yelled with more hope than conviction. "The motor's still running!"

The engine could be heard receding in the distance, and then, far away, it suddenly sputtered and stopped.

Melva ran up to them near the broken fence. "What in the name of heaven—?!" She was about to go on, but Orlean suddenly said, "Shhhh," and she stayed silent.

Then the faint noise Orlean had heard came again. It was the distant sound of the engine coming back to life. She and Wayne looked at each other, and both of them became aware of finally starting to breathe again.

Half to himself, Wayne said, "He stopped 'er, an' got 'er fixed."

Realizing what had to have happened, Melva said, "Did he kill the cow?"

"The cow's not dead," Orlean said. "—I think it fainted."

The sound of the motorcycle's engine was growing now, and a little later Clair swung off the street and drove slowly into the yard. He brought the scratched and dented cycle to a stop near them and shut off the motor, still sitting in the seat. The ugly bruise on his right forehead was nothing compared to the look of immense embarrassment and anguish that had replaced the usual smile on his face. "—Everything got stuck all at once," he finally said. Then, with a faint shrug, "—Damn it t' hell anyway."

Neither Orlean nor Melva was used to such strong language, but it wasn't said in a bad way. To Orlean, forgetting the words, it sounded more like a quiet sigh of distress, a sad recognition of one more problem in what might very possibly have been a life of hard times.

"You're hurt," she said. "Your forehead is bruised."

He grinned ruefully. "Long as it's my head, there ain't much t' worry about. —They say it's made outta iron."

"Boy," Wayne put in, "you sure did stick on t' that there machine. Most riders woulda bailed out, or come off, in the first ten feet."

"Well, somebody had t' stay aboard an' find out where it was goin'." Clair grinned with a little more feeling. "Otherwise, this cycle coulda wiped out half the community up the street."

"If you'll come in," Orlean said, "we can soak that bruise with a cold rag."

"That's right," Melva nodded. "At least it'll maybe cut down the swelling."

"No, but I thank you." Clair now got off the seat and kicked the resting rod down so it would stand by itself. "I gotta rope that cow t' hold it for the time bein', and then fix up this fence."

"I'll go explain what happened t' Mrs. Sheppick," Wayne said. "It's her cow, and she's kinda deaf or she'd have already been out here."

Mrs. Sheppick wasn't too upset about the fence. It was built so poorly that the cow itself had broken out fairly often, just by backing up and scratching its rump on it. She gave them a hammer and nails from a nearby shed. And by the time dark had settled in, the fence was back in better shape than it had been before, and the spotted cow was on its feet, wandering about in a puzzled fashion.

Orlean came out of the house, where she and Melva were fixing supper, as Clair and Wayne were getting ready to go. Standing in the yellow light cast from the kitchen window, she said, "I sure am sorry about all this. —But I guess I'm mostly glad that you didn't get hurt too much."

"The bike got hurt worse," Clair said. "But I can fix it okay."

"If the two of you would like to stay for supper, Melva says there's plenty."

"Well, we sure thank you, but I don't think so."

"—A glass of water?"

"No, thanks."

"—My name's Orlean."

"I know." He rolled down his sleeves and started to button them. "Kinda like,—the city of New Orleans."

"Yes."

He smiled. "When ya come t' think about it, I guess we both got kinda funny names, somehow."

Again she found herself smiling back at him. "I guess so."

"Well—I'll be seein' ya."

"—I hope so—Clair."

"Next time I make a delivery, I promise not t' plow through two wood fences t' do it."

She still wasn't quick enough, or yet sure enough of herself, to reply in the same light, casual vein. All she could say was what she meant. "Thanks for bringing the salt. —And what you did on your bike, before it got out of hand, was really graceful and beautiful."

His infectious grin came across his face again and he said, "You gotta admit that it was that last part that was the real lulu." And then the grin turned into a low laugh. "Maybe what you said about me before is true."

"What?"

"Slammin' head-on through fences like that, an' bein' a laugh-a-minute, maybe I really could go t' work for a circus."

He swung onto the seat and Wayne got on behind him with a small, smiling wave to Orlean. They drove out of the yard and away, and it was only when she could no longer hear the engine that Orlean at last turned and went back into the house.

4

Among My Souvenirs

A few mementos rest,
Within my treasure chest,
And though they do their best,
To bring me consolation . . .

I count them all apart,
And as the teardrops start,
I find a broken heart,
Among my souvenirs. . . .

AL HAD put in a hard shift up at the mine that day, and when he got home after dark he was too tired to be his normal, joking self. He washed up and ate in a heavy, unspeaking silence, and then went straight to bed.

Margaret hurried in a few minutes later, after a long session of playing Mah-Jongg with friends, gulped a few quick bites and then dashed off to meet Darrell at the Gem Theater.

So it was that Melva and Orlean wound up quietly doing the dishes together, Melva washing and Orlean drying.

Finally, Orlean said, "—Do you like him?"

Melva rinsed a plate before answering. "I wouldn't want t' go anyplace on a motorcycle with him."

"But isn't he handsome?"

Melva started washing another plate, studying it with frowning thought. "—Handsome is as handsome does, honey."

"But he *does* handsome, too."

Melva handed Orlean the plate and started to wash the gravy bowl. "Both him and Wayne are fine-looking young men. —But Clair strikes me as being maybe, maybe too much of a smooth talker, too much of a slicker for a girl like you, despite those innocent blue eyes of his."

"Him a slicker?" Orlean smiled at the plate she was drying. "He's hardly the patent-leather hair and waxed moustache kind."

"I'm just saying that there's something more to him,

31

—something more experienced about him than the other young men around here. And I don't want you to be hurt. You been hurt a lot more than enough, already."

"No more than you, Melva,—or the others."

"Yes, more. Somehow, it's different with you, little sister." Melva hung up the washcloth as Orlean finished drying the gravy bowl. Then Melva turned and put her arms around Orlean, hugging her gently to her breast. "I wish, sometimes, that things weren't the way they are in this world, honey. I wish, somehow, that I could just reach in and pull the sadness out of you." She smiled through suddenly damp eyes. "I'd be like a dentist pulling a sore tooth. It would hurt like fury for a little while, but then the pain would start to go away."

Orlean returned Melva's hug warmly, laying her head against her big sister. But her eyes, troubled as they were, were still dry. "I'm fine, Melva. Please don't worry about me."

Overcome by her own inner feelings, Melva sniffed slightly, almost half a sob, and was instantly impatient with herself for this. "—It's a funny thing," she said, "I've been with you all your life. And I've never, ever seen you cry one tear for anything but joy."

"—I love you, Melva."

The gave each other a final, hard hug, and then Melva stepped back and forced a small, wry smile. "I don't know what, if anything, will ever come of it. But I'm glad you went downtown for that salt today. At least, whether he's a slicker or not, you finally said a few words to a young man."

"Only when he slowed down on his bike long enough."

Melva's smile widened. "Well, we'd better get some sleep." And then, "I hope that little scamp Margaret isn't out too late."

At the door to her and Margaret's small back bedroom, Orlean turned briefly. "About that salt, Melva. —I know we didn't need it."

Melva shrugged slightly. "A little extra salt can always come in handy. Now you go on to bed, young lady."

When she was finally settled in bed, Orlean turned up the kerosene lamp so that it threw a little brighter light. Then she reached under the bed for the small tin box in which she kept the few treasured things she possessed. Opening it, she took out an ancient, faded red rose that had been pressed long ago in the family bible. Her mother had performed a miracle, many years before, by somehow making that rose grow. Of course, the family had been living in Granger then, which was farther away from the mill, toward Salt Lake. But even there the air was still poisonous, and her mother's one living rosebush had been such a rare and unique thing that people had come from far around to look at it and admire it.

There was a round, smooth pebble from the shore of a lake she'd once visited. She could hold its cool smoothness in her hand and close her eyes, and feel once again the brisk, fresh breeze from the clear water, see once more the tiny, happy whitecaps running and playing with the teasing winds over the nearly sky-blue surface of the lake.

There were a few letters and old Christmas cards, a tarnished little-girl necklace, and a childhood ring that didn't fit anymore. But now she took out the one thing that she was really looking for in the tin box.

It was a slightly creased photograph of her mother and father taken just after they were married. Her father with a quiet gentleness in his strength. And her mother with a quiet strength in her gentleness.

And now, though they were still young and alive in Orlean's eyes, they were gone. Father, an oak tree of a man, from an unexpected, totally unbelievable heart attack. And then mother, simply because without him at her side, she had no further wish to live.

Gently, Orlean replaced the photo and then put the tin box back under the bed. She turned the kerosene lamp far down, so that it was almost completely out, but not quite. Then she lay back to watch the dim, vague shadows from the lamp playing flickering games of hide-and-seek with themselves on the ceiling above.

All right then, Orlean silently demanded of herself, what's wrong with me?

Why couldn't she be happy-go-lucky and full of easy-going fun and laughter, and silly and carefree like everybody else?

Why couldn't she cry? Though it seemed to her just then that somebody had once said something about,— tears that sometimes flowed backwards. Maybe hers did. Maybe, in some strange way, she cried backwards. In any case, whatever there was inside of her, it sure did hurt a lot.

And why was she such a darned coward? Ever since she could remember, she'd sat off on the sidelines, dreading the idea of being suddenly and frighteningly brought to the center of attention. In school she'd even hated spelling bees, and she was a good speller. She hated school dances, and she was a good dancer.

Maybe hate wasn't the right word. She didn't actually hate anything. Maybe feared was the word. And in that case, softer words like shy and timid were easier to think of and use. But the first hard word, coward, came to Orlean's mind once again, and it made her frown briefly at the shadowed ceiling.

Was she afraid of things? Or was she just, somehow, different?

She remembered back to the time when she was ten, and she'd had a giant windfall of an Indian-head nickel from Uncle Charlie. With one penny or two pennies, you just naturally went to the penny-candy store. But with that much money, a whole nickel all at once, there was only one thing to do. You waited impatiently for Saturday, and then you went to the movie at the then brand-new Gem Theater.

Orlean had gone in with a lucky few other kids who happened to also be rich on that particular Saturday

night. By the time the movie let out it was already
dark, and it was a long, lonely walk home to Shield's
Addition, the cluster of small houses on the far edge of
Magna where Orlean lived.

On the way up the street some of the other kids
started acting foolish and a little rough, yelling and
throwing rocks at each other in the dark.

Orlean, just walking along by herself, was suddenly
stunned and nearly knocked forward to the ground. As
her mind gradually cleared, her ears and head began
ringing and beating with shrill, throbbing pain, and she
realized numbly that she'd been hit on the back of the
head with a rock. A moment later she knew that it had
been a very sharp rock. For when she leaned weakly
against a fence and put her hand up to the pounding
hurt, the hand came back covered with blood.

At no time did she cry out in anger, or for help, or
even make any small sound of pain. And soon the
other children, unknowing, were long gone in the dark,
their shouts and calls fading away in the distance.

One slow step after the other, often leaning and
resting against a dimly seen fence or a shed along the
way, Orlean made her painful way toward Shield's
Addition.

By the time she saw the lights of home, she could
hardly stay on her feet. But then, finally, she managed
to get to the front of the house.

And at that time, much of her attitude toward the
entire scheme of things that would come to pass in her
life and in her world, forever, became very clear in a
shy and bittersweet way.

Her parents had company. Two Mormon Elders
were with them in the lighted parlor, talking about
something, making points with the movements of their
hands.

Orlean couldn't disturb these important people, embarrass them with her blood-clotted hair, with the fresh
blood that was still seeping down onto the back of her
dress. So, in respectful silence and with rapidly fading
strength, she made her way around one dark side of

the house to the back door. Then, as noiselessly as possible, she went into the unlighted kitchen and sat quietly in a chair at the table.

That's all she remembered until she became dimly aware that she was in her mother's lap. Her mother was rocking her back and forth, crooning a soft little tune as tears ran down her cheeks. The kitchen was lighted by a lamp now, and her father was standing over her, staring down at her with a face of granite sadness.

"Thank God," he whispered as her eyes opened. "—There you are."

"Oh, baby," her mother said, swiftly trying to blink back her tears, "why didn't you cry, or let us know you were hurt?"

"I,—I just didn't want t',—be a bother t' anybody."

"Bother?!" Her mother hugged her so fiercely that it hurt. "You almost bled to death before we found you."

"That shyness of yours," her father said gently, "is a thing that you'll have t' learn t' get over. There's times for boldness, 'Lean. An' sometimes even a good loud holler for help ain't outta line."

Orlean could tell that her head had been washed and bandaged, and she saw that she had been dressed in her nightgown. Feeling better here in the warmth and security of her parents, she said, "I'm sorry, Pa. I just,—hated t' disturb you, an' embarrass you an' Ma with company."

"You funny little dickens," her mother said, rocking her gently back and forth in her lap. "You just love so awful much,—that you can't help but put all others before you. And you stand back and quiet, an' never ever complainin',—even when you're bleedin' your life blood out."

Then the little, ten-year-old Orlean had gone off to sleep again, safe in her mother's arms and her father's presence.

Oh, *God,* she missed those two, the sixteen-year-old

Orlean thought to herself now as she stared at the dim, dancing shadows on the ceiling. Melva married. Margaret, from all signs, about to be. The brothers, who for whatever reasons had never been very close, gone off and away somewhere to start their own, distant lives. And what was she, Orlean, to do? She couldn't stay with Melva and Al too much longer. They were willing, and kind, but they had to have freedom for themselves, and for their family that would be coming in time.

A recurring dream came to Orlean. Horses. Wild horses. Beautiful beyond belief, thundering by swiftly and silently in her mind. To the best of her memory, she'd first had this dream when she was five. And it came back to her again and again, each time as vivid and wonderful as before.

There was this mystical and magic place far away and high up in the mountains. Not just any mountains, and certainly nothing like that stained and scarred mountain with the mill on it. These mountains were green and fertile, with the songs of birds everywhere, and snow-capped peaks on the distant heights. The valleys were verdant, and filled as far as the eye could see with every imaginable kind of gay and happy wildflowers. And above all among these other breathlessly lovely things, there were the majestic wild horses, proud, swift, beautiful and invincible. Sometimes, in her dream, the horses would race right up into the sky, and go galloping across the clouds themselves, as though the clouds were great, white, fluffy fields stretching endlessly and forever in the heavens.

There was something else in Orlean's dream, a mysterious and warm presence that she could never quite see or place. Whatever, or whoever, it was, it was protective and good. But it was always just barely out of sight, somewhere beyond the next hill, or hidden from her view at the far end of a green valley below.

Finally this dream took Orlean's mind away from the sorrow of her mother and father.

And, at last, she slept.

5

Great-grandpa

Great-grandpa,
When the West was young,
Barred his door,
With a wagon tongue.
For the times were rough,
And the Redskins mocked,
And he said his prayers,
With his shotgun cocked.
He ate his bacon,
And his corn-pone fat,
But his great-grandson,
Woulda starved on that.

CLAIR DROPPED Wayne off in front of the small Huffaker house, where from behind a few scraggly trees faint light from the house showed vaguely.

Getting down from the seat, Wayne said quietly, "—You ain't comin' in?"

Clair shook his head, his face impassive. "Nah. —I'll see ya tomorrow."

Understanding, Wayne nodded and clasped his big brother's shoulder with brief, strong affection. Then he turned and went toward the house. Clair started to turn his cycle around, but Wayne got to the front door first. From inside the house, a strident female voice could be heard demanding, "Why are you so late?! Have you been out galavantin' around with that brother a' yours again?!"

Going easy on the throttle, Clair drove slowly back down the street as quietly as possible, his throat thick with a sad, choked feeling.

A few minutes later, he turned off the now fairly wide-awake Main Street and parked his bike in an alley behind the three-story Panama Hotel, one of the two largest buildings in Magna.

The Panama was a combination hotel, speakeasy and whorehouse. When Clair had arrived in town a week ago, and finally realized that he just couldn't stay at his own home with his own family, he'd gone looking for a room. And they'd had a small place, not much bigger than a closet, in the back of the Panama Hotel.

Big Bertha Pearl, the hugely built owner and proprietess of all three businesses under that roof, had taken a liking to Clair and let him have the tiny room.

"What can ya afford for it, kid?," she asked, her massive face almost hidden by a headband filled with drooping peacock feathers, and her fat, mottled neck completely hidden by countless overlapping strings of pearls.

"Nothin'. —Ain't got a job yet."

She could see that the young man was not apologizing, or backing down, but just stating a simple fact. "Well then, what can ya do?"

He took a long breath, thinking hard. "You got a pool table in the speak downstairs. I got t' be pretty good at rackin' up poolballs for customers over t' Park City."

Big Bertha Pearl nodded. "Then you got a nighttime job an' a room, kid. They work out even."

"What hours, ma'am?"

"About ten t' twelve. B'fore ten they're too busy drinkin' t' shoot pool, an' after twelve they're too drunk t' see what the hell they're doin' anyhow." She twirled a long loop of pearls idly, frowning at him. "An' I ain't no ma'am, kid. I'm Big Bertha Pearl."

Suddenly unsure of quite how to address this formidable woman properly, Clair simply nodded.

Big Bertha Pearl now stood up, all six feet and two hundred pounds of her. She and Clair were on the same eye level, but she outweighed him by at least forty pounds. "Now you're back in town, kid, why ain't you stayin' with your family?"

"It's,—personal."

"How old're you?"

"Nineteen."

"Bullshit! How old're you?"

His young eyes gathered the strength to match hers. "—All right, I'm sixteen. Seventeen pretty quick."

She shook her head ponderously, her strings of pearls shifting slightly with the movement. "Jesus Christ! I've gone an' hired myself a goddamn baby! You best look someplace else."

Clair said very quietly, "I been known t' settle a few arguments on them pool tables over t' Park City. An' I'm a hard worker."

Something about the quiet confidence of the young man touched a responsive chord in Big Bertha Pearl. "—Get your room key from the bartender, an' ya start t'night." Then she said, as an afterthought, "—An' I guess ya can just call me Big Bertha, if ya want to."

Now, going straight up to his tiny room this night, Clair lay down on his back with unutterable sadness and rested on his bed for a while, his expressionless eyes wide open. Finally, about nine o'clock, he went across the street to the Tip Top Cafe for a lonely, flavorless chicken-fried steak with hard peas and dry mashed potatoes and a lukewarm glass of milk. And then, promptly at ten, he started racking the pool table at The Smokehouse, the speak in the basement of the Panama Hotel.

He worked his full two hours, often hiding an almost angry impatience when his practiced, pool-trained eyes would see half-drunk miners trying the wrong shots, or just plain missing so badly that you couldn't even tell what they were shooting at in the first place.

The two top bootleggers from around there came in. Old Poison Pete and his fat son, Little Pete. They laughed and joked with some friends at the bar, and they bought drinks for everyone around them. Big Bertha Pearl joined them after a while, and Poison Pete playfully slapped her on the butt, which was sort of like hitting a Mack truck on the rear bumper with a fly swatter.

A little later on, while Clair was racking up a fresh eight-ball game, Sheriff Pistol Pete walked in and joined the others crowded around the bar. Clair couldn't help but think just then that it seemed like damnere everyone in this town was named Pete. One thing for damned certain, he decided in silent, grim humor, was that if the Clairs were matched up for general battle against the Petes, the Clairs would sure as hell be in trouble. There was only one of them in the world, and that was him.

Poison Pete wandered over to the pool table and offered everyone there a drink. And in his depressed, half-angry frame of mind, Clair accepted along with the others. Big Bertha Pearl frowned, but she didn't say anything against it.

It was Poison Pete's own booze that he offered around, calling it "simple, good old home brew," and it tasted to Clair like gasoline with a dash of iodine in it for flavor.

"Drink y'r glasses down!" Poison Pete told everyone. "The secret a' Magna havin' the best booze in Utah is that the water around the mine here's so goddamn awful that anything ya do to it's gotta be an improvement!"

Clair finished two of Poison Pete's drinks, and then Big Bertha Pearl was at his side. "It's midnight," she said, "and your work day's over. —Maybe you ought t' turn in."

With a tongue that suddenly felt like an oily radiator cap, Clair muttered, "—I think,—maybe y'r right."

Not only feeling sad and exhausted, but painfully drunk, he finally made it upstairs. Luckily, when he fell down, his room was so small that almost the only place he could hit was the bed.

He switched off the bare electric light and lay there in the dark for a long moment. Only then, finally, did he come to grip with his real agony. Not his scratched and dented bike. Not the wooden-tasting dinner. Not Poison Pete's guaranteed-to-kill or die-trying whiskey.

His real agony had to do with the strident voice he had heard from within the house earlier that evening.

Clair was fiercely proud of the pioneers he vaguely knew of way back in his family, those early, brave people who had crossed the Great Plains and mountains to settle in Utah. They were men and women he could understand, respect and finally love, even though the passing of time had made them only dimly seen, powerful figures on a vast, much too quickly disappearing landscape. Some of them had even been descendants of Thomas Jefferson. He guessed, then, that he must be too. His forefathers had plowed the very first furrow that had ever broken into the hard, hostile earth of a Utah field. They had started the first printing press that ever tried to give news and hope and wisdom on a printed page to the struggling people of this new, huge land.

In his heart, Clair wished he had been born one of those pioneers. But he had been born more than fifty years too late.

And born into a family divided, a family that had put him out before he was quite old enough to even know what being put out meant.

His mother, for reasons known only to her, perhaps not even really known to her, had decided that Clair should not be born, long before the moment he was born, the fifth child in a family of seven.

Clair's first memories were painful ones, impossible to understand. The older children, Marvin, Sherril, Ken and Evelyn, would come home from kindergarten and grade school at noon for lunch. Clair was still too young for school. All the children would line up hungrily in the back yard and their mother, Enzy, would give them food, usually sandwiches or soup. And wherever he was standing in line, she would ignore Clair, simply leave him standing there with no food and, even worse, no word. Marvin, the oldest boy, quickly became aware of this, and whenever he could, he would get Clair behind the garage and try to share his own food with his little brother.

Grateful, Clair had taken one bite of Marvin's jam sandwich the first time it happened. But with the feelings welling up inside of him, he could hardly choke it down, because his mother hadn't just given it to him normally, and with love. And after that, he pretended not to be hungry.

Or Clair's first important school holiday, May Day. That year, as school was coming to an end for the summer, the Huffaker family was a little more solvent than usual because Frank had a steady job, selling paint. So that morning mother Enzy Huffaker gave each child down the line, one after the other, an unheard of fortune of thirty-five cents to spend for candy and rides when the school bus delivered them to Liberty Park in Salt Lake City. She gave each child, even little Wayne, a quarter and a dime.

Except that she passed by Clair as though he weren't even standing there before her. No money. No look. No word.

Even at sixteen now, Clair could get choked up with bewildered grief wondering what possessed that strange woman, the woman who more than any other he was supposed to love, and wanted to love.

His father, Frank, went almost as much against Clair's ideals about parents as his mother. Frank was overweight and always tired, a vague dreamer of half-dreams whose ideas were never fully formed, or strong. Enzy, in her harsh voice, would tell him to do everything. And Frank would do it. Or plan vaguely on doing it, depending on the energy he had at the time.

He was not an unkind or cruel man, but he would never go against her, even though a son of his was for no known reason being systematically crucified.

He might ask, "Say, how come ya didn't give little Clair thirty-five cents t'day, like the other kids?"

She would answer something like, "I have seven children you put upon me, Frank. *Seven!* An' I slave my hands t' the bone all day long tryin' t' raise 'em! Now don't you go an' start tryin' t' tell me how t' do it! Right now, while you're standin' here a' arguin', baby Lois's screamin' her lungs out f'r her diaper t' be changed!"

And even though one-year-old Lois might not be making a sound, Frank would feel overwhelming guilt and distress, plus the deep-rooted fearfulness that all long-married husbands have of easily outraged wives. And he would mumble, "Well, a' course,—whatever you say, Enzy dear."

Neither one of them would have remembered such a thing as the thirty-five cents any longer than that.

But Clair remembered, and it wouldn't have been any different in his memory, better or worse, if it had been thirty-five million dollars. He'd worked all week after school, cleaning up the garage and pulling weeds in the back yard, both hoping to please, and hoping for a nickel or maybe even a dime on May Day.

When the school bus had pulled into that magic place that was Liberty Park, right in the middle of Salt Lake City, there'd been more kids there than Clair had ever seen before in his life, so many that at first little Wayne was afraid to get off the bus. All of the schoolkids from every place in Salt Lake County were there. There were acres and acres of tall, spreading trees and lawn, and every kind of ride in the world to go on for a nickel apiece. There was a big lake with an island in it, and you could go for a ride as a passenger in a speed boat, or even hire and take out your own rowboat all by yourself. There was a Ferris-wheel and a Loop-the-Loop, and loud, happy music was booming out from a Merry-Go-Round that was whirling dizzily around with gaily painted horses going rhythmically up and down, moving proudly on their gleaming brass poles.

Near the Merry-Go-Round there were two long, low buildings that smelled good, even from the bus, where you could buy everything from hot dogs to any flavor of soda pop, or cotton candy or popcorn or candied apples.

Ken rushed off like he'd been shot from a cannon, but the other kids stayed near Clair, knowing he had no money and wanting to share with him. Wayne even wanted to give Clair his whole quarter and dime, and then just go around with him.

But Clair told them no. "Listen," he said, "I don't wanta be stuck with all a' you hangin' around with me all day. I'm goin' off on my own, an' I'll meet ya back here at the bus."

And then he turned around and quickly lost himself in the thronging crowds of other school children.

At first he was still feeling so sad and hollow-chested that he couldn't pay much attention to anything, but just walked on and on, unseeing among the laughing, celebrating children. But after walking aimlessly for a long time, he finally willed himself to stop feeling sorry for himself and start paying attention to the things that were around him. And he found that there were many things at Liberty Park that were free. There were the beautiful trees and grass, that were unlike anything in Magna. You could sit by the lake, and put your hands in it. There was a huge house with joining squares of clear glass for a roof, where the sun could shine through, and inside were hundreds and hundreds of plants and flowers that he'd never seen before, or even imagined.

And best of all there was a zoo that you could walk through without having to pay any money. There were all kinds of birds in it, plus foxes and deer, coyotes and wolves, all in their separate cages. At the far end, there was even a big, brown bear lazing in the sun.

Later in the day, Sherril and Wayne finally found him there by the bear cage. They were hurrying along, and Sherril was gingerly holding a partly melted vanilla ice cream cone.

"We been lookin' all over for ya," Sherril said. "We brought ya this vanilla cone."

"Yeah," Wayne said. "You must be starvin' by now."

Sherril thrust the melting cone forward in such a way that Clair had to take it, but he just held it in front of him.

"Ain't ya gonna eat it?" Wayne asked.

"Ya better," Sherril told him, " 'cause we sure ain't."

"Ya ain't?" Clair turned toward the cage and held the cone out. "Hey, you, come 'ere."

The big bear lumbered toward the offered cone, and

Clair threw it between the bars so that it landed on some grass near the bear's forepaws.

With a few throaty rumbles and great delight, the big bear laid down with the cone in its forepaws and started to lick at the ice cream.

Sherril and Wayne were looking from the happy beast to Clair with puzzled frowns, so Clair said, "Somehow, I just don't feel hungry."

Even now, lying in the Panama Hotel only half-awake and with a head that felt like it had been hit with a sledgehammer, Clair was fiercely proud that it was the bear who had got the last nickel's worth that had ever almost come to him from the tight, pinched face and purse of his mother. Ever since that time he'd never accepted anything from either his mother or father, and in his entire life he never would. As a child after that May Day, half starving, and with flapping, hole-worn shoes, he'd tried to run away three or four times. But he was still too young to be taken seriously by anybody, and always some well-meaning person would haul him back to his "home" where Enzy would scream senselessly or slap him while his father mumbled unheard words of advice.

The first and only time he could remember his mother smiling at him was when she smiled very thinly and told him that she and his father had decided to curb his rebellious ways by sending him to live with relatives in Wyoming.

Clair thought briefly of those many times and many places he'd known since he was first sent away at about the age of seven.

They included Evanston, Wyoming, Salt Lake City, and a dozen points in between. But, unexpectedly and beautifully, almost everyone he'd stayed with had been warm and wonderful to him. Big, fat, loving Aunt Maine. Quiet, uncannily wise Mrs. Legget. And the iron matriarch with the warm sparkle in her eye, Grandma Brown. He'd always managed to earn his own way, though, wherever he'd been. Working at jobs ranging from sweeping out stores to lumberjacking.

They had turned out to be good, rich experiences. But what with moving around a lot it hadn't been an endless piece of cake, especially with that damned name, Clair. Everybody thought it was a girl's name, and God, the rough fights he'd got into! From Logan to Park City, from Ogden to Strawberry, from Murray clear up to Big Piney. And he was almost always outnumbered, too, just naturally being a loner. There was that running feud with those four tough Mexican kids up in Ogden who decided that they were going to cut him up or kill him. Luckily, when they'd come upon him in the alley behind where he was going part-time to school, he'd been prepared. He went among them with a pair of brass knuckles recently acquired from a pawn shop on South Street for a dollar-fifty. The knucks had been a good investment, for the first kid he got a good swing at on the jaw, dropped his knife and went down like he'd been hit with a crowbar. When he leaped back up, his hand on his jaw, blood was spurting like a fountain from his mouth and nose. He'd rushed off blindly, half-yelling something in Mexican, and the other three followed him.

Clair hoped he hadn't hurt him too bad.

It was only when they had all disappeared down the alley that Clair realized he himself had been cut on his left side and was bleeding too. Another couple of inches in, and he might have been dead.

He still had that dropped knife, the kind with one long blade that flipped open when you pushed a small button on its side. He kept it next to his brass knuckles in his duffle bag.

About a month later he'd been sent to Salt Lake for the summer, and there he'd seen the most impressive man he'd ever known.

The man was visiting Grandma Brown and way, way back in time he had been an older friend of Clair's Grandpa.

Clair couldn't remember his name, as a mere boy was more than likely never even introduced. But what a big, rugged barn-door of a man! He had to be well over seventy years old, and he had to weigh nearly two hundred and fifty pounds, yet he still had a young eagle's eye, and a step so light that it looked like he could have jumped clear up into the sky if he'd wanted to.

And his hands! Big, gnarled branches of wrists ending in wide, hardworked and a thousand-times-hurt fingers. Fingers that had become more and more powerful and beautifully lined with every hard piece of work, and with every hurt.

Finally that night, the old giant of a man looked at Clair with those eagle eyes of his and said very quietly, "—Your Grandpa was one fine man, son."

Then he stood up, touched Clair's shoulder with a massive, gentle hand, and was soon gone, forever.

Thinking all of his thoughts about the people, places and times in his life, and wishing not for what was, but for what ought to be, Clair at last went to sleep.

6

Sentimental Me

Look at me again, dear,
Let's hold hands and then, dear,
Sigh in chorus,
It won't bore us . . .
I am not the kind that merely flirts,
I just love and love until it hurts.
Oh Sentimental me,
And poor romantic you,
Dreaming dreams,
Is all that we can do. . . .

Two nights later business was slow at The Smoke-house, and Bull Barstow, boss of the bull gang up at the mill, came over to the pool table.

"Ain't got nobody t' shoot with," he grumbled. "How 'bout you?"

"I just work here."

"Ain't nothin' doin' anyhow. Say, four bits a game?"

"That's pretty steep."

"Two bits then."

"Well, I guess one game wouldn't hurt."

Shortly after midnight, Clair knocked at the door of Big Bertha Pearl's office and went in. She looked up from some work on her desk and said, "Yeah?"

"Bull Barstow asked me t' play some pool."

"Well, why not? It's quieter'n a Mormon's confession t'night."

"—I won five dollars off 'im."

"Five bucks?!" Big Bertha Pearl studied him for a moment. "You ain't a hustler?"

"No. Just a pretty good shooter."

"How come ya didn't just pocket the money an' keep your mouth shut?"

"—I was on your time. Seems like, maybe the money's yours."

"You're crazy. You won it."

"Sure is easy money."

She shrugged. "Ain't no such thing as easy money, finally."

"Sure seems like it right now."

"—You wanna shoot sometimes, on slow nights?"

Clair grinned, "If it's okay, you bet!"

"Okay. But don't never murder the customers. An' don't never bet on the come with money you ain't got."

That night marked the beginning of some of the happiest-go-lucky, carefree months Clair had ever known. In any given week he never did worse than break even. And nine times out of ten he'd wind up with some extra dollars, each one seeming the size of a giant, shiny cartwheel, because for the first time in his life he could just up and spend it any old way that he happened to want to, without even thinking twice about it.

But he already knew one thing he wanted to buy with that first windfall from Bull Barstow. The next Sunday, his day off at the grocery store, he drove into Salt Lake with Sherril in his brother's new Ford Model A Sedan. It was a gloriously warm and sunny day in Salt Lake, and they drove with the canvas top down, the engine tooling along smoothly.

"How 'bout if we drive on up t' The Laughing Lady for a drink or two?" Sherril suggested.

"Good idea."

"Just t' help stave off the sunstroke, a' course."

"Boy," Clair said, fingering the car's polished dashboard idly and watching some people cross the wide street before them as Sherril stopped for a signal, "this sure is the life."

"It damn sure is." Sherril took a long, deep breath. "Like bein' right in the middle a' that big old Big Rock Candy Mountain itself."

"Well," Clair grinned, "I don't see no cigarette trees around here, but will ya settle for a Lucky Strike?"

"Sure will."

Sherril drove on, as Clair lighted up for the two of them.

It was dusk when they got back to Magna, and Sherril stopped to drop Clair off in front of Melva and Al's house. Clair got out with a large brown paper bag under one arm, and started toward the house as Sherril drove away.

Clair knocked at the back door and a moment later Melva, still in her go-to-meeting church clothes, answered it. "Well, hello there."

"Evenin', ma'am. —Is Orlean home?"

"We just got back." Melva raised her voice a little, "It's for you, 'Lean."

Melva stepped away from the door and Orlean appeared in a pretty yellow and white dress, her eyes widening when she saw who it was. "—Hello." And then, "—Won't you come in?"

"No, thanks." He nodded slightly down toward the paper bag in his hands. "Not groceries this time. Just somethin' I thought you might like."

She said numbly, "—Something,—for me?"

"Yeah. Here, I'll help ya get it out, but be careful."

She stepped to him and in a moment was holding the gift, staring at it speechlessly. It was a clay pot with four beautiful, already full-grown red geraniums planted in it.

All she could finally manage to say was, "—How,—could you know?"

Not too sure what she meant, he grinned and shrugged. "Well, that one ya had when I was here b'fore was almost a goner."

"—You saw it."

From the doorway Melva said, "Those are real, real nice. —Do you two want t' sit in the parlor awhile, and talk?"

"No, thanks," Clair said.

Orlean put the flowers down, very gently, on the step and then turned back to Clair. "I'd,—sort of like to take a little walk. —If you would."

"Sure. That'd be swell."

Out of habit with Margaret, Melva almost said, "Don't be too late." But instead she said, "—You both have a nice time," and closed the door.

Quietly strolling through the growing darkness

toward Main Street, Orlean said, "No matter how long
I live, Clair, I'll never forget you bringing me those
flowers."

"I wish I coulda had 'em wrapped in colored paper,
but that place in Salt Lake only had paper bags." Then
he said, "Sure is a nice night for a walk."

"I'll bet you've seen all kinds of nights, all over."

"Well, a few. —I'm workin' nights at The Smokehouse, you know."

"That saloon?"

"Speakeasy. It's not the kind a' place you'd know
much about, I guess."

"No. But any place you liked, I bet I would too."

They were at Main Street now, with its long line of
bright lights leading to the dark mountain beyond.

"Would you like to go to Turk's Drugstore for an ice
cream?" Clair asked.

"I'd like that."

Even though the town was in a roaring mood
tonight, with big miners crowding the sidewalks and
loud laughter, shouting and music blaring from every
other doorway, Orlean felt safe and protected with
Clair. Instead of an ordeal it was suddenly, somehow,
an adventure.

They ordered two dishes of vanilla ice cream at
Turk's, and sat in wire-backed chairs at a tiny table to
eat it.

"How long have you had your,—Indian?" she
asked, not being able to imagine him ever not having
it.

"About three months. I got a great deal on it from a
friend of mine who's in the state penitentiary now."

"In jail?!"

Clair nodded. "He held up a gas station. They
caught him on his cycle, that Indian, about four blocks
away."

Orlean took another bite of ice cream. "I've read in
the magazines about getaway cars. But never about
getaway motorcycles."

Clair grinned. "I'd been savin' every penny I could

to buy a cycle, even goin' without eating t' help put a little bit aside. He knew about that, so on his way t' the pen, he let me have it for the forty-five dollars I'd saved. He wasn't too bad a guy."

Carried along by sincere curiosity, she said, "Have,— have you ever been in jail?"

Clair laughed. "No."

She was instantly embarrassed by her question, but then Clair asked, "Have you?" and she started laughing along with him.

On the walk back home, Orlean said, "Sometime, would you like to come over and have supper with us?"

"Well, I'm not too much on those family sort of things."

"Oh."

"Ya see, I been kinda on my own, all those different places, for nearly ten years."

"It must have been exciting. But, didn't you miss your family?"

"Oh, I guess so, sort of, once in a while." He added proudly, "But all my big brothers're doin' real fine. An' my big sister, too. Evelyn's turned out t' be a real beauty, an' I got a hunch you two'd be good friends in nothin' flat."

"Wayne's real nice, a lot like you. Tell me about the others."

"Marvin's married an' moved up t' Canada on a real good job. He's practically a college graduate in electricity. Builds power plants. An' Sherril's just married. He's a top electrician up at the mill. Right now Ken seems t' be kinda goin' in circles, but he'll straighten out."

"—And Evelyn?"

The tone of pride in Clair's voice became even greater. "Would you believe it, I introduced her to Miles, her husband."

"That's nice."

"Miles is even older than Evelyn, about twenty-three or so, and we got t' be friends in Salt Lake last year. So one time when Evelyn came in t' spend the day, I got them t'gether." He smiled half to himself. "I just knew they'd hit it off."

They were at the front of her house now and Orlean turned, smiling back at him in the dim moonlight. "That must make you feel really good."

"Yeah, it sure does."

"—Well,—"

"I'll see ya up to the door."

"Thank you."

"Say," he said as they crossed the dark yard, "you doin' anything special, about two weeks from now?"

Orlean's heart started beating strongly, but she tried to seem as casual as possible. "Do you mean, Sunday after next?"

"Yeah."

"Well, that day, there's just church, that's all."

"I gotta warn ya it might go on kinda late. Some of us 're goin' out t' the Salt Palace Pavillion by Smelter Town."

Turning toward him at the door, Orlean felt her heart acting up so much that she was almost afraid Clair would hear its loud beating. "The Salt Palace?!"

He nodded. "A big place out t'ward the Great Salt Lake."

"Oh, I know!" She added uncertainly, "It's just that I've never ever been there."

"Me neither," Clair shrugged. "But Sherril an' Miles have, lots of times, an' we're all goin' out cause it's Sherril's wife's birthday." He hesitated. "Do ya think ya could come?"

"Oh, yes!"

"Good." He smiled and put out his hand. She slowly put her own small hand in his, and he pressed it firmly but gently for a moment, then softly released it. "Well, good night."

"Good night, Clair."

He turned, rather quickly, and walked away with long strides into the dark.

When the sounds of his footsteps could no longer be heard, she leaned down and touched the geraniums on the step briefly and gently. Then she opened the door and went in.

Melva, Al and Margaret were all at the supper table, and her place was set and waiting for her.

"Guess what?!" she said, letting loose of some of the excitement within her. "Clair asked me to go to the Salt Palace with him!"

"*Wow!*" Margaret said.

Orlean looked at Melva. "It's okay,—isn't it?"

"I've heard that it's a pretty fast place," Melva said quietly. "—But of course it's okay, honey, if you want to."

"I sure do!"

As Orlean sat down and started to put some food on her plate, Al said in a slightly teasing way, "He sure must have real fancy ways, that young man a' yours."

Orlean couldn't stop her cheeks from reddening. "He's not 'my young man,' Al."

"Don't be too sure a' that," Margaret said with intense sincerity. "Darrell's been my steady beau for five whole months an' *we* sure ain't never been out t' the Salt Palace Pavillion! Besides, 'Lean, Melva told me all about them pretty new flowers out on the doorstep."

Al looked up from eating, delighted at this new ammunition. "Flowers? He brung ya flowers?! Was this here dandy by any chance wearin' spats an' a silk top hat?"

"Now you stop teasin' her while she's eating, you big bully," Melva said.

Later, when Orlean and Margaret were just about to go to bed, Al couldn't resist one parting shot. "You know what the man says, 'Lean. It's okay for a young couple t' go for a walk t'gether at night,—as long as they don't go too far." And as usual, it was he who burst into loud laughter at his own joke.

"Oh, you, Al!" But Orlean was grinning slightly as she disappeared quickly into the back bedroom.

When Melva and Al were alone in the kitchen, he said quietly, "Ya know, honey. T'night's the first time I ever recall seein' little 'Lean smilin' like that. —Sure is nice."

Melva looked at him warmly. "With all your bluff, an' corny jokes,—I guess you're not the worst husband a girl ever had."

Late the next night Sherril came into The Smokehouse after his shift at the mill. He joked with the bartender as he got a drink at the bar, called a happy hello to Big Bertha Pearl, and then took his drink over to the pool table where Clair was racking a game of nine ball.

As the players started shooting he said to Clair, "Well, how'd them posies go over?"

It took Clair a thoughtful moment to quietly answer. "—It was like,—well Sherril, you'd a' thought I'd brought 'er the Taj Mahal, 'r somethin'."

Sherril grinned and said dryly, "I take it she liked 'em okay."

"More'n that. I swear I thought she was almost gonna cry. But after a minute she was okay, an' we took a little walk."

Sherril took a sip of his drink and made an exaggerated face at the taste of it. "Ya ask her?"

Clair nodded. "She said yes."

"That's sure gonna be one hell of a ritzy, rootin'-tootin' night, Clair. An' with her bein' a little Mormon girl from Magna, ya think she'll be up t' that kind of a hot old time, without cryin' for her momma, or wantin' t' go home?"

"She ain't got no momma," Clair said, his voice suddenly hard. "An' it seems t' me that we're from Magna, too, Sherril."

Sherril, who lived on fun and laughter and could never stand the idea of hurting anyone, was immediately and painfully sensitive to Clair's changed tone of voice. "Hey, hold on there, kid brother! It's just that it's gonna be a real special night, an' I sure do want for you t' have the best good time that ya can."

"Yeah, I shoulda known that," Clair said, his quiet voice becoming warm again, soothing Sherril's hurt feelings. "—I'll tell ya," he went on. "In a way, she seems t' be scared a' her own shadow. But underneath, I got a feelin' she has more grit, maybe, than both you an' me put t'gether."

Relieved, Sherril grinned. "Hell, havin' more grit than me's the easiest thing in the world." He finished his drink and said cheerfully to the pool table at large, "What am I wastin' time here with all you ugly bastards for, when I got that gorgeous redhead a' mine waitin' for me with a drink up at home?"

A couple of shooters said things like, "You lucky devil," and "If she gits tired a' your homely kisser, send 'er down here."

Clair said, "Give Vivianne my best," and then Sherril was gone.

Toward the middle of the next week Melva came into Swenson's and ordered a supply of groceries to be delivered. Clair put that delivery off until the end of the day, near closing time.

Then, as he was putting the last of the two big bags into the wire basket behind Swenson's bike, Wayne came to the back door giving out onto the alley and said, "Want me t' go along with ya?"

"No, thanks."

"Okay." Disappointed in not being able to go with his big brother, Wayne started to take off the long white apron he wore in the store. As Clair began to pedal away, he called, "See ya in the mornin'," and Clair waved back at him, then turned out of Wayne's sight on Third East.

When she heard the faint thumping sound at the kitchen door a few minutes later, Orlean somehow knew that it was Clair, and she hurried to open it. Melva hadn't ordered eggs that day, so he only held a large bag in each arm, and there was no sack between his teeth.

He smiled and said, "Glad t' see no broom, this time."

"Come in!" She hurried to clear a few things off the table so that he would have enough room to put the heavy bags down.

After he'd put them on the table he turned to her, taking off his cap. "Well, that's a relief. —That's the last delivery I got."

"It is?"

"Yep." He hesitated. "Means, I'm kinda off work now,—for a little while, anyway."

Equally hesitant, Orlean said, "—Oh,—well." And then, almost without thinking, she blurted out, "Would you like a cup of coffee?"

"Coffee?!" Clair realized he'd overreacted, so he shrugged, trying to cover up his surprise. "—You got any, here in this house?"

"Oh, yes." Orlean was suddenly aware that she couldn't implicate Melva or Margaret, so she added as casually as she could, "I keep it around, and I drink it all the time. Just as long as the others,—don't know."

"Well. —In that case, sure. I'd like nothin' better'n a good cup a' coffee."

A kettle of water was already hot on the stove and Orlean, who'd made at most a dozen forbidden cups of coffee in her life, couldn't help but be pleased with herself by somehow remembering and knowing the two main questions about coffee. "Milk?" she asked proudly, "—sugar?"

"Black, thanks," Clair said.

That was a relief. Orlean wouldn't have ever been able to guess how much of either to put in.

Over their two cups of coffee, she finally said, "Clair, do you know,—what the other girls will be wearing to the Salt Palace Pavillion?"

Clair shook his head. "No."

She toyed with her cup a moment, and then she said quietly, "—You must know a lot of,—of real smart girls, in Salt Lake and all."

"Well," Clair said, flattered, "I guess I do know a few."

"What I mean is,—if you wanted,—to change your mind about taking me—"

Clair thought about that for a moment, perplexed, and then he suddenly grinned and frowned at her at the same time. "I'm takin' you, Orlean, and you can wear a tent for all I care. Now is that fairly clear?"

"—Yes, Clair."

Later, while she was rinsing the coffee cups out, Clair wandered into the front parlor. In one corner, next to the sofa, there was a beaten old guitar leaning against the wall. She came into the parlor then, and he said, "Does anyone play that?"

"I do," she said. "But not much."

"Could ya,—play somethin'?"

"Gee, I don't know," she said. "I haven't touched it in ages." She picked the guitar up and touched the strings singly and thoughtfully, adjusting the tuning knobs slightly to make the sound right. "I guess I could try, anyway."

Uncertain at first, and then with growing confidence, she started to pick out chords. And finally she began to play, with simple, quiet feeling, "I'll Take You Home Again Kathleen," humming the tune in a soft, low voice.

She'd almost finished the song when there were the sounds of approaching voices in the yard, and hearing them she stopped abruptly.

"Nothin' I ever heard ever sounded nicer," he said. "I always have liked that 'Kathleen' song a lot."

She smiled, leaning the guitar back in the corner. "I'm glad. I always have, too."

Melva and two older, primly dressed church ladies came in the front door as Orlean opened the back, kitchen door for Clair.

"I'll pick ya up Sunday, about seven," he said as he went out.

A moment later Melva came into the kitchen to make some cocoa for her guests. "Comin' up t' the house, I thought for a minute I heard some music."

"I was playing a song for Clair."

Melva got the box of cocoa down from the cupboard. "I was beginnin' t' think you'd never again pick up that old guitar. —Get me the sugar bowl, will you?"

7

The Big Rock Candy Mountain

I'm headed for a land that's far away,
Beside the crystal fountain,
I'll see you all this comin' fall,
In the Big Rock Candy Mountain.
Oh, in the Big Rock Candy Mountain,
You never change your socks,
And little streams of alcohol
Come tricklin' through the rocks,
There's a lake of stew, and of whiskey too,
You can paddle all around them in a big canoe.
Oh, the birds and the bees,
And the cigarette trees,
And the rock an' rye springs,
Where the whang-doodle sings,
In the Big Rock Candy Mountain. . . .

ON SUNDAY, for the first time she could remember, Orlean didn't go to church. Neither the morning nor the evening meeting. She was too busy finishing the new dress she was making, fighting against the seven o'clock deadline while the hands of the clock on the kitchen shelf suddenly seemed to be twirling around as fast as a spinning top. And Melva and Margaret, because of staying to help her, were late even before they started out for the evening meeting.

But Orlean was ready a little before seven, and then the clock's hands came to a complete stop, now not seeming to move at all. Finally she went into the parlor to sit and wait, her hands folded in her lap. After four or five minutes that were more like four or five hours, there was the sound of a light step on the front porch and a soft knock at the door. For a brief moment, as she hurried to the door, the terrifying thought occurred for the first time to Orlean that they might, just possibly might, be going on Clair's motorcycle. And the way she was dressed she couldn't last on a motorcycle for fifty feet.

Opening the door she was immediately relieved to see a sedan parked in the dark before the house, its headlights on and its engine idling quietly. And then Clair stepped into the door's light. He was wearing dark blue pants and a black jacket, with a gleaming white shirt topped by a dark blue bow tie. The tie was slanted at about the same rakish angle that she'd always seen him wear his leather cap, and it looked much better that way to her, somehow, than if it had been stiffly and properly straight.

From Clair's point of view, he couldn't help but think for a fleeting moment that he'd never before seen the young woman now standing in the doorway. Orlean's long dark hair was parted in the middle and fell in soft, waterfall waves to her shoulders, gently framing her face and making her wide brown eyes seem even larger, and faintly, heart-tuggingly wistful. She wore a long, simple white dress with a white knitted shawl over her shoulders. And the single color off-setting the white was a long, happy, yellow silk scarf that was loosely tied around her neck, its two ends falling gracefully before her down to below her waist.

"Well," he said, smiling and groping for the right words, but not being able to find them, "—I see ya decided against wearin' a tent." Her welcoming smile faltered and he added quickly, "I mean, you are a knockout!"

Her smile returned, wider than before. "I'm all ready."

"Let's go."

He shut the front door as she stepped out, then took her elbow to help her to the car. He opened the car door for her to get in, then closed it carefully and went around to get in the driver's side.

As he put the car in gear and started up the street she said, "This is a beautiful automobile."

"It's Sherril's. We're all gettin' t'gether over at his place." Then, after a moment, he said, "Listen, Orlean."

"Yes?"

"There'll be a big crowd at the Pavillion, an' lots of drinkin' an' smokin' an' all, t'night. But I only want you t' do what ya feel like, an' not t' do what ya don't feel like." He paused. "So if anything should some up that ya don't like, just remember that you're with me."

"—I'll remember."

A short time later, Clair pulled to a stop before a well-kept house that was freshly painted and had a new white picket fence around it. He helped Orlean from the car and to the front door where a pretty, orange electric light fixture was turned on. Clair knocked but didn't wait for an answer, opening the door for Orlean to go in.

She entered and Sherril raised a glass toward her from behind a curved bamboo bar in one corner. "Welcome!" he smiled. "Come on in an' make yourself comfortable!"

Wayne and a pretty young girl about his age were seated on a sofa, and as Wayne stood up a little shyly, Sherril said, "I'm Sherril Huffaker, Orlean. I've seen you downtown a couple a' times, but we never met. You know Wayne, an' that big dummy comin' in b'hind ya. An' this here's Guila, from out in Hunter. She's been puttin' up with Wayne, off an' on, for nearly a month now."

Orlean and Guila smiled at each other, and at that moment Vivianne came breezing swiftly out of the kitchen, a drink in one hand and a plate of finger sandwiches in the other. She was a stunning, willowy redhead who exuded good nature and happiness. She was wearing an elegant green dress unlike any that Orlean had ever seen, with shiny silver sequins across the bodice, and a narrow slit that went up to her knee on one side of the skirt. Orlean had heard somewhere that she was from one of the big cities in the state of California, and she probably knew all about the most up-to-date fashions. "You're Orlean and I'm Vivianne," she said, hurrying to put the plate of food on the bamboo bar. "We're really glad you're coming with us!"

"Happy birthday, Vivianne," Orlean said.

Vivianne touched her forehead in mock anguish. "Twenty-two! From now on I swear I'm kissin' out birthdays! Here Orlean, let me put your shawl in the bedroom."

"What're you two drinkin'?" Sherril asked.

"Oh, nothing for me,—yet," Orlean said.

"I'll take a gin an' grapefruit juice," Clair told him.

As they sat down on a matching sofa facing the one Wayne and Guila were seated on, Orlean tried not to be too obvious about how interested she was in the unusual furnishings. Almost everything, including the window drapes, seemed to be done in red velvet. Even the soft, deep carpeting on the floor was a rich rust-red. A lamp on the end table near her was particularly fascinating. The lampshade continually, slowly rotated on its base, and the turning shade, with the light within it, was painted all around in different, colorful, forest-fire scenes. So if you looked at it long enough, it actually seemed like you were watching a small but real forest fire, with living flames burning and silently roaring through the painted trees.

Vivianne came back in and Orlean said, "Your parlor is just lovely, Vivianne."

"Thanks." Then with an infectious laugh Vivianne said, "We're trying our best to make it so modern we can start calling it a living room!"

Sherril brought Clair his drink and Vivianne said, "I might as well take another one, especially since I've sworn off ever again having another birthday."

"Guess outta pure loyalty I gotta join m' bride." Sherril went back behind the bar to start the new drinks.

"If you're gonna keep bringin' up your birthday like that," Clair said, "I guess we might as well give ya your present." He took a small package tied with a ribbon from his pocket. "This is from Wayne an' me." Wayne gave him a quick glance, which Clair ignored. "An' it's from Orlean an' Guila too, just t' make sure there's a lot of love with it."

Smiling and excited, Vivianne took the small package. "Oh, thank you! *All* of you!" She untied the ribbon quickly and opened it. "It's gorgeous!" she exclaimed, taking out a red, enameled pin that was a tiny replica of a ballet dancer.

"Well, everything else around here is red," Clair grinned. "And Sherril's one big fear is that you just might dance 'im t' death."

"I'll wear it tonight! It'll be perfect on my green dress."

Sherril handed Vivianne's drink to her across the bamboo bar. "Somebody might mistake ya for a Christmas tree."

There was another knock on the door and Miles and Evelyn arrived from Murray, carrying a big, pink-ribboned bottle of champagne for Vivianne.

"The damn stuff is supposed t' be imported from France," Miles said gruffly.

"But it's more probably made by some Frenchman in a basement in Salt Lake," Evelyn laughed.

As introductions were being made, Orlean began to feel more and more out of place. This was a sophisticated, worldly and unutterably handsome group. Both Clair and young Wayne could easily be mistaken for matinee idols. And Miles and Sherril were finely dressed, prosperous, good-looking men. But Evelyn! With a sister like her, what would Clair ever be able to see in any other girl? Vivianne was really stunning in a colorful, flamboyant way, but Evelyn was a true beauty, a dark-haired, dark-eyed princess whose every move and every look was filled with regal grace. She had on a classic, simple black dress with just the right amount of her throat showing to wear one perfect strand of large pearls.

But then, when she and Evelyn were introduced, Evelyn came quickly over and hugged her warmly. "I'm so glad to know you, Orlean."

Orlean found herself saying, and meaning it, "—I'm glad to know you too, Evelyn."

Wayne said, "Me an' Guila got t' be goin', or we'll be late for the movie. Anyway, Vivianne, we just stopped by t' wish ya happy birthday."

"I want to thank both of you for the pin."

"Well,—" Wayne hesitated. "It was mostly from Clair."

Shrugging, Clair said, "It's equal, from all of us."

Wayne and Guila left, and Vivianne said, "We'll save the champagne for the Salt Palace, but before we go, let's have one more dash of liquid poison from behind our new bamboo bar." She smiled at Sherril. "It's his birthday present to me."

"It really adds to the room," Evelyn said.

"Hell," Miles snorted, "any bar really adds t' any room."

"It's Hawaiian," Vivianne told them. "Just like they have over there on the beaches at Waikiki."

"I don't mind the seven dollars a month it costs f'r the next fifty years." Sherril grinned. "But it sure was a hard hardship comin' up with that two-dollar cash downpayment."

This time around, Orlean accepted a grapefruit juice, just to have something in her hand, and she noticed that Evelyn only took a tiny bit of gin in hers.

Half kidding, Miles said, "Why don't we take my Packard instead of your Ford, Sherril, an' go first class?"

But Sherril couldn't be baited. He thumped his fist on the bar and said, "Right! Nothin's too good f'r Vivianne on her birthday! We'll go in your fancy god-damned gold chariot!"

They all got into Miles' big Packard sedan some time later, and it was after nine o'clock before they at last drove up to the brilliantly lighted entrance to the huge Salt Palace Pavillion beyond Smelter Town. From the rising mountain ground here, as they got out of the car they could see the vast, heavy-waved Great Salt Lake shimmering dully in the moonlight at a far, dim distance to the north.

There were more cars parked here than Orlean had ever thought existed. Long, unending row upon row of cars stretched out before them and to both sides until they were lost to sight in the far darknesses around the brightly lighted area.

Clair took her hand in his and they walked with the others up a gravel path to the wide stairs leading to the front door. There was a big, hard-faced man in front of the door, but he recognized Sherril and Miles, and waved them all inside with a small, pleasant bow of his head.

Orlean had never been in such a gigantic place. There seemed to be, and maybe were, thousands of people swarming about in the huge ballroom, a great many of them laughing and talking at crowded tables, and many others swaying back and forth under a massive chandelier hanging over the dance floor at the other end of the great room, that seemed to her to be at least a full mile away. And even beyond the dancers under the chandelier, there was a large orchestra playing loud, blaring music that managed impossibly to carry clear to the front door where Orlean could make out vaguely that they were playing "There's Yes Yes in Your Eyes."

Vivianne, happy and laughing, seemed to know a great many people there, and as they were led to a table she waved the be-ribboned bottle of champagne she'd brought, and called out gay greetings to friends along the way.

The head waiter seated them at a table near a window and not too close to the dance floor. "This table's a hot decision," Vivianne approved. And then, to Orlean, "Last time Sherril brought me here we were right by the orchestra, and much as I like music, you couldn't hear yourself think. I was almost sittin' in the drummer's lap!"

"From the looks he was givin' ya," Sherril grinned, "he wouldn't have minded that idea half way."

A waiter came over to take their orders. "Set-ups before dinner?" he asked.

"Would you like ginger ale?" Clair asked Orlean. "Or a juice?"

"Orange juice, I think," she said.

A little later the waiter came back with their set-ups and a silver bucket of ice on a stand to chill Vivianne's champagne.

Orlean wasn't sure just what a set-up was, but now it became clear as Clair, Sherril and Miles all took out pocket flasks. The set-up was whatever mix each person wanted served with ice in a glass. Then hard liquor was added from a flask to complete the drink.

Clair put his flask out on the table and said, "This is from Big Bertha Pearl's own private stock of home brew, if anybody wants t' try some of it."

Sherril said, "You got yourself a customer. Her private stuff's the best booze in Utah."

"Sounds good to me," Vivianne smiled.

But Miles shook his head. "Me an' Evelyn'll stick t' this Scotch."

The two men poured whiskey for themselves and their women, and then Sherril handed Clair back his flask. Clair looked at Orlean, and his question came out sounding more like a statement. "You don't want any a' this, do ya?"

She smiled and shook her head. "I think I'll wait and have some champagne, later, for Vivianne's birthday."

Clair nodded, starting to pour some whiskey into his ginger ale. "That's a real fair deal."

"You bet it is," Vivianne laughed, both her voice and laughter starting to be just a little on the giddy side. "Everybody's got to at least taste it, since I've sworn off birthdays forever."

Evelyn raised her glass. "Here's to a hundred more," she smiled, "but we'll keep every one of them a secret."

Vivianne clicked her glass lightly against Evelyn's. "The rate I'm sailin' along tonight," she giggled, "I just might wind up drinkin' a toast t' each and every one of those next hundred years!" Then with a quiet look at Sherril, she added, "—And to spendin' every one of them with this good man."

At her sudden, unexpected and touching change in mood, there was a warm, silent moment that was felt and shared by everyone at the table.

"Hell!" Sherril finally said. "Up t' now I didn't plan t' live all that long." He stood up, putting his hand out toward Vivianne. "But if we are goin' to, we better start gettin' in shape right now."

"I do believe he's asking me to dance!"

"An' nobody in history ever had t' ask you twice."

She stood up, her hand in his, and they made their way through the tables toward the dance floor. As they got there, the band finished the song it was playing. And then, as the leader now started shaking his baton in swift, jerking movements, they began a fast, ear-splittingly loud version of "Ain't We Got Fun!"

The dance floor erupted in wild movement, and Clair frowned, trying to keep track of Sherril and Vivianne in the frantic crowd. "Boy, if they flap their arms around much faster," he said, "they may take off just like birds, an' fly right up t' the roof!"

But in the suddenly booming roar of music, no one heard him. So he and Miles shrugged at each other, and they both refreshed their drinks.

Evelyn leaned over close to Orlean and said, "I've been wanting to get a chance to tell you, that I just love your dress."

"Oh," Orlean smiled, "I'm so glad! I just didn't know what to wear! And Clair wasn't too much help. He said I could wear a tent as far as he was concerned."

"That sounds like him," Evelyn laughed. "But whatever he says, tents are definitely out this season." She touched the end of the sleeve of Orlean's white dress. "Did you make this yourself?"

Uncertain thoughts rushed swiftly through Orlean's mind. She was still not at all sure of herself, and still overwhelmed at being here for the first time in the elegant Salt Palace Pavillion. And she would rather lie down and die on the spot than in any way embarrass Clair. Perhaps embarrass him by having not had, and having to make, her own dress for such an important night, and then saying so to this worldly, absolute beauty who was Clair's older sister. But then she also remembered what Clair had said, about above all her being with him. "—Yes, I made it." She smiled and added, "As a matter of fact, I just finally finished it about fifteen minutes before Clair came to get me."

"I thought you'd made it." Evelyn touched the sleeve of Orlean's dress, gently, one more time. "It's much too nice to have been bought at a store." Then she smiled and said, "I made this dress that I'm wearing, too. —Do you like it?"

"I really do, Evelyn. And wearing it with those pearls, I think it's the prettiest thing I've ever seen."

They spoke more, suddenly sisters themselves in a quite way, and Orlean learned that Miles owned trucks and equipment and a gravel pit that helped to make roads all through Salt Lake County. Then, a little breathless, Sherril and Vivianne rejoined them.

The menu at the Salt Palace Pavillion was a long, wound-up roll of paper that you had to pull down on, so that it came unrolled and you could read it. But with all its elegance, about the only thing listed on it was T-Bone steak, so that's what they all had.

Just before they'd finished eating, four or five loud men came by the table. Orlean wasn't used to people who drank, so it came as a small shock to her that the people she was with were just happy and laughingly full of fun and life because of drinking, while for the same reason of drinking these strange men were hostile and arrogant as they stopped and stared openly at the women at the table.

In a slurred voice, the biggest man said harshly, "You lucky boys sure got yourselves a purty bunch a' fillies!"

Sherril grinned at him easily, though he was prepared for anything. "An' you sure got terrific taste! How 'bout a drink?"

The big man said, "I'll just plop m'self down an' take that drink with this here lady!"

His friends laughing, he started to sit beside Orlean on the arm of her chair.

"I wouldn't do that," Clair said, standing up.

When he was standing near the big man it was obvious that Clair was greatly outweighed, but he was about the same height, and within his slenderness there was the feeling of tensed, steel cables.

"You gonna stop me?!"

Very quietly, Clair said, "That's right."

"Listen, buster! Ya wanna step outside?!"

"No," Clair said levelly. "But if you push it, I sure will."

They stared at each other for a long moment.

The big man finally shrugged and dropped his eyes. "Ah, the hell with it!"

He and the other men left the table, and Clair sat back down.

Orlean put her hand on his and said in a small voice, "—I was scared."

Clair grinned at her. "—Me too."

But she didn't believe him.

"I tell you," Vivianne said, "I gave the air to parlor snakes like them a long time ago. Just one good bozo, like us three lucky girls got, an' the rest of them cookie-dusters can go jump in the ocean." Then she smiled and said, "Say, it's about time t' open the champagne!"

Sherril opened the bottle with a loud popping sound, and began to pour. Clair looked at Orlean, and she nodded with a faint smile, so he held her glass out for Sherril to fill it along with the others.

"Happy birthday again," Evelyn said as they raised their glasses, and Sherril added laughingly, "Here's t' *no pain,* with *champagne!*"

As Orlean sipped and then put her glass down, Clair said, "Do ya like it?"

"—Yes." And then she nodded. "Yes, I do."

Clair and Miles lighted cigarettes, and Miles leaned over to light one for Vivianne. Orlean watched Sherril, his hands not too steady, as he began rolling his own cigarette, and Clair grinned and said, "Sherril's really takin' to the fancy life t'night."

"Oh? —I always thought store-bought cigarettes were supposed to be fancier than homemade ones."

"Not this kind," Sherril said. "It's a real potent

tobacco clear from Mexico that I smoke on special occasions." He added with grinning pride, "It even got me the first half of a nickname a' mine."

"What's that?" Orlean asked.

Sherril ran his tongue over the cigarette paper. "Marijuana Huffaker."

Clair said, "It's hard t' tell which hits him hardest, that stuff 'r booze."

Sherril lighted it and took a long drag. "—Don't never do nothin' t' me."

"Not much. After a couple a' them smokes, he always starts t' get cross-eyed."

Sherril took another deep puff. "Not me. —But sometimes the rest a' the world starts t' get a little cross-eyed."

"Either way you handsome brute, maybe we'd better get in a couple of dances while we can," Vivianne giggled, "before you start thinking there're two of me!"

"You're on!" Sherril stood up. "God knows just one red-head like you is enough t' handle."

They left as the other two men stood up, and Miles said, "Well, how 'bout you an' me doin' the same, Ev?"

She smiled up at him. "I was beginning to think you'd never ask."

As they also left now, Orlean looked up at Clair, but at the moment he seemed to be looking vaguely somewhere else, and he sat back down beside her.

He made an unconsciously rather elaborate ceremony of lighting another cigarette, and then finally said, "I,—I sure am glad you like that champagne."

"I am too. —I'd have had some anyway, to celebrate with Vivianne. —But it really is good."

"Would,—you like some more?"

"Yes, a little, thank you."

He poured for her, then added a large amount of the whiskey from his flask into the glass of mix before him. Orlean's eyes went past him to the couples quickly gyrating on the dance floor to the loud music. "Sherril and Vivianne, and Miles and Evelyn, sure seem to be having a nice time out there, dancing."

"Yeah, they sure do." Clair glanced at the dancers and then back at the glass before him. "I—was never too much for them fast, modern steps."

Orlean studied him a thoughtful moment and then said, "I agree with you, Clair."

"You do?"

"Um-hmm. Take that Charleston they're doing now. It's a lot better sort of dance for a girl, than for a man."

"Yeah," Clair nodded, relaxing, "I always did favor the good old steps."

Then, as though the orchestra was reading Clair's mind, the fast music suddenly stopped, and they started to play something soft and slow that was faintly familiar to Clair.

"—Like a waltz?" Orlean said.

Clair gripped his glass as though its very weight would make it impossible for him to stand up. "Well,— t' tell the truth, I ain't even waltzed,—in quite awhile."

"Why don't we try?" she asked hopefully. "I can remind you how it goes, and it's real easy."

"Well,—" Clair hesitated.

"Besides, they're playing a song we both like," she encouraged.

Still not recognizing or hardly even hearing the music, Clair managed to say, "—Okay." He stood up and held Orlean's hand in his own suddenly damp palm to take her to the dance floor.

The first few moments were sheer, sweating agony for Clair as he realized for the first time how hard it was to fake a waltz. Trying to grin slightly, he mumbled, "I'm the only fella I know who even steps on his own feet."

"But I can tell that it's all starting to come back to you," Orlean said, gently leading him. "Just remember the rhythm. One, two, three. One, two, three."

After a short while Clair said, "I think I'm gettin' the hang of it. —Again."

A little later Clair became so confident that he now began to lead Orlean, who was as light as a leaf in his arms, and seemed to know every move he was going to make before he knew himself. Soon Clair felt as though the dance floor had changed from an overheated torture chamber to a great, happy and carefree place to be. And relaxing, he started really hearing for the first time the music they were playing. "Hey!" he said. "That song's 'I'll Take You Home Again, Kathleen'! The same thing you hummed an' played on the guitar!"

She nodded, smiling up at him. "I'm glad you asked me for this dance,—because I really love that song, and the name Kathleen."

"If ya think about it," he said, smiling back at her in his new-found confidence, "it could just about be named after you."

"It could?"

"Sure. Orlean and Kathleen sound a whole lot alike, t' me." As the music now reached the right point, he spoke in a half-singing voice along with it, "I'll take you home again, Orlean."

Laughing, she said, "Well, I sure hope sooner or later, that'll be true of tonight, at least."

"If I got a choice," he grinned, "I'll hold out for later."

The music stopped and the band then struck up a blasting rendition of "Don't Bring Lulu."

Suddenly hesitant again, Clair said loudly enough to make himself heard, "That's pretty rambunctious."

Understanding, Orlean simply nodded in agreement, and they went back to their table. "Whew!" she at last said, sitting down, "I was ready for another sip of my champagne, anyway!"

"If you're not used t' that stuff," Clair told her in a gentle voice, "it can kinda sneak up on ya."

"Shouldn't I have any more?"

"Well, I guess if you just finish that second glass it won't hurt."

"All right." She frowned in quiet thought. "—But I really do like it."

Miles and Evelyn came back to the table, and later Sherril and Vivianne returned, both of them flushed and gaily excited from their dancing.

Over newly-made drinks they all joked and laughed together happily for a long while, and then Evelyn finally said, "Clair, you and Orlean looked just wonderful out there on the dance floor. I didn't know you danced."

"He's a very good dancer," Orlean said.

"Talk about dancin'." Miles shook his head slowly. "Sherril, you an' Viv can keep on goin' forever. You ought t' join the marathon dance t'night, an' easy win yourselves that goddamned five-hundred-dollar prize money!"

"No—sirree!" Vivianne gave Sherril a hug with one arm, raising a glass in her free hand. "Real dancin's got t' be only for the love of it, an' not ever for any prize."

"Unless the prize is a redhead," Sherril said, "in which case I'd,—dance on m' hands on the ceilin'."

"Well, hell," Miles shrugged. "I just think ya could win it, is all."

Orlean finished the last few drops of champagne in her glass. And then, hardly realizing it, she said, "I know what Vivianne means."

Everyone looked at her, waiting for her to go on, and she was suddenly at a hopeless loss for words. But the band saved her then, instantly thundering into a roof-shaking roar of jazz that made conversation nearly impossible through the entire Salt Palace Pavillion.

Laughing and inexhaustible, Sherril and Vivianne quickly headed for the dance floor, and soon after Miles and Evelyn followed them. Clair called a waiter over, and Orlean realized that he was trying to pay the bill. But she gathered from his shrugging frown that it had already somehow been taken care of by Sherril.

After the last, crashing sound of music, a new, smaller orchestra started to replace the first one. It was after midnight, and the marathon was now about to begin. Orlean saw that the new dancers were being given large numbers on pieces of cardboard to wear around their necks. And what a difference there was between them and the happy, other couples who were now coming off the floor. Most of the newcomers were shabbily dressed, but more than that their faces and even their spirits seemed somehow to be shabby and wan, each pair of eyes filled with a vacant hopelessness all of their own.

She knew that this was the time to go, and when she looked at Clair she saw that he understood it too.

On the drive back to Sherril's all three of the men, and Vivianne too, had a few drinks from the flasks.

Finally after late goodbyes, while the others were having a nightcap at Sherril's and Vivianne's house, Clair drove her back home in the Model A sedan.

But when he parked quietly in front of Melva's house, despite the unheard of hour, she didn't feel like getting out of the car.

Clair sensed her feeling, and shared it, and not knowing quite what else to do he lighted a cigarette. "—I hope ya—had a good time."

"Oh, I did!"

"I'm sorry,—about that fella tryin' t' sit beside ya."

She smiled in the darkness of the front seat that was lighted only dimly by the tiny, glowing tip of his cigarette. "You were so brave about that bully! —And so afraid, about dancing."

"I've run inta' bullies before," he said. "But t' be really honest, Orlean, I never did get out an' dance, b'fore."

"I know that."

She could feel his sudden, probing look in the dark, and she said, "But you really are good at it. All you have to do, is to not be afraid of dancing."

He was silent for so long that Orlean thought he

might not speak again. But then he said, "You told us you knew what Vivianne meant, about not dancin' for a prize. —What was it you were thinkin'?"

Choosing her words as carefully as she could, she said, "—In a way, dancing is kind of,—like life itself." She paused, trying to explain exactly how she felt. "With either one, you have to do it because you just plain want to do it, and love it. —Not because of some kind of a prize that somebody might maybe hand you say, at the end of the road."

Clair thought about this and then took a long breath that was like a sigh. "—I guess I better take you in."

"I guess so."

They walked to the front door where a lamp had been left just barely burning inside of it to give a tiny light.

At the door, Orlean turned and asked quietly, "Was tonight, the first time, that you ever danced with a girl? —Really?"

"Well." Clair was glad it was dark, so she couldn't see the plain truth on his face. "—Pretty darn close to it."

But she knew the truth, even in the dark. "I'm glad. —And I was probably more scared tonight than you were."

"You? Scared?"

"Melva and Margaret have tried to teach me a little bit. —But you're the first man I ever danced with, too."

"Well, I'll be damned," he said very quietly. "You sure had me fooled on that score."

"—Will I see you then, again?" Her large eyes were softly luminous and sweetly wistful as she looked at him in the dim moonlight cast from above.

"If I got anything at all t' say about it, you sure will." He paused, and then a few good and right-sounding words came to him. "—I don't know why, Orlean. But every time I see you, it's like the first time that I ever did see you, and it's somehow like something happening,—all over again."

She smiled, then reached up to kiss him quickly on the cheek. And in the next moment she was gone, swiftly disappearing through the front door and into the house.

After a long, quiet moment, Clair turned and walked slowly back to the Model A waiting silently and patiently for him to return and drive away on the dark, dusty street.

8

My Heart Stood Still

I took one look at you,
That's all I meant to do,
And then my heart stood still.
My feet could step and walk,
My lips could move and talk,
And yet, my heart stood still.
I never lived at all,
Until the thrill of all,
That moment, when
My heart stood still. . . .

THERE WAS a brief, briskly-cool Indian summer that year, and on three or four Sundays Clair took Orlean out past the tiny settlement of Bacchus and far up on the no longer used, rough and pitted old wagon trail into Starley's Canyon.

Melva disapproved of these Sunday trips for two reasons. One, Orlean was missing church more and more, and even worse didn't seem to mind it at all. And two, they went on Clair's motorcycle, which Melva still couldn't help but consider a minor work of the devil.

But both of her disapprovals were held back, shown only with a slightly raised eyebrow, or voiced only by an occasional, faint sigh. Because, still and always, the far most important thing was Orlean's happiness. And Melva had never in her life seen her little sister so happy as she was now. Even her confidence had grown, and while she was still shy, it was no longer the painful, tongue-tied shyness of before.

From Orlean's point of view, that first ride behind Clair had taken more courage and blind faith than she'd ever known she had. But he'd driven slowly and carefully, feeling her frightened arms holding tightly around him, until gradually she'd become more relaxed and secure. It wasn't too long, as a matter of fact, before Orlean started urging him to higher speeds and tricky turns, but he would never try anything with the slightest risk to it while she was aboard.

On the last of their trips to Starley's Canyon, the brisk Indian summer was already giving way to the cold threat of a bitter, hard winter coming down from the high, northern mountains.

Orlean was wearing an old pair of Levis that Wayne had outgrown and given to her for her cycle riding. She had on a warm jacket, and the rakish, leather cap that Clair had gotten into the habit of loaning her for the rides. On the two-mile, deserted straightaway between Magna and Bacchus Clair opened the cycle up a little, so that as she held onto him, Orlean's long, dark-brown hair trailed out gracefully behind her from underneath the leather cap.

And finally, as they mounted farther up into Starley's Canyon, it became, as always, like entering a whole new world. Gone were the flat, dull grays and blacks that made up Magna and the barren mining-mountain beside it.

Here there was a happy, breezy battle of endless color between the thickly growing trees dressed in their shimmering, deep-autumn leaves. There were even large clumps of hardy, green grass, and here and there vivid, eye-stunning patches of yellow, red and blue wild flowers.

And the air! Since the very first time Clair had brought her up here, Orlean had compared each breath she took with the light, invigorating taste of the champagne she'd tried at the Salt Palace Pavillion. There was a clean, cool, refreshing similarity, but it was this air, finally, that tasted better.

They stopped at a high meadow with a tiny brook running through it, and the sounds of many birds singing from within the trees.

Orlean got out some sandwiches and hard-boiled eggs she'd brought along in the saddlebag of the motorcycle, and they sat next to each other by the small stream to eat.

"—Do you know?" she said. "We're only a few mountains away from Magna, and the mine."

"Yeah?"

"An eagle could fly from here to there,—in ten minutes."

"Never talked to an eagle about it, but I guess that's

about the time it'd take." Then he added, "—It sure is different here, all right."

"I just wish we could,—just stay right here, forever."

"Be kinda hard, with winter comin' on," he grinned. "Unless we took up trappin' for a livin'."

"I'd be willing."

"A big, hungry bear'd git ya, for sure."

"Not with you around." Then she said abruptly, "Do you still,—know,—many of the other girls, from all the other places you've been before?"

"You sure can change a subject fast." He hesitated. "No. I only ever really knew a couple, anyway. An' not for long." He paused again. "I guess,—you're the only one I ever sorta just, started goin' around with,—in a kinda, regular way."

"Do you know why?"

"No." He thought a moment. "It's just a somehow natural thing."

She moved closer to him. "That's nice."

Clair put his arm around her. "It sure seems like it t' me."

After its few, beginning threats against the brief Indian summer, winter suddenly roared in with swift, white fury, its howling winds bringing one freezing blizzard after another. With ashes from stoves, and salt, and heavy, tromping boots, Magna fought against the cloaking whiteness, the dark, poisonous smoke from the mill and the smelter helping to turn the snow there into brackish and shrunken, heavy black sludge. No car was without snow chains on its tires, and even with them they often became hopelessly stuck in the deep snow or icy sludge, or a combination of both.

In these hard winter times travel was limited, and for a young couple to simply and vaguely go outside of an evening was impossible. So under these conditions, Clair finally agreed to having supper now and then with Orlean, at Melva and Al's. But Clair would never come without bringing a gift. The first time it was a bottle of Big Bertha Pearl's best wine, which in a

Mormon home was a mistake. It was accepted with
mumbled appreciation by Melva, who then quietly put
it out of sight in a cupboard. In his own loud, good-
natured way, Al helped by clapping Clair on the shoulder and saying, "We'll keep it around f'r case a'
snakebite!" After that, Clair brought other things, usually a box of chocolates. And even though they were
"family" evenings he enjoyed them, especially when
Margaret and Darrell, happy and carefree in their
bubbling young, and obvious love for each other, were
there too. And sometimes, best of all, they would go
into the parlor after supper, where Orlean would strum
the guitar and sing for them, a thing she hadn't done
for a long time.

The high point of that first part of winter was when
Sherril and Vivianne decided to go on an overnight trip
to Wendover, and asked Clair and Orlean to go with
them. That was a great hardship for Melva, because
Orlean had never in her life spent a night without
being with someone in her family.

When finally it was made clear to Melva that Vivianne would personally look out for Orlean, and that
the late November roads to Nevada weren't too bad,
she at last, although still reluctantly, agreed.

Wendover was a wide-open town on the exact border between Utah and Nevada. Half of it was in one
state, and half in the other. And when they got there,
Clair explained to Orlean how to gamble. With his
explanations in mind, Orlean gambled his quarters on
blackjack, and then at roulette, and at about midnight
she was seven dollars ahead. In the meantime he'd
only lost two dollars, so they came out five dollars
ahead, which was enough for them to take Sherril and
Vivianne to a good dinner.

There was an all-night photograph place there, and
Clair thought the two of them ought to have their
picture taken. So they did, and that picture was the one
souvenir that Orlean brought with her when she got
home late the next day.

A very relieved Melva and she were alone in the kitchen, having a secret cup of coffee together, when she took out the photo envelope and handed it to her big sister.

"A picture?"

Orlean nodded soberly. "—Taken last night."

Melva opened it, looked at it, and muttered, "Oh, my *God!*"

What she was looking at was a very clear photograph of both Clair and Orlean locked up in a jail cell together. Both of them were holding bottles in their hands and had obviously just been arrested. Clair was frowning angrily, while Orlean looked unutterably innocent despite the bottle in her hands, casting her anguished eyes upwards, as though asking personal guidance from the Dear Lord to help her get out of this awful predicament.

"What *happened?!*" Melva cried. But Orlean was already laughing, so that Melva knew it wasn't as bad as it seemed to be.

"It's just a joke! They can take your picture so that it looks like anything! We could have been fat people in funny swimming suits on the beach, or standing in front of the Eiffel Tower!—Or we could have even been pirates, or about to be hanged as horse thieves, if we wanted to!"

Melva took a long, relieved breath and then looked back at the picture of the two of them imprisoned. "—Well!" She took a sip of coffee and coughed a little so that she would have a moment to catch up with her little sister. "—Which pictures, in all of them different, crazy things, did you most want t' be in?"

"Just any one of them. Or maybe even all of them," Orlean said. And then she shrugged thoughtfully. "You know, Melva, none of them could ever be anything but right,—just as long as Clair was there beside me."

Christmas seemed to come that year as suddenly as winter itself. On Christmas Eve, Clair nosed his motorcycle slowly through the snow and eased it up to park it near the dimly lighted kitchen door.

Orlean opened the door and let him in, flushed with

happiness and excitement. She was there alone. Margaret had gone with Darrell to an early church meeting, and Melva and Al were stopping off before church to visit with friends up in Shield's Addition.

"Do you want coffee?" she asked.

"Well," he nodded, "that sounds—"

"First come and see our Christmas tree!"

Taking his hand, she led him quickly through the kitchen to the parlor, where a few candles on a tiny tree in a corner shed dim light through the room. There were strands of popcorn draped around it and its candles, and some colorful pieces of cut-out paper in the shapes of pointed stars and quarter and half-moons and jagged-edged suns tried, with surprising success, to make a small universe of that even smaller tree.

"That really is pretty," Clair said.

"See this?" Orlean touched the largest, silvery-metallic star that gleamed brightly at the top of the small tree, gaily reflecting the lights of the burning candles below.

"Yeah. —It really is nice."

"I made it." She grinned mischievously. "And everybody in the church ward thinks it's the prettiest star around."

"Well," Clair hesitated, wondering at the mischief on her face. "Why shouldn't they?"

Her grin turned into a small, happy giggle. "I made it from the best thing I could find, Clair. It's the bottom of an old coffee can!"

He smiled, shaking his head, and then started laughing along with her. "I'm surprised ya didn't politely offer them all a drink of that wine hidden in the kitchen."

"Oh, darn!" She snapped her fingers. "I knew I'd go and forget something!"

"You sure are in a good mood." He hugged her warmly. "But first of all, little girl, you, Merry Christmas."

They kissed for a long moment, and then she stood back, smiling. "I think I finally got your present right!"

"Got it right?"

"Just in the nick of time! Let's go back into the kitchen!" She quickly put out the candles, and then went before him into the kitchen, adding with a shake of her head, "It seems like I'm always just barely finishing things in the nick of time!"

Sitting at the kitchen table, Clair frowned and repeated to himself, "—You finally got it right? —I know! You've knitted me a purple pair of socks."

Making their coffee at the stove she said, "No."

"Then,—a purple pair of mittens?"

"All those things are wrong. I can't knit."

"You can't?" He frowned again. "—You didn't, by any chance, make me a bracelet out of the tin left over from that old can?"

"You'll never guess!"

"Well, at least, I know ya got it right."

Orlean could hardly wait to empty her cup, and then she said eagerly, "I know it's still not Christmas, but can I give it to you now?!"

"You sure the heck can!" Clair started to get up, but Orlean said, "No, not at the tree! You have to see it in here, where there's good light!" She hurried into the parlor and returned with her hands behind her back. Then, at the last moment she stopped a step away from Clair, suddenly uncertain and hesitant. "—I,—maybe, it isn't right,—after all."

Clair reached out and touched her arm gently. "—Hey, you," he said with soft patience. "—Can I please have my Christmas present?"

She nodded slightly, then slowly brought her arms around from behind her holding a beautifully wrapped package about the size and shape of an oversized but very thin book.

Smiling, he said, "It's got t' be a book a' dancin' instructions."

Orlean shook her head very slightly and handed it to him.

Now holding it, Clair said thoughtfully and seriously, "—A picture of you?"

"—No."

Clair opened it and looked at it. For a long moment he didn't speak. And then finally, in a very low voice, he said, "—My God." It was a large, magnificent pen-and-ink drawing of a proud rider on a splendid, rearing stallion. It was so life-like that he could almost hear the great stallion snorting defiance, could almost feel its mighty hoofs thundering against the earth. And though it took him a moment more to realize it, Clair at last saw that it was he himself who was that proud rider.

As though it were someone else speaking, Clair heard his own voice say, "—You,—did this?"

Orlean nodded a little, standing beside him, and then at last said, "—Do you like it?"

Still holding the drawing in one hand to look at it, he put his other arm around her, his tight hug wordlessly telling her the answer.

After a long silence, Clair put the drawing carefully down on the table within its wrapping paper. Then, with his other arm still around Orlean, he pulled her gently down onto his lap. In a low voice, and with the shadow of a grin, he said, "Well, little girl, you sure have gone an' wrecked me."

"I have?"

"Yep. After that present a' yours,—there ain't nothin' I can ever give ya back."

"Well,—you could try."

"Okay." He sighed and took a small package wrapped in yellow paper and tied with a yellow ribbon from his pocket. "This is the very best item that Woolworth's had t' offer."

Quickly Orlean unwrapped a small box and then opened the box. "—*Oh!*" she murmured, taking out a finely-made, delicate gold necklace with a gold, heart-shaped locket on it, and holding it to the light. "Oh, Clair!" she went on breathlessly, almost frightened by the gleaming gold necklace in her hands. "This must have cost you a *fortune!*"

"The heart part opens," he said.

She hesitated before opening it. "—Is it a picture of you?"

"Funny," he smiled. "That's the same question I asked you before. —In both cases the answer's no."

She opened the locket. Inscribed on one side of the heart was the name "Orlean." And on the other was "Clair."

Slowly, unable to speak, she closed the locket.

Then, when she finally thought she might be able to at least whisper without her voice betraying her, she turned in Clair's lap, handed him the necklace, and asked, "—Would you,—put it on me?"

Later, with the Christmas tree candles burning low, they sat in each other's arms on the sofa, watching the flickering candle-flames dimly lighting the shadowy parlor.

At last Orlean shifted slightly in Clair's arms and looked up at him. "—What are you thinking?"

"Oh,—" He leaned down and kissed her on the forehead. "Lots a' things. Like, maybe, goin' t' some kinda school, so I could get a really good job."

She laid her head close against his chest. "You could do *anything* you ever wanted to."

"Hmmm!" He grinned in the shadows. "You should talk,—drawin' the way you do."

"You didn't mind? —Being on a horse, instead of a motorcycle?"

"Hadn't thought about it. —But I like it best, just the way you did it."

She kissed his shirt softly. "—I'm glad."

After a long moment, he said quietly, "Orlean?"

"Hmmm?"

Then, after another long silence, he said very carefully, "I guess I'm going to have to be the first one to say this." He paused. "—I love you."

Her small body against his became absolutely still, as though everything within her had suddenly stopped in the middle of a breath, and only the warmth of her remained. Then, after an eternity of stillness, Clair faintly felt her begin to breathe again. In a small child's simple, questioning way, she said, "—Why, Clair?"

"I don't know. —I just do."

She looked up at him in the shadows, soft tears glistening dimly in her eyes. "—I've loved you, ever since the very first time that I ever saw you."

He raised her in his arms slightly, so that he could kiss the tears in her eyes. And then, as he hugged her gently back and forth in his embracing arms, he said quietly, "I guess, maybe, I felt that same way you did, at that same time."

"No," she said gently, blinking and smiling up at him through the tears he hadn't quite kissed away. "It took you longer, Clair."

He shrugged. "—Might be, a little bit."

"And—I was afraid, you'd never feel,—the way I do."

"—Afraid?"

"—I wouldn't know what to do, anymore, without you, Clair."

"Then,—don't be afraid," he said, holding her close.

"Tell me a thing," she said. "—How do you start to depend on a man even more than your life itself,—and yet not want to make him feel unhappy, or responsible for all that?"

"Easy," he said, holding her closer and warmer. "The man makes himself responsible, if he's any man at all."

After a minute, Orlean said, "Those candles are burning pretty low on the tree."

"I'll get them." Clair left the sofa and crossed the parlor to blow out the flames. So that when he returned to sit beside her, the room was now totally dark, except for a tiny patch of yellow coming from beneath the closed door to the kitchen.

Curling up in his arms again, she said, "—Can I be your girl, then?"

"I'll take it under consideration." He drew her closer to him. "—Even if you can't knit."

9

Home, Sweet Home

'Mid pleasures and palaces,
Though we may roam,
Be it ever so humble,
There's no place like home.
A charm from the skies,
Seems to hallow us there,
Which, seek through the world,
Is not met with elsewhere. . . .

CLAIR AND Orlean spent all the time they could together during the holidays, and they even stayed up all night on New Year's at a small party at Sherril and Vivianne's, so that it was daylight before Clair finally got her back to Melva's kitchen door.

"Good night," he said. "Or good mornin', dependin' on how ya look at it."

"I like both."

"Yeah. They do both have a natural ring to 'em,—said b'tween us."

"I'll see you here for supper?"

He nodded, then grinned wryly. "Seems like I'm practically livin' here, these days."

"Melva and Al don't mind." She smiled, "And I sure don't. —Besides, they're going out tonight after supper, anyway."

"That's nice of 'em."

She stood on tiptoe and kissed him. "—If you behave, you can help me with the dishes."

He kissed her back. "And if I don't behave?"

"In that case," she smiled, "we'll probably forget all about the dishes." Then, still smiling, she turned and hurried into the house.

And through the coming weeks, it was the same. Whatever time Clair had off from his two jobs was spent with Orlean. They went to a few movies at the Gem Theater, and one night, he even took her to what he called "a smoker," along with Sherril and Vivianne."

"What's a smoker?" she'd asked.

"It's where everybody goes and smokes."

"—Oh."

He laughed. "Maybe you'll like it and maybe you won't, but it's something that everybody ought to at least try once."

"All right,—if you say so, Clair."

Both Clair and Sherril were prepared for the night with flasks and some cigars. They drove to a big building on the outskirts of Salt Lake. Inside, it was crowded and deafeningly noisy, with the smoke of a thousand cigars making the air an almost solid blue haze. There were long, packed rows of benches set up around a raised, brightly lighted and roped-off platform in the center of the huge room, and Orlean suffered silently through two brutal wrestling matches and two bloody prize fights before, finally and mercifully, it was time to go.

On the drive back to Magna, Clair said, "Did you really hate it as much as it looked like you did?"

"Ohhh!" She shuddered slightly. "More."

"Well," Clair shrugged. "I guess it's all a part of learning about life." Then, feeling slightly guilty, he said, "Tell ya what. You were a good sport t'night. So the next thing we do will be anything you want to."

"—Anything?"

"Absolutely."

"Good." She grinned faintly in the dark back seat of the car. "—We'll go to church."

After a long, quiet moment, he said, "—Church?"

"Church." And then she added, "—It's all a part of learning about life."

They'd gone to church and Clair had suffered silently through the seemingly endless meeting.

Afterwards, walking back to Melva's, Orlean clung to Clair's arm on an icy stretch of road, and smiled up at him. "Did you hate it as much as it looked like you did?"

"I just loved it." He grinned down at her. "And

believe it or not, I even saw the light. —I ain't never again takin' you t' no more smokers."

On a darkly overcast Thursday evening, with the heavy threat of a coming, hard snowfall in the air, Clair finished his last delivery of groceries and returned the bicycle to the alley behind Swenson's. Then he gunned his Indian to life and drove through the growing dark to Melva's place.

Orlean heard the motorcycle's engine and opened the kitchen door, calling out before Clair got to it. "Come on in! Boy, it's going to be a cold night!"

"Anybody else home?"

"No." She helped him off with his chilly-feeling leather jacket. "Not for an hour or so."

As almost always now, when they were alone, they had coffee together at the kitchen table.

There was a soft, warm silence as they sipped their coffee, and then Clair said rather suddenly, "For a long time now, I been meanin' to ask you somethin'."

Orlean looked up with slightly startled eyes. "What?"

He laughed. "I didn't mean t' scare ya." Then he said, "But how come you never buy any coffee, and yet always have it on hand?"

She smiled at the question, almost with relief. "I guess it's okay to let the cat out of the bag. Melva and Margaret drink it, too. So, every now and then, when anyone's in Salt Lake, they pick up one or two cans."

"Well, I'll be darned," Clair grinned. "This innocent-lookin' place is just one step away from bein' a Chinese opium den."

Orlean smiled at him slightly, her eyes faintly troubled.

"Hey," he said, frowning a little. "—I promise never t' tell,—no matter how much they torture me."

Her smile widened, but her eyes were still not smiling with her lips.

Suddenly very serious, Clair said, "—What is it, Orlean?" He waited a brief moment and then went on. "There's somethin' on your mind. I been feelin' it for a little while, now."

But still she didn't answer. She looked at him with warm, loving eyes, and then her eyes lowered to quietly study the top of the table between them.

Still frowning slightly, Clair took another sip of coffee. "Don't ya think ya could, tell me? —Hell, honey, the way it's gotten t' be, I'm practically a member of the family."

At these words, she looked back up at him, trying vainly to muster a faint smile. "That,—sort of, touches on it, Clair."

"What does?"

She tried again, without much success, to smile at him. "The family part. —I'm going to have a baby."

There was a sudden, deafening silence in the kitchen, and for a long moment the only thing Clair was really aware of was the steady, slow beat of blood thumping through his left temple.

Finally, as though with someone else's very quiet voice, he said, "If I heard you right. And I think I did. What you meant t' say is,—*'we're* going to have a baby.'"

For the first time now, listening to the quiet words that Clair was saying to her, faint tears began to dampen Orlean's eyes. "—We are?"

Clair nodded and reached his hand across the table to place it gently down on the top of hers. "—But from what little bit I know,—you'll wind up doin' the lion's share."

She turned her hand under his and clasped it, their palms touching together with a sudden, tight, almost fierce warmth, and their eyes meeting with silent, level love across the table.

Finally, Clair said, "That's been a heavy burden f'r you t' carry all alone. Why didn't ya tell me?"

She shook her head slightly, brushing the dampness

from her eyes with her free hand. "At first I didn't know, for sure. And then,—I don't know."

"You are sure though, now?"

She nodded. "I guess I've been afraid of,—well, don't you feel mad, Clair, or scared, or kind of,— trapped?"

He squeezed her hand and managed a small grin to help offset his answer. "I sure do."

"—Which one?"

"All three." He put his other hand out to now clasp her small hand between both of his. "But mostly I feel like, say sometime next week, gettin' married. —If ya will."

Orlean just barely managed to hold back a small sob. "That's a *terrible* reason for you to have to ask me to marry you!"

Clair stood and pulled her up into his warmly embracing arms. "Hell, honey, it's the best reason in the world. That baby'll be born outta pure, simple love, an' that's sure the best way." He kissed both of her cheeks gently, and then grinned lovingly down at her. "B'sides, any old excuse t' do it is as good as another, if ya really feel like spendin' the rest of your life with one special person, in the first place."

"But you were thinking of going to school, of learning, of—"

"Hey," he interrupted quietly. "It seems t' me I just asked you t' marry me, and somehow got cut off there with no answer."

She hugged him hard, her head against his chest. "Oh, *yes!* But you know that!"

Gently, he raised her face up toward his, and they kissed for a long, soft moment. Then he sighed a long, slow sigh, and smiled. "—I never did get engaged t' be married, b'fore."

"—Neither did I."

"—Kinda,—feel like celebratin', just now."

"Me too." Suddenly she smiled beamingly up at him. "And we can, right here!"

Orlean hurried to the cupboard and reached high up to get the unopened bottle of wine that Clair had brought to the house long before.

"Well, I'll be,——" Clair said. "I'm marryin' a very good provider."

They opened the bottle and Clair poured two glasses of wine at the table. And then they lifted their glasses, looking at each other without yet drinking.

"What can ya drink to, at a time like this?" Clair said in a low voice.

"——I don't know."

Moving his glass gently from side to side in his fingers, slightly shifting the suddenly precious and meaningful wine within it, Clair said, "I don't, either. ——Do ya drink t' life, or happiness, or a good marriage?" He hesitated. "God knows it'll be a long haul up there, in front of us. ——The way the world goes, hard an' cruel sometimes darlin', I'd guess there'll be some times when both of us would be willin' t' drink t' just not hurtin' so much, anymore." He paused for a moment, and then his infectious grin started to show itself on his face. "But t' hell with whatever them tough times there are ahead, that'll just naturally be comin' our way." His grin broadened. "You an' me just bein' there t'gether will,——will make everything a thousand times worth anything."

Clair took a long breath. "That's my wish, for this celebratin' wine." And then he said, "Before we drink, ——have you got one?"

Orlean hesitated, thinking deeply of what Clair had said. And then, finally, she spoke quietly. "Yes. I don't know why, or exactly what it means. ——But I thought of it, when you brought me back here on New Year's, and it was already daylight." She stopped and smiled shyly at Clair. "——Some words came to my mind then, that I can't explain, but that I can't get out of my mind. ——When we walked to the door, and when you kissed me.——"

"——Yes?"

"Those words, and the way I felt just then, keep coming back to me. —And right now, I'd like to drink both to what you just said,—and to those words that I can't forget."

They both raised their glasses, and Orlean said very quietly, "—One time,—I saw morning come home."

Later, Melva suddenly came from out of the bitter night and into the warm kitchen with a great gust of cold, blizzard wind, quickly forcing the door shut behind her. Shaking snow from her coat, a package under her arm, she turned to see Clair and Orlean at the table with the open bottle of wine and two glasses before them. Orlean moved to help her, as Clair stood up.

Orlean took the package as Melva shrugged out of her coat. "Wine has never been on that table before," she said. "Did both of you get snake-bit at the same time?"

"Melva," Clair said. "I asked Orlean to marry me, and she said she would."

"Well." Melva hung her coat on a coat-hanger in the corner and said a little brusquely, "I think it's about time."

Then, her back to them, she went to the window, seemingly looking out into the dark for something that wasn't there.

"—Are you glad, Melva?" Orlean finally asked.

Still turned to the window, Melva said, "—If there's another glass, I'll have a small drink of that wine with the two of you, before Al comes home."

It was only when Melva came into the light a moment later, to join them at the table, that Clair and Orlean saw the tears on her cheeks.

Before starting to work at The Smokehouse that night, Clair went to see Big Bertha Pearl in her office. She could see that he had something crucially important on his mind, and she frowned up at him from behind her desk, shifting the massive strings of pearls around her neck. "You look like ya been hit over the head with a twelve-pound sledgehammer."

"I'm,—gettin' married."

She hesitated just long enough to blink once, before answering. "Man usually gets about that same look you got, either way. You better sit down, 'r you'll never last long enough t' make it."

He sat on an overstuffed chair as she came around the desk to sit facing him thoughtfully on a nearby sofa.

"I guess,—the whole idea's just startin' t' sink in," he said.

Studying him quietly, she said, "You sure ya want to Clair? Because,—if certain things're forcin' a marriage that ain't wanted, there's ways t' get around it."

Clair felt his forehead become warmer. "—There's nothin' I ever wanted so much in my life."

Big Bertha was silent for a moment, and then said, "She the one who drew that picture a' you, ya got hangin' up in your room?"

Clair nodded. "Didn't know ya'd seen it."

"Well, I did. An' just judgin' from that alone, I can double guarantee she sure does think the world a' you." Big Bertha hesitated. "—Maybe, almost, even more'n she ought to, Clair."

He looked at her, his eyes faintly surprised and questioning.

"Hell," Big Bertha smiled, "that little girl drew you like a perfect goddamned conquerin' hero,—a Sir Galahad who's already more'n likely found himself half-a-dozen Holy Grails." She paused again. "That's a hard measurement t' live up to."

"The best I can do,—is my best."

For the first and only time, Big Bertha leaned forward and patted Clair's hand twice with her own, heavily bejeweled fingers. "I guess that's just about exactly what you will do." Then she leaned back and was suddenly her normal, businesslike self again. "You came t' see me for two reasons. The second part is t' tell me you're quittin'."

"—I'm sorry about leavin'. But I do have t' get a real job, now."

"Sure ya do." With such a tiny hint of sadness in her voice that Clair didn't hear it, she went on, "No more time f'r you t' just kick around like a kid anymore, an' sorta gradually figure out just what the hell direction y'r goin'." She shrugged, the heavy pearls moving slightly on her neck. "Right now it's gettin' a job, an' full speed ahead. What ya got in mind?"

Clair said, "They ain't hirin' much these days, but I guess I'll try up at the mine t'morrow."

For a moment, Big Bertha looked down silently at the flowered carpet on the floor. "Well, looks like every man ever born around here winds up goin' t' work at that mine, sooner 'r later. —Ya sure that's what you want, Clair?"

"What else is there?"

"Yeah," she sighed. "I guess it is just about the only game in town."

She went back to her desk and quickly wrote a short note on a piece of paper, then put it in an envelope and sealed it. "When ya go up there t'morrow ask t' see Ray Corman, an' give him this."

"Ray Corman?"

"Superintendent Raymond Corman, in the Administration Office. —An' don't let nobody else open the envelope." She handed it to him. "Need any money, Clair?"

"No."

"—Didn't think ya would. An' workin' here or not, go ahead an' use your room as long as ya need, or ya want."

He put the envelope back on her desk. "You're probably the best lady I ever ran into. But the way I am, I can't take nothin' from nobody." He started from her office, then turned and said, "Thanks, anyway."

She came to him and held out the envelope once more. "You take this, an' take care a' yourself."

Still, he hesitated.

"—An' mostly, Clair, you take good care a' the girl who drew that picture."

At these last words, Clair finally nodded, and then took the envelope. "I'll do m' best."

The next morning Clair got some time off from Mr. Swenson and walked up the long, steep path to the mine, where he asked the man at the check-in point how to find the Administration Office. It was a gray, one-story building just above the two facing lines of fine houses that made up the B & G Row, and slightly below the vast, metal work-buildings, smoke-grimed and noisy, looming higher up on the side of the mountain.

On a board hanging from a wall in the entrance of the Administration Building, Clair read down the list of names until he came to "Corman, R. (Supt.) Room 125." Finding the door numbered 125, he hesitated before it briefly, and then knocked.

From within a loud, impatient voice called, "Yeah?! It ain't locked!"

Clair entered the room, taking off his leather cap and closing the door behind him. It was a small room with a plain wooden desk, a few filing cabinets along one wall. Seated at the desk, a window partially open behind him, was a heavy, surly looking man wearing a white shirt with a tie loosened at his throat. "Well?"

"Mr. Corman?"

"Yeah? What ya want?!"

"I'm lookin' for a job."

"You're wastin' your time. We ain't hirin'."

Clair paused, almost ready to turn and leave. Then he stepped to the desk and put the sealed envelope on it. "I was told t' give ya this."

Corman frowned, then ripped it open and read the short note, his frown deepening. After a silent moment, he very systematically and carefully tore both the note and the envelope into very tiny shreds and dropped them into his wastepaper basket. Finally looking back at Clair he said, "—Maybe, if we tried, we could find somethin'."

"I'm willing t' start at any job ya got up here in the mine."

"This here ain't the mine," Corman said gruffly. "This here's the mill. The mine's thirty miles north, up t' Bingham. An' the smelter's off over t'ward Garfield an' Smelter Town."

"Well, yeah—"

"An' they're all joined t'gether by our own railroad, which I'm super of. How d' ya feel about railroads?"

"Good. —Real good."

"You got any school?"

"Eighth, nearly ninth grade. I can read an' write, an' there ain't many arithmetic problems I can't figure out pretty quick."

"Maybe, just maybe, we could use another electrician's helper on them tracks." He nodded to himself, still locked within his constant frown. "Guess we might could put ya on sometime next week."

"Well, Mr. Corman, that sure does sound good t' me."

During the next hectic week everything seemed to happen, and have to be done, at once. Clair explained to Orlean what little he yet knew about his job. "It's seven days a week, an' long days. But it pays twenty-four dollars a week!"

"That's almost a hundred dollars a month!"

"An' I think I found us a house we can live in."

"A whole house?!"

"Well, the house has only got one room, but it's a nice room. It's got a good stove in it. And even runnin' water inside."

Slightly worried, she said, "How much is it?"

"Nineteen dollars a month. That might be a little high, but I think we can fix it up real nice. An' I told 'em it was no deal until you'd seen it."

She saw it, and liked it, and then there were a thousand more decisions to make and things to do.

Clair didn't want a church wedding, but compromised at the idea of being married by a Mormon bishop named Hartkee in the bishop's own house. Melva and Margaret helped Orlean work on her wedding dress, mostly just changing and simplifying her white, earlier Salt Palace Pavillion dress. Her two sisters also tried to help Orlean get the small, one-room house cleaned and partly furnished and as ready as possible.

The first time she and Melva went there, Margaret said, "House? Melva, this ain't a house. It's a garage with the garage door sealed up."

"Don't you never say that t' nobody else," Melva told her. "An' give me a hand with this curtain for the window."

Sherril and Wayne worked with Clair over the weekend to get the rusted old potbellied stove in one corner of the room, with its smudged, wire-held tin chimney sticking up through the ceiling, working again. And both Clair and Orlean bought a very few, needed things for the house.

Finally, on the evening that they were to be married, Clair picked Orlean up at seven o'clock, wearing his new, dark-blue J.C. Penney suit. Sherril and Vivianne were waiting for them in the car on the street as Orlean opened the front door, her eyes radiant.

Wetting his lips slightly, Clair said, "—You ready t' go?"

She nodded wordlessly, and a few minutes later the four of them entered the parlor of Bishop Hartkee's home.

The bishop and his wife were a warm, down-to-earth couple in their fifties. Both of them hugged Orlean and Hartkee shook hands with Clair, nodding cordially toward Sherril and Vivianne. "Well, well," he said, "I baptized this little girl, Orlean Bird, never dreamin' I'd also have the privilege and honor of goin' on an' joinin' her in Holy Matrimony." He smiled at Sherril. "Well, Sherril, we don't seem t' see each other too much these days, but I reckon this very pretty lady beside you is your new bride, Vivianne, and sure as shootin' this nervous young fella is your brother Clair."

Faintly ill at ease, Sherril nodded. "That's right, Bishop."

"He's my best man, Bishop," Clair said.

"Well, you just make yourselves all comfortable and relax. I never lost nobody yet at a weddin' ceremony. Here, let me take your coats."

"Would any of you," Mrs. Hartkee asked, "care for a fresh-made cranberry juice cocktail, in view of the occasion?"

It seemed the only right thing to do, so they all accepted. And a moment later, cranberry juice in hand, Clair got Orlean a little away from the others and said in a low voice, "Listen, I don't want you t' worry about it, but I'm busted."

Her eyes widening in distress, she touched the gold-heart locket she was wearing around her throat and whispered, "I was afraid you spent too much on this."

"No, that was worth more than anything. But after buyin' that little gold ring, an' some a' the plates, an' some knives an' forks, an' that second-hand table an' bed we had t' get, it all sure adds up."

"Oh, I know!"

"I only got seven dollars left. Two ones, an' a five. But with them givin' us cranberry juice an' all, I sure hope it'll add up all right."

"Oh, Clair," she said, grave concern in her eyes. "I'd rather die than for you to be embarrassed."

"Guess all we can do is see what happens." He managed a small grin. "Right now we'll get married. An' then if it turns out we couldn't afford it in the first place, we'll grab the marriage license and make a run for it."

Bishop Hartkee came over to them with two small paper forms to fill out. "This is nothin'," he said easily. "Just put your names, an' dates a' birth, an' like that. Why don't ya sit at the table here? You'll find pens in the drawer."

Part way through the forms, as the others talked a little off to the side, Clair glanced over at what Orlean was writing and suddenly reacted with a sharp, deep breath.

"What?" she asked him quietly.

"You're two months *older* than I am!" he whispered.

"Me?!" She looked over to make sure of what he had written. "Well, we're both just getting started into seventeen. —Do two months really matter?"

"—No. It's just a surprise, an',—"

"In any real and true way, Clair, you're a hundred years older, and smarter, than me."

"—Well," he grinned, "we both just survived the shock, so I guess it's okay."

When Bishop Hartkee was ready for the small, quiet ceremony, it took place just there, in the warm parlor, with a Book of Mormon and a Bible that the bishop placed on that same table.

He read some written words from each of his two Good Books. Then, very sincerely, he quietly spoke his own words about Marriage, about Life and Happiness, about Forsaking All Others, and about being Together in Sickness and Health. And finally, most important, he spoke of Loving and Cherishing, until Death Shall You Part.

Though they simply felt each other and their nearness so much that they didn't really hear most of the quiet words, Clair and Orlean both managed to murmur "I do" at the right time.

"With this ring, I do thee wed."

Sherril gave Clair the simple gold ring they'd bought at the last minute in Salt Lake, and Clair put it on Orlean's finger. It seemed to fit easily and securely, and to belong there.

"I now pronounce you Man and Wife. You may kiss the bride."

Their kiss was very soft and brief. And then it was done.

While Bishop Hartkee's wife was trying unsuccessfully to persuade Sherril and Vivianne into having another glass of cranberry juice, Clair spoke to the bishop.

"—How much do I owe you, sir?"

"The marriage license itself costs two dollars."

"I see." Clair paid him the two dollars. Then, with a glance at Orlean, he said, "But,—there's got t' be some cost t' you, sir."

Bishop Hartkee shrugged, looking vaguely down toward the table. "Well, in cases of marriages like this, here in my home, I usually just charge the new husband a minimum fee of five dollars."

Clair and Orlean looked at each other, and Clair slowly took out his very last remaining money, the five-dollar bill, and handed it to him. "It—was worth more, sir."

Bishop Hartkee took the five-dollar bill and said, "Thank you." Then he added casually, "There's another thing that I usually do at a time like this."

"Yes, sir?" Clair said.

"I also usually give that same five dollars to the new bride, as her first wedding present." He pushed the bill into Orlean's hand. "Now both of you go on and get out of here. It's gettin' late for a Mormon bishop. And God bless the two of you."

They drove to Sherril's where there was a party already started. Melva and Margaret had walked up with Al and Darrell, the four of them bringing a cake Melva had baked. Miles and Evelyn had driven in, and Wayne and Guila were there. And tonight, there were two bottles of champagne, though Orlean's sisters, and Al, settled for soft drinks.

Orlean was so happily and explosively filled up with the idea of having just been married to Clair that she didn't even quite know or care where she was, or what was happening, and she hardly noticed the second glass of champagne that was poured for her.

All she knew was that at one point she turned to Clair and said softly, "Can we go home?"

And he said equally softly, "Yes."

Sherril took them down, and left with a small wave of his hand as he drove away up the street.

They walked toward the door through some new-fallen snow, its hardening surface crunching back coldly at them under the weight of their steps.

At the door she stopped and quietly said, "—I've never,—gone into a home, like this, before."

"—Neither have I. I'm supposed t' carry ya, I guess."

"Do you want to?"

"Well,—yes. If I can do it without slippin' on the ice out here, an' injurin' us both on our wedding night." He opened the door, lifted her easily and stepped inside, then kissed her gently and put her down. Striking a match he lighted the kerosene lamp on the table. As the light glowed higher, Orlean shut the door against the cold and looked around her. There was one frostbitten window near a small sink. The old pot-bellied stove was giving a small hint of faint yellow heat glowing bravely and dimly from the uneven cracks of the stove's square door. A small bed, a wobbly table and two chairs were in the center of the room. And other than that, only the kerosene lamp on the table, that Clair had just lighted.

"It sure still ain't much." He shook out the match as it started to burn his fingers.

"Clair," she said, softly.

"Yeah?"

"—I've never loved any place as much as this, in my life."

10

Casey Jones

Come, all you rounders, if you want to hear,
A story 'bout a brave engineer.
Casey Jones, he mounted to the cabin,
Casey Jones, with his orders in his hand,
Casey Jones, put his hand upon the throttle,
And he took a farewell trip,
Into the promised land . . .
Casey Jones, there's two locomotives,
Casey Jones, you oughta' jump,
Casey Jones, two locomotives,
There's two locomotives that's a goin' to bump. . . .

IN TIME, spring began to make its gentle but irresistible advances toward the icy giant of winter. And then, almost as though it had all magically happened in one day, winter was gone, leaving only snow-capped high peaks in the distance as a silent reminder that it was never defeated forever.

And then summer was suddenly there, balancing the past winter's freezing cold and ice with its newly arrived blistering heat and dust.

The time was passing so quickly for Clair and Orlean that they hardly noticed it. Neither of them had ever been so happy or so busy in their lives. And September, the time the baby was due, seemed to be rushing toward them with unbelievable speed.

With Clair working seven days a week, usually about a ten-hour day, they didn't have much time together, but the time they did have was constantly new and warm and rich.

From his very first day of working on the railroad, Clair had begun to study any books on electricity and railroading that he could find, as often as he could at night by the light of the kerosene lamp on the table. And whenever he could, Sherril, a master electrician, would stop by to help him in his learning.

One night while she was doing the dishes at the sink, Orlean felt a sudden, inner movement for the first time in her swollen stomach and almost dropped the plate in her hands. "Clair!" she said. "The baby moved!"

Looking up with startled eyes from where he was studying at the table, he really did drop the book in his hands, and hurried anxiously to her. "Are you all right?! Does it hurt?!"

"—No." She put her hand to her stomach. "It just,— surprised the dickens out of me."

"Here, sit down."

"No, honestly I'm fine."

"You sure?"

"Yes, just fine."

After a moment he took a deep breath. "—What did it feel like?"

She paused thoughtfully. "It felt like a hiccup,—only farther down."

Finally, both convinced and relieved, Clair grinned. "Do you think it was you, or the baby, who hiccupped?"

"Oh, you!" she smiled. "Let me finish the dishes."

She turned to the sink and he went back to his book. Working with her back to him, she said quietly, "Clair?"

"Yeah?"

"—It won't be long, now."

"No, it sure won't."

Then she continued, still quietly. "I saw your mother today, on Main Street."

He lowered the book and looked toward where she was drying dishes, her back still to him. "—Oh?"

"She crossed the street, so we wouldn't pass by each other."

"Maybe, she just didn't see you, or even know who you were. But,—she does act in, kinda funny ways, sometimes."

Orlean finished drying the last cup and put it on the sink before turning slowly toward him. "Clair, why haven't we ever been in their home? Why,—weren't they even at our wedding party?"

"They were asked, honey. Through Wayne."

"Oh. —I've always known, of course, that there's something terribly wrong between you. And a lot of times I've had to bite my tongue to keep from asking you to tell me about it."

He shrugged, frowning sadly. "I,—wouldn't even really know, quite where, 'r how t' begin."

"Oh, darling!" she said quickly and gently. "I'm not asking you now, either! But, they're about to become grandparents for the first time in their lives. And,—they'll be the only grandparents our child will have." She paused briefly. "It would be so unfair for them not to have a chance to know and love each other."

Clair nodded silently at her words, but Orlean could see the look of deep, thoughtful sadness in his eyes. So she smiled at him, her smile dismissing the subject, and sat in the chair beside him at the table. "—Well then, dear husband, have you learned very much sitting here with these books, while I've been slaving over a hot sink?"

A faint grin began to toy at the edges of Clair's mouth. "—At this point, dear wife, there is no question but what I know everything there is in the world to know about electricity."

"Everything?"

"Absolutely. I have now finally even figured out how t' spell 'electricity,' which is, generally, considered t' be the hardest part of all."

"—Wow." She nodded gravely. "How come, with all you know about electricity, dear husband, we are still sitting here with a kerosene lamp?"

"Because with all I know, dear wife, it's safer."

Orlean picked up a slender blue notebook that Clair had been writing in, and opening it read, " 'Clair Huffaker. Signal Department.' " She tilted her head slightly to one side. "That's very good, so far."

"Thought you'd like it."

Then, with a growing frown, she continued reading. " 'Thickness Gauge of Relay. —Ten-thousandths to Twelve-thousandths of Trunion Play. —Fifteen-thousandths from Armature to Cores. —Ten-thousandths in Wipe from Pickup to Normal.' "

"It gets even more fascinatin'," Clair told her.

She shook her head slightly and continued reading. " 'Thirty-thousandths between Carbon and Contact on

Polar Relay. —Polish Trunions and Adjust Carbons.' "
Then she closed the notebook and put it down. "—I
think I've learned enough for one night."

Clair's grin had become broad and easy. "At least ya
know what I really am, now. I'm an official Carbon-
Adjuster an' Trunion-Polisher."

"It certainly is an honor to meet you."

"Don't let it go t' your head."

About a month later, fairly late in his workday,
Clair got an order at the Signal Department Office to
take a One-man up the tracks to the mine at Bingham
and repair a relay signal that had been reported out of
order. This was the part of his job that Clair liked best.
The One-man was a small, completely open, gas-
powered inspection and emergency vehicle that could
literally fly along the tracks when it was opened up to
its top speed. Except for its four, small iron wheels, it
looked almost like a Model A Sedan with the car's
body taken off and its seats removed. It was just big
enough to carry a limited amount of emergency equipment in the front and one or sometimes two men
standing at the back and driving it.

Clair signed out for the tools he'd need and walked
up the path with them to the sidetracks where a One-
man was waiting. He checked the gas and oil, and then
started the engine, idling it at first.

A little later he was speeding up the gradually
sloping railroad tracks toward far-off Bingham, the
cooling September air playing with his hair under his
leather cap. About twenty miles along the way there
was a warning signal of a train coming down toward
him, and he pulled his One-man off onto a spur to wait
for it to pass. A few minutes later there was a growing
thunder in the distance, and the earth began to tremble
slightly. Then the ore train came roaring into sight
through a rocky canyon on its swift, downhill trip to the
mill at Magna. Behind the big, powerful locomotive
there were about fifty huge iron cars, each loaded high
with large boulders of rough, rock ore from the mine

that were to be broken down, crushed and processed at the mill. As the massive train rumbled by, now shaking the earth so strongly that the One-man's engine stalled, Clair waved off toward it, and the fireman and engineer on the passing locomotive waved back. And then, in a final, receding thunder of sound and speed, the train had gone by and the way was clear again.

Clair backed his One-man off the spur onto the main track and started up toward Bingham again. A few minutes later, he entered the first tunnel, the entrance signals telling him that it was all clear. It was a long, dark tunnel, running from one end to the other about five miles under a high ridge of mountains. He came out of it, briefly, into the daylight at the top part of the town of Bingham. Here, steep, high cliffs fell almost straight down into a razor-like narrowness at the bottom of the long canyon, where often there was only room between the cliffs for one small, mountain-hanging house and the tiny road itself winding patiently up toward the hidden mine above. Clair had heard that Bingham was the longest, skinniest town in the world, and from this present point of view there was every reason to believe it was true.

Soon he was into the second, shorter tunnel. And when he emerged from it, the world suddenly, instantly became a thousand times larger to his eyes. He came out on the "Pit," the largest open-cut copper mine in the world. It was one, gigantic hole, huge enough to have taken mountains out of the way, that over the years had been dug into the earth. On any one of its countless, down-reaching, railroaded levels, an entire ore train at the far side of the Pit looked tiny enough to pick up in one hand. An immense, ore-dislodging and mountain-shattering blast of dynamite could be set off at the other end of the Pit, and it could only be recognized by a finger-tip puff of quickly disappearing white smoke and, seconds later, a vague, distant sensation that was more of a faint curiosity than a sound.

Clair drove his One-man down to the seventh level and found the faulty signal, a yellow-flasher indicating

caution. The problem was simply a wire dangling away
from its contact, probably jarred loose by the millions
of tons of ore trains constantly lumbering by. Clair had
it fixed in minutes, and started his One-man just in
time to get up the track and out of the way of a huge
ore train that rumbled slowly by, guided into its
slowness by the now working yellow-flasher.

By the time Clair got back down through the five-
mile-long tunnel, where it was eternally pitch-black
night, the sun had set and daylight was almost gone.
And he at last brought his One-man to a stop at the
mill in the full darkness of night.

He walked down to the Signal Office and filled out
his report, then went out to the nearby toolshed to
check in his equipment. Old man Kilmer, who ran the
toolshed, carefully and methodically checked in Clair's
gear. He then, almost as an afterthought, said, "Oh,
say, Huffaker. There was a message come in f'r
you."

"Yeah?"

"Yeah. —Seems like y're wife's havin' a baby."

"Goddamnit, why didn't ya *tell* me?!"

"I just did."

But by then Clair was already gone. He raced headlong down the long, dark path toward the dim lights of
Magna in the distance below, and by the time he got
there his heart was beating at the inside of his chest
savagely, and his heavy, rapid breaths were burning
and choking against each other in his throat. But still
he kept on running, and the few people he passed on
Main Street looked at him curiously. A little later he
turned up on Fourth East, and finally, almost ready to
fall down, he arrived at his small home.

Melva was standing just outside the door, and light
was coming from the window. Clair came to a stop in
front of her and managed to say, "—How is she?"

"She looks a lot better than you do." Melva smiled.
"—It's a boy."

The door opened and Dr. Sloan came out, ready to
leave. "Fine boy, Clair. Why don't you go on in?"

Both he and Melva walked away, and Clair, taking off his cap, opened the door and stepped inside.

Orlean smiled quietly up at him from the bed, holding a small, nearly invisible lump of life wrapped in a blanket in her arms.

Cap in hand, Clair stepped slowly over to the bed. And finally, in a low voice he said, "—Well."

"—Everything's just fine," she said. "—Would you like to meet your son?"

Clair reached down and touched the sleeping boy's forehead gently. "—I guess we'll have t' teach 'im t' shake hands."

She smiled again. "Melva was here all the time, and then the doctor came. It was a lot easier than I'd thought it would be."

Clair nodded slightly, still a little exhausted and dazed. "—How old is he?"

"About two hours."

He leaned down and kissed her softly. Then he said, "Could ya drink some coffee, if I made it?"

"Sure."

A little later they were sipping coffee, and Clair had pulled a chair up beside the bed to sit near her. "I guess," he said, "now that we know its gender, we'll have t' give the little rascal a name. Actually, I've thought of at least a hundred. But I kinda think 'Wayne' would be nice."

"Clair," she said.

"Yeah?"

"No, I mean the name 'Clair.' That's the name I want to give him."

Frowning and deadly serious, he said, "You got t' be jokin', honey. That'd be a terrible thing t' do to a two-hour-old kid."

She just smiled slightly, without answering.

"Listen," Clair went on. "D' you know how much trouble a kid can get into with a sissy name like that? Without even tryin'?"

There was still no answer.

"B'sides, even worse, that'd make him a Junior. An'

I don't want no kid a' mine t' have t' go through life bein' a 'Clair' an' then a 'Junior' on top a' that." He hesitated. "How 'bout John, 'r Robert,—'r Chester?"

"Darling," she said softly and quietly. "You can call him whatever you want. —But I'm going to call him Clair."

"Well," he said with a faint, slightly defeated grin, "that could get t' be kinda confusin' for 'im."

"And being your son, he'll never be a 'Junior' to anybody. —Except to one man. You."

Clair reached over and touched the still sleeping baby's forehead once more. "—The size he is right now, I guess the name 'Little Clair' wouldn't be too far wrong."

She blinked back the beginning of a tear. "—Then, it's all right, with you?"

"Yeah. —Sure it is."

"—Thank you, Clair."

He took her hand and held it in his. "—Ya know, honey. —If they made butterflies outta iron,—you'd sure be one of 'em."

Two months later, Melva stopped by in the early evening on one of her daily visits. Orlean was wearing her good blue dress with the white polka dots on it. Her hair was richly brushed and held softly with a yellow ribbon. She was getting Little Clair ready for something special, putting a red, knitted cap on the boy that Evelyn had made for him.

"Well," Melva said, "it looks like he's gettin' ready for his first big night out on the town."

Orlean adjusted the red-knit cap at a rakish angle on his head and said, "As soon as Clair gets home, the three of us are all going to go meet his parents. —This little tyke's grandparents."

"That's nice, 'Lean."

"Clair's really excited." Orlean's own excitement showed in her voice. "Funny, Wayne sort of had to make an appointment for us to go see them."

"Well, it's not too hard t' see, that Clair and his folks aren't all that close."

Orlean tickled the baby under his chubby cheek, making a face at him, and he grinned back in toothless appreciation. "You'll make them get back together, won't you!"

Clair got home a few minutes after Melva had left, and he was not only excited and nervous, but exuberantly happy about something. He kissed Orlean, then growled into the baby's ear until it was giggling convulsively.

Finally Orlean found herself laughing helplessly along with the contagious laughter of the boy, and then she at last managed to say, "—Are you going to go on growling at that poor child all night?"

"My dear woman," Clair said, kissing the boy's ear and standing up. "You are not speaking to an Electrician's Helper anymore."

"Was I before?"

"In my experience," he grinned, "I have found that life comes in two flavors, good and bad,—with maybe a dash of pistachio in-between."

"When did you make that up?"

"Just now." He hugged her, sweeping her slightly off her feet. "Honey, I'm an Electrician's *Assistant!* And I'm not making twenty-four dollars a week anymore, but twenty-*eight!*"

"Oh!" she said, hugging him back. "And what a *wonderful* time for it to happen! Your parents will be so proud of you tonight!"

"—I hope so." Clair hugged her again, then washed quickly and changed into his blue J.C. Penney suit.

"You sure are getting fancy," Orlean said.

"Have to, t' keep up with the two a' you."

They walked the eight or nine zigzagging blocks across town to where Clair's parents lived. Clair carried the baby all the way. But on the front porch, before knocking, he handed the small bundle of sleeping life to Orlean. Then, neither hard nor soft, but just firmly, he knocked at the door.

Mr. Huffaker answered the door, paunchy and uneasy, and smiling at the same time in his shirt sleeves. "Well, well, well, just come right on in and make yourselves right at home. You'll be little Orlean. I've known your family for years. What a cute little fella ya got there."

"How are you, Dad?" Clair said.

"Oh, just fine, just fine! Enzy'll be out in just a minute, now." And then, suddenly, he seemed to run out of any other words to say.

They were all standing in the middle of the parlor, now wrapped in the middle of the sudden silence. Orlean finally smiled and said, "—I'll just put the baby down, Mr. Huffaker."

She went to the sofa and laid him down on it, gently resting his head on a pillow that was there.

And then Enzy came into the room.

The first thing that she seemed to see was the baby on the sofa. She walked directly to the child, ignoring everything else, leaned down and jerked the pillow out from under its head. "He'll dirty it! And this is my good pillow from San Diego!" She glared at her husband. "You should know better than let her put him on it, Frank!"

"Well, I didn't think,—"

"You didn't think!" She turned, and leaving the room said, "I'll go get him an old one!"

In the stunned silence, Orlean picked the baby up and said very quietly, "—Let's go, Clair."

Clair looked at his father and said, "It's best, Dad."

The older man's heavy-lidded gaze fell to the floor. "—Maybe so."

On the walk home, Clair took the baby to carry him, and Orlean held his arm, walking close to him on the dark street.

"Honey," he said. "—I'm sorry."

"—Don't feel too bad, Clair."

"I'm fine. —Just, kinda worried about you."

She held his arm tighter, walking even closer to him

on the deeply shadowed street. "Somehow, tonight made me think of some words that come from way back in my memory, and make me know more about why you're as strong as you are."

"What are the words?"

"—I asked God for strength,—and He gave me problems."

And then, soon, they were home.

Another winter, and then another, came and went, and all the seasons were filled with rich, warm times. The boy learned to walk early, and soon after that decided that the only way to get from one place to another was at a dead run. Soon he was talking, too, and whenever he had anything to say his words came out of him on a dead run also, excited and mispronounced and spilling swiftly out of him in an eager stream of enthusiasm.

In the spring following that second winter, two important things happened. First, the savings they'd been putting aside reached the unheard of sum of three-hundred dollars, enough for a downpayment toward buying a two, or maybe even a three-room house. And second, Orlean became pregnant again.

To celebrate, they left Little Clair with Melva one night and went with Sherril and Vivianne to the Hotel Utah in Salt Lake for dinner.

On the way home, Orlean was half dozing against Clair's arm in the back seat of the car when he leaned down and touched her forehead with his lips. "Honey?"

"—Mmm?"

"Try t' make it a girl this time."

"Why?"

"I'd sure hate t' have another guy named Clair, all in one family."

"—I'll try." She smiled and then dozed off again.

The next morning Clair got another order for an emergency repair job at the Bingham mine. "What's the trouble?" he asked the dispatcher.

"Hell, I ain't real sure. Looks like there's about three signals ain't workin' up t' the Pit. Might be a whole series a' relays on the blink." He shrugged. "Just go on up t' the Pit an' check 'er out, if it takes ya all day."

"Okay."

A little later Clair was speeding up the sunny, wind-swept tracks on his One-man. About fifteen miles along the way a signal warned of an approaching train, and he drove off onto a spur. Soon the giant locomotive and its quarter-mile-long trail of huge ore cars thundered swiftly and deafeningly by, shaking the earth as it passed.

Clair and the engineer waved to each other, and within a few minutes Clair was flying up along the tracks again on his One-man. Still making good time, he came into sight of the downhill mouth of the five-mile tunnel. The signal showed the tunnel was clear, so he sped into the entrance and was almost instantly surrounded by the eternal, black night within the long, narrow tunnel.

Clair switched on the single, small headlight on the One-man. Not that it did much good, but he could at least see a few yards of the gradually winding track before him, and could make out the darkly-damp, glistening walls rushing by a few feet to each side of him.

It was hard to estimate time and space within this unchanging, endless darkness, but Clair guessed he was about halfway through the tunnel when, for no knowable reason, he had a chilling, terrifying premonition of something being in the tunnel before him. Perhaps it was the tiniest hint of a faintly changing rhythm and feeling of the rails beneath the small iron wheels of the One-man.

But by then it was too late.

And what happened next took place in less than ten seconds.

Now the earth did begin to shake. And then there was the noise, a million crashing thunderbolts of screaming noise from the darkness ahead striking Clair with such force that it seemed the incredible power of sound itself would tear away his fiercely straining grip on the One-man and hurl him off of it.

An instant later there was the light. A giant, dazzling ball of flaming white light that suddenly loomed into sight and sped toward him hugely and blindingly from around the curving track ahead.

In a brief moment of icy, calm clarity that grimly accepted inescapable death thundering down upon him, Clair realized that the signal relay problems were not at the Pit only, but that they extended many miles down the track, to and including the warning signal at the tunnel entrance. And as the locomotive hurtled toward him, he realized in that same instant that not only was there no time to jump, but with the tunnel walls so close to each side of him, there was no place to jump.

And then there was the horrendous crash.

Yet to Clair, suddenly, there was no longer any more sound or feeling. His world simply went violently, soundlessly and, mercifully, painlessly insane. He was flying and spinning wildly through the air, smashing up against the tunnel ceiling, then smashing again crushingly against the side of a giant, speeding ore car, then careening off and crashing into the wall of the tunnel.

And then, oblivion.

In the cab of the huge, speeding locomotive, there had only been the vague sensation of a faint, brief thumping.

Cupping his hand against the engineer's ear, and shouting as loud as he could to be heard, the fireman yelled, "You feel somethin', just then?!"

The engineer nodded and shouted back, "Last train musta dropped a big rock off onta the rail!"

Somehow, lying on his back, Clair opened his eyes numbly and saw monstrous ore cars thundering above him, their giant iron wheels sparking and screeching by so close to his shoulder and head that he could have reached out and touched them without hardly moving his hand. Then, as though it belonged to someone else, he noticed that one of his legs was lying across the track, being run over again and again by the huge, screaming iron wheels. With one hand, he tugged weakly at the bloody pants encasing what was left of his leg, finally pulling it from the track.

Looking up at the ore cars roaring overhead, Clair wondered vaguely if one of the big, high-loaded boulders would fall off and crush him.

And then, again, oblivion.

11

Red Wing

. . . She loved a warrior bold,
This shy little maid of old,
But brave and gay he rode one day,
To battle far away.
She watched for him day and night,
She kept all the campfires bright,
But far, far away, her warrior gay,
Fell bravely in the fray.
Oh, the moon shines tonight on pretty Red Wing,
The breezes sighing, the night birds crying,
For far 'neath the stars her brave is sleeping,
While Red Wing's weeping,
Her heart away. . . .

"Red Wing," words by Thurland Chattaway, music by Kerry Mills © MCMLVII by F. A. Mills. Copyright renewed. Assigned to and used with permission of Shawnee Press, Inc., Delaware Water Gap, Pa. 18327.

THERE WAS a loud, fast knocking at the door, and Orlean crossed the room, from where she was taking a loaf of fresh-baked bread from the stove, to answer it.

Sherril was standing in the dark there, the muscles in his usually smiling face held so tight that he almost looked like a stranger. Wayne was just behind him, eyes already red, but fighting bravely against further tears.

"What is it?" Orlean asked quietly, though the look of them almost made her heart stop beating.

"—Clair," Sherril managed to say.

Already Orlean was feeling those bitter, stinging tears that flow backward, but her eyes stayed dry and her voice was calm. "Is he dead?"

Sherril wet his lips. "Don't know. —He had a real bad accident in the main tunnel. They just told me and I come an' got Wayne, an' you."

"Where is he?"

"Ambulance is takin' him t' Saint Mark's in Salt Lake. Ya better get ready as fast as ya can."

"I'm ready." Orlean scooped up Little Clair from his crib and grabbed a blanket to wrap him in on her way out the door. They walked quickly to Sherril's Model A sedan parked in the street with its motor still running.

Wayne helped Orlean into the front seat with Little Clair in her lap, then hurried to get into the back seat as Sherril shifted into gear and sped away.

Arranging the blanket warmingly around her half-asleep son, Orlean said in a still calm and quiet voice, "—Do you know what happened?"

"Not a whole lot." Sherril slowed very slightly, and then sped on through a stop sign. "Him an' his One-man got run into by a ore-train comin' down outta Bingham." He rubbed the back of his hand roughly against his cheek. "Nobody even knew about it for a damn long time. It was a goddamned miracle that he was still alive when they finally found 'im."

Orlean said in a low voice, "—He's awfully strong."

Speeding along, Sherril glanced briefly at Orlean then turned his attention back to the road ahead. "—You know I sure do love you, Orlean. And all that any of us can do right now is t' hope. —But from what I been told, chances're awful slim of him even makin' it t' the hospital." He hesitated and cleared his throat slightly. "—Just don't build up your hopes too high, is all I'm tryin' t' say, honey."

Again she said, in a low voice, "—He's awful strong."

And nothing more was said until they got to the Hospital of Saint Mark in Salt Lake.

Sherril and Wayne each held one of the main double-doors open to let Orlean carry her sleeping boy into the hospital entrance, where there was the instant, heavy and nauseating smell of chloroform.

Sherril whispered briefly to the stiffly starched nurse at the reception desk, and then he told Orlean and Wayne in a hushed voice, "He's here. —He's still alive." Sherril took a deep breath. "He's bein' operated on right now."

Orlean seemed to only be able to say one single thing, and she now repeated it quietly for the third time. "—He's very strong."

"Nurse says there's a waitin' room," Sherril said. "Up on the third floor."

The waiting room was small and airless, with one closed window and a few straight-backed chairs in it.

And here the constant odor of chloroform in the air was even more sickening.

Orlean sat down with Little Clair in her lap, and the men sat near her.

"Can I,—ya want me t' hold him awhile?" Wayne asked.

She shook her head silently.

It was a long, almost wordless night. Sherril chain-smoked cigarettes, and once in a while he walked down the hall to whisper to a night nurse sitting there, but she never seemed to know anything. Sometime after midnight he said softly, "—I guess no news is good news. He must be holdin' on." And then, "—You okay, 'Lean?"

She nodded, but still said nothing.

Daylight was beginning to show faintly through the single window when a haggard, slender man of about fifty, wearing a rumpled gray smock, quietly entered the room.

"Mrs. Huffaker?" he asked.

"—Yes."

"Your husband is doing as well as can be expected." He hesitated. "But there is a,—problem."

At their voices, or perhaps the slightly increased tension in Orlean's arms, the little boy began to wake up. Orlean handed him toward Wayne and said, "Please." Realizing that she didn't want the child to hear, and perhaps understand, Wayne took him gently, and Orlean and Sherril went out of the room with the other man.

In the corridor he turned to them, briefly rubbing his exhausted eyes with one hand. "I'm Dr. Hughes."

"Will he live?" she asked.

"It's too early to know for certain. Frankly, it's a miracle that he's survived through the night. We've had to give him enormous amounts of blood, but he seems to be reacting well to it. He has a concussion, and several fractures."

Orlean took a long, deep breath. "—The problem?"

He hesitated. "Young lady, perhaps you should come to my office and sit down."

"I'm all right, Doctor."

"Very well. —His right leg is practically completely severed, a few inches below the knee. I'm afraid we'll have to remove it."

After a moment, she said, "—There must be *some* chance of saving it,—isn't there?"

"Mrs. Huffaker, I have to be honest with you. It isn't a—clean severance. It's rather as though three or four inches of the bone and muscle tissue have been completely pulverized and crushed. I believe one or more train wheels passed over it. There's a very real danger of gangrene, or blood poisoning. Not to even mention countless months in the hospital, plus the huge expenses. And given only one remote chance in a million of saving it, amputation is medically the only possible answer."

She looked at him quietly. "—Is it my decision?"

"You're his wife, young lady."

"—Try to save his leg."

There was a long moment of silence that was finally broken by a short, frightened wail from the child in the waiting room behind them, who now awakened and was bewildered by his strange surroundings. Orlean turned and went back in to comfort him.

Sherril said, "I'm his brother, Doctor. —How come, in the name a' God, didn't he bleed t' death all that time he was in the tunnel?"

"He would have, except that his pantleg somehow became twisted around his thigh tightly enough to form an accidental but fairly effective tourniquet."

Sherril shook his head at this and exhaled a long, hard breath. "Boy, seems ya sure can't never tell what this old world's got t' offer, good or bad, at any damn minute."

Dr. Hughes nodded very faintly and tiredly. "His concussion alone could have been fatal. Your brother has an incredible will to live,—amazing strength."

Sherril glanced briefly back toward the waiting

room, where Orlean had now soothed the frightened child. "That's all she said the whole night. —About him bein' so strong."

Dr. Hughes looked toward the room with thoughtful eyes. "How old is that little girl he's married to?"

"Nineteen, I think."

"—Your brother's not the only strong one in that young family." Then he turned and walked slowly away, down the long hospital corridor.

A few minutes later, while it was still before sunup, Melva and Margaret came into the waiting room. They'd just learned about the accident from Al, who had dropped them at the hospital and gone on in the car he'd borrowed from a friend to tell Miles and Evelyn.

As Sherril started to quietly tell them about how Clair was, Melva gently took Little Clair into her own lap, and Margaret began to unwrap a still-warm bowl of oatmeal that they'd brought along for the boy.

But Orlean just couldn't bring herself to listen one more time right now, to spoken words telling again of what had happened to her Clair. She stood up, faintly aware of the muscles in her back aching from the long night of sitting in the straight-backed chair.

"Can Wayne or me go an' get ya somethin', 'Lean?" Sherril asked quietly.

"No thanks," she murmured. "I'll just walk down the hall, for a little bit."

As she approached the desk on the third floor, the night nurse said, "Mrs. Huffaker?"

"Yes?"

"I just got a paper that you have to sign."

Orlean took the piece of paper, but couldn't make herself concentrate on the finely printed wording. "—What is it?"

"It's a regular form, holding the hospital and doctors blameless in case any problems should develop with your husband, later."

"I'm sorry," Orlean said numbly. "I still,—don't quite understand."

The nurse took the form back from her and studied it for a moment. "What it's mostly about is right here. '—ill-advised medical procedure, due to the high contingent possibility of gangrenous infection.'" She glanced at Orlean quietly, and then read a little more, explaining to Orlean. "—You won't let them perform an operation that they think they should. And as the patient's next of kin, you've got final say."

"Yes?"

"If you don't sign this, they'll go ahead with—the surgery. And if you do sign it,—then the full responsibility for whatever happens, is yours." She looked at Orlean with troubled eyes. "Usually these here form things are about an outbreak of chicken pox or something. But this one's so important,—I wish I hadn't even been the one that read it to you. —You ought to talk to somebody, to friends, or—"

"If I sign it, they can't cut his leg off. Is that right?"

"That's right. But they're good men, afraid of gangrene, and—"

Orlean took the paper and picked up a pen from the desk. With a trembling hand she signed it, and then handed it back to the nurse.

Perhaps not meaning to, the nurse caused one more, final pang of fear and doubt. She said quietly, "—Did you ever see a man with gangrene?"

And Orlean, with the very last of her emotional strength, said, "No. But you never saw my Clair on a motorcycle, or waltzing."

Moving away from any more talk, Orlean walked at another angle in the hospital. She came to a staircase and went down it, and then down another, and then there was a door.

She went out and found herself alone at the back of the building. There was no one near, and no one in the stands of dimly seen trees across the fields before her. And the growing brightness of sun had still not yet come up over the mountains to the east, so that there was a calm, darkish-gray light in the sky above.

The half-moon was still there, pale and timid, ready to retreat before the coming light. And here and there around it, tiny sparks of stars struggled bravely to survive a moment longer.

Alone and very afraid, she looked into that strange, morning sky, knowing that she had never seen another quite like it, nor ever would again.

"—Please, God," she said, gazing into the high-above heavens and speaking only in her mind. "Let him be well."

The stars winked back at her with small, twinkling and winking promises, but no real answers, and the dim, silver moon said nothing at all.

So she looked at the deeper void, in between the lights.

"Please God," she said again, speaking once more only in her mind. "Can you understand that you've finally made something,—that I love more than you? I don't know, but that must be a good thing on a God level. To be able to make something better, or more loved than yourself.

"Right now, he's dying upstairs. —Please, Dear Lord, don't let him die.

"I'm a good Mormon, God, and he's not. And I'm willing to trade me for him, so it would probably be a pretty fair thing for you, if you'd like to consider that.

"But your stars and the moon aren't paying attention to anything I'm trying to say, and maybe you don't have the time to, either. They're starting to go away.

"I'll tell you one last thing, God. —If you decide to let him live, you won't be sorry. I'll promise to come with him, when you choose the time, and then you'll have the two of us, both working together for you."

The twinkling stars were now long dimmed and gone, and the moon was fading away as the sun started to top the eastern mountains. And now, finally, Orlean stopped speaking within herself to her suddenly very near God. Never before, even in church, had she felt His presence so invisibly close and so real as it was out here under the softly, slowly changing sky.

After a long moment, she turned and went quietly back into the hospital.

For nearly a week Clair stayed near the thin border between life and death, sometimes weakening, then fighting back with some feeble inner strength, though in all that time he never regained consciousness.

Finally, Dr. Hughes came by the waiting room and said to Orlean, "If you don't get a little rest, I'll have to hospitalize you too."

"—I'm fine."

"I doubt if you've had more than two hours' sleep a night, if that. —What about your little boy?"

"My sisters are taking good care of him."

Dr. Hughes sighed and bit his lip slightly. "Look, young lady, will you promise me to go home and get a good, long sleep, if I break a regulation or two, and let you see your husband?"

Orlean stood up quickly. "Oh, *yes*."

They walked farther back along the corridors than Orlean had ever been before, and a nurse on duty near some double doors frowned up at them, but seeing Dr. Hughes, said nothing.

Before entering a final room, the doctor said, "We can only stay a minute, and be very quiet."

They went inside silently.

There were many beds in the long room, most of them hidden from sight by surrounding cloth drapes that fell from the ceiling to the floor. Nurses and a few doctors were moving about with nearly soundless efficiency.

Dr. Hughes separated the fourth curtain on the right, and they entered the small cubicle it formed. Clair was lying flat on the bed under a sheet, with only his face and one arm exposed. A thin tube led down from an overhanging bottle to a needle in that arm. His forehead was wrapped in a bandage that went completely around his head. And though his right leg couldn't be seen, the swelling of the sheet there showed how heavily bandaged it was. His breathing was almost inaudible, and irregular.

Silently, Orlean stepped a little closer to look down at his face. It was so pale, and heartbreakingly weak.

She stood there looking down at him for a long, silent moment. And then with no warning, no other movement of his face or lips, Clair's eyes opened for the first time, and he looked up at Orlean.

Dr. Hughes inhaled sharply, in his sudden surprise.

Clair's eyes stayed open for only two or three seconds, studying Orlean with totally clear awareness. But that brief time was long enough for him to see her quick smile. And then his eyes finally, slowly, closed again.

The doctor touched Orlean's arm gently, and they moved away.

The moment they were out and starting back down the corridor, Dr. Hughes shook his head wonderingly, "My God!"

"He woke up!" Orlean said happily. "He knew me!"

"But it happened just at that very moment when you were standing by him for the first time." The doctor shook his head again. "My colleagues might consider me certifiably insane, but it looked to me as though, somehow, in some unexplainable way, he simply *felt* that you were standing there near him."

She thought about this for a quiet moment and then said, "—Doctor?—Isn't his waking up, even for just that little while, a real good sign?"

"Yes, it is. It's not a guarantee of anything, most certainly including his bad leg. But it is very encouraging." They arrived near the waiting room, and he added, "You promised to get some sleep."

"I will. I can, now. —And then I've got an awful lot

to do." She touched his arm softly. "Thank you, Doctor."

In the next three weeks Orlean could only see Clair twice, and each time for just a few seconds. Once he slept through the brief visit. On the other visit his eyes opened, but he was too weak to speak. All he could do was smile faintly when she touched his hand with hers.

And then finally, early one evening, Dr. Hughes came into the waiting room and said, "I've just been talking to him."

"You have?"

He nodded. "Your husband seems to think, all of a sudden, that he's a healthy young lion. We've moved him into another ward, where less intensive care is needed, and visitation privileges are better."

"Can I see him? —Talk to him?"

He nodded again. "For perhaps ten or fifteen minutes. But if he seems to be getting weak, make it shorter."

A few minutes later, her heart pounding with quick eagerness, she walked up to beside Clair's bed. He looked at her and grinned faintly. "—Hey, there."

She sat silently near the bed and took his left hand in her own, a warm, good dampness growing in her eyes.

After a moment he grinned again. "—Us Trunion Polishers,—sure can tend t' be, kinda clumsy,—sometimes."

She squeezed his hand very gently. "—Even downright reckless, sometimes,—if you ask me."

His weak hand squeezed back faintly. "I don't know, because of all that stuff wrapped around it. But they tell me my right leg,—might not be too handy, anymore."

"Oh, Clair!" She lifted his hand and leaned forward to kiss it, tears suddenly coming down her cheeks. "It'll be all right! You'll be just fine!"

He smiled slightly, turning his head a little on the

pillow. "Hey!—You're the one—ain't supposed t' cry, unless you're happy."

"I'm crying because I'm finally talking to you!"

"I know that, honey." His voice now became a little stronger. "An' I can tell ya for sure that I'm gonna live all right. But what with Little Clair, an' the next baby comin', I got t' get up an' movin' around, one way or another. —I ain't at all sure that we c'n afford the luxury a' tryin' t' hold onto my goddamned, beat-up old right leg."

"Don't say anything like that," she said quietly. "Don't even think it."

"The doctor told me the odds, honey, an' the likely costs. —We got t' think a' the family first."

She squeezed his hand hard this time. "You *are* this family. And we *can* make the whole thing work. We've got that three hundred dollars saved. And the Copper Company is paying you fifteen dollars a week compensation while you're here."

"They are?"

"They didn't want to, but Sherril went with me to the State Industrial Commission, and they *have* to."

"Well, I'll be damned."

"And I've moved close to you in Salt Lake, and got a job."

"You've what?!" He almost lifted his head from the pillow.

"They're getting more telephones here in town every day, and they need operators. I took a two-day course, and I'm earning between twelve and fourteen dollars a week."

After a frowning, stunned silence, he said, "What about Little Clair?"

"Your Grandma Brown offered to take care of him while I'm working. —And she did a pretty darn good job of taking care of you, when you were a little boy."

"Jesus Christ," he muttered. "—There *nothin'* you ain't thought of?"

"Not much," she said. "—I'm terrific."

He looked at her for a long time. "I guess you knew I wouldn't be too happy about that leg bein' cut off. And if this works out—I guess, maybe, I'll owe you a dance."

Smiling at him, she said, "Could the music be, 'I'll Take You Home Again, Kathleen'?"

Suddenly, and very quickly, he was beginning to tire. "—You're forgettin'," he said, "—for us it's—'I'll Take You Home Again—*Orlean*.'"

"—I've never forgotten, darling."

His eyes starting to close, but a tiny grin working at the edges of his mouth, he muttered, "While you're out doin' all them things,—there's just one helpful thing I can do—hangin' around here in this hospital,—that you can't do."

"What's that?" she asked softly.

"I c'n,—take up knittin'." And then he drifted away, falling into a deep, heavy sleep.

But his breathing was strong and evenly measured.

She gently put his hand back down on the bed. Then she stood up and walked quietly from the room.

12

The Prisoner's Song

Oh, if I had the wings
Of an angel,
Over these prison walls
I would fly,
Into the arms of
My sweetheart,
Oh, there let me live,
And let me die. . . .

CLAIR HAD never known until now what a deadly enemy time can be, or what a cruel prison a hospital bed can be. Long, endless weeks finally became deadly months, and then even spanned the seasons themselves, until a cold, deep winter had come and was now almost gone.

It was nearly a year later, on a dreary, late afternoon, when Clair raised up in bed and struggled to arrange a pillow behind him. Then, finally sitting upright and leaning back against the pillow, he reached for a cigarette on the nightstand near him and lighted it.

Sometime, today. —Sometime later today, he might know.

Inhaling deeply, he closed his eyes hard against the bitter thought of another failure.

Jesus! Damnere a full year of being a goddamned, helpless cripple! And it had to have been just as tough, maybe worse, on Orlean, working and worrying about him endlessly, one damn long day after the other. Hell, it would have been a whole lot better for her if he'd just been killed, clean and outright, in the first place. The Copper Company would have given her a little money, at least, for him dying on the job. And a girl like Orlean could have already gotten married again, easy, instead of being saddled forever with a hopeless, bedridden half of a shell of a man like him. Goddamn his pantleg for twisting around him in the tunnel and stopping the bleeding. Why couldn't his goddamn pants have minded their own goddamned business anyway?

It just wasn't fair for her. Though it went against

everything within him, he'd even had the thought of jumping out of the window, so that he'd stop being such a problem. But he couldn't have made it to the window, and he was now in a ward on the second floor anyway. "Hell," he'd told himself grimly. "You dumb sonofabitch, you'd just wind up breakin' your other goddamned leg, too." So, *damnit,* there wasn't a thing he could do about it. Especially while those doctors kept rebreaking his goddamned crooked leg, over and over again.

He inhaled again, knowing even with his eyes shut that his hand was trembling slightly.

Maybe this time, today. Maybe, finally, the leg would be right. But it sure as hell never had been, yet.

Smoking and waiting with closed eyes, he thought back over the foreverness of time he'd been here.

Their second baby, a little girl that they'd named Delores, had been born. And Wayne and Guila had gone off and got married. When Wayne had come in to ask what Clair thought about the idea, Clair had suggested that maybe his little brother was too young. But then Wayne had gently pointed out that he was now the same age as Clair had been when he married Orlean, so that had been that.

Soon after, Darrell and Margaret had gone and taken the same step, and Margaret and Guila were as happy as kids at Christmas time fixing up the little places they'd moved into.

In those endless months, Clair's father had once come to see him, heavy-jowled and uncomfortable. He'd sat and folded his hands before him, and made a big point of clearing his throat. "—Uhh, Enzy, y'r mother, sends ya her love. —She's just been so danged busy,—lately."

"Sure, Dad," Clair said quietly. "—I understand."

The older man studied his chubby fingers that he'd folded together in his lap before him as though to give each of them a kind of weak, mutual support. "—I just may go in the furniture business,—out t' Magna,—but I dunno yet, f'r sure."

"That sounds real nice, Dad."

"Well,—I just wanted t' stop by,—an' make sure you're doin' okay."

Clair couldn't find it in him to mention that for a long time he'd been in agony, and near death. He just said, "—Thanks, Dad."

"Gotta go, now. Y'r brother Ken's waitin' down in the car." The old man unfolded his fat fingers and stood up. "Ken says he's sorry he ain't seen ya yet. But he's been purty busy, too. An' right now there's,—kind of a parkin' problem downstairs."

"—Sure, Dad. —Thanks for stoppin' by."

The old man had nodded vaguely, without quite looking in Clair's direction, and gone out of the room.

And, almost as if to offset that, a few days later Big Bertha Pearl had paid him a visit.

She came in, her pearls swinging at her throat, and frowned down at him without sitting in a chair. In a voice that was almost a whisper for her, she said, "You dumb sonofabitch. Why don't ya look where you're goin'?"

"Well, I *did* look."

"That's no goddamned excuse at all!" She touched his hand with her big fingers, all loaded with massive rings, and spoke with quiet sincerity. "Listen, kid, I'm in a hurry with a long ways t' go, and I got money. Tell me,—what d' ya need?"

"Nothin', thanks, Big Bertha."

"That's all you ever need, is nothin'!"

"Well,—"

"An' here ya are, all whacked out, an' down on your luck," she said almost angrily, "an' ya *still* say ya don't need nothin'!"

"Hell," he grinned, "don't lose y'r temper at me. —I ain't well!"

She took a long, resigned breath. "I been keepin' close track of ya, through Sherril an' all."

"—Wish ya wasn't goin' away?"

"Got m' reasons. —I likely won't see ya again."

"Well,—thanks f'r gettin' me that job, up t' the mill."

"Sure. Look where it's got ya." She lowered her eyes, blinking as though something were caught in them, and turned quickly away, her pearls swinging on her neck. Then she turned quickly back and said, "—I'd ever had a kid, maybe kinda like you,—I wouldn't a' been too disappointed."

And then she was gone.

Clair now lighted a second cigarette from the glowing butt of the first one, and stubbed out the butt. Outside, the dim, gray afternoon light was fading.

Anytime, now.

He didn't know if he could stand the idea of them breaking his leg once more. The way they did it made it seem more like he was in a torture chamber than a hospital. Carefully arranging his leg just so. Raising that big, ugly, heavy iron-ball slowly up high above it. And then, suddenly letting it fall. Five times now they'd done that,—and five times the bone had started to grow back together more crooked and impossible to use than before. And each of those times it had seemed a crueler way to do it, and was harder for him to face all over again.

"Hell," Clair muttered to himself, shrugging slightly against his fear. "Guess there just ain't no real polite way t' bust a fella's leg."

Then he tried to force himself to think of something else.

A nurse turned on the lights in the ward, and a moment later Orlean came in and kissed him softly before sitting near the bed. He could see at once that she was as nervous as he was, but was pretending not to be.

"Well," he grinned. "Fancy meetin' you here."

"I just thought I'd drop by," she smiled. "—Since there wasn't anything better to do." Then, as casually as possible, she added, "Guess there's,—no news yet?"

"No, not yet," he said easily. "Doctor spent most a'

the mornin' takin' off the cast, an' takin' X rays an' all." He grinned and shook his head. "Damn leg musta been photographed as much as Charlie Chaplin by now. —But I ain't at all sure whether it's his pictures 'r mine that come out the funniest." Her eyes dropped from his and he said quickly, "Hey, honey, I was just kiddin'. —Maybe it'll be okay this time. I got a feelin' that it really will, at last."

She now slowly raised her eyes to meet his, nodding and smiling faintly.

And then Dr. Hughes came quickly to the side of the bed, holding some reports in his hand. In a strained, unusually low voice, he said, "—It worked."

It was still a few more weeks before Clair could leave Saint Mark's, weeks in which he spent every waking hour moving about more and more, at first with the help of crutches, gradually building up both his own normal strength and the strength of his leg, and relearning his lost sense of balance in walking.

Toward the end of that time, Orlean became faintly vague and mysterious about everything except how well the children were doing. But Clair was usually so exhausted during her visits by his efforts to build his weakened body up, that he was hardly aware of her elusiveness. All he knew was that she was quitting her job, that Sherril had lined up some sort of a part-time job for him, and that they were moving back to Magna.

Then, finally, there was the sunny, clear spring day when Orlean and Sherril came to take him from the hospital.

In the lobby, Dr. Hughes came over to them and handed Clair a small, shiny piece of curved, flat steel about the size of the bottom of a man's foot. It looked like a large spoon on one end, joined to an even larger spoon on the other. "Going away present," he said. "If your leg or foot starts to get tired, put this in your shoe."

"Sure is nice,—but what is it?"

"Arch support. The arch in your right foot is almost nonexistent."

Trying to find some words to thank him for everything, Clair said, "Doctor—I,—" But then his voice started to break, so he made his voice stronger and said, "Sure hate t' wind up with a funny foot, like this."

"Mercury had funny feet," Dr. Hughes said. "They had wings on them, and he was the fastest runner in Roman mythology."

Clair looked at the flatly curved piece of steel in his hand. "—Thanks for the wing, Doctor."

The doctor kissed Orlean on the cheek, and walked quickly away.

Then Sherril went to bring his car around, and Clair and Orlean got into it.

On the road back to Magna, Clair frowned and said, "We didn't pay nothin' on our way out of Saint Mark's. How come?"

Sherril said, "—Paid, beforehand."

"How the hell—?" Clair paused briefly. "We *had* t' be short."

"We covered most of it, Clair," Orlean explained. "Dr. Hughes worked for practically nothing. And we only owed two hundred dollars more."

Clair frowned from one of them to the other. "Where the hell did ya come up with the other two hundred dollars?"

"Easy," Sherril said. "I finally sold your Indian."

"My cycle?" Clair asked.

"Yeah."

"Much as I love them wheels," Clair said, "they wasn't worth half that. —Who the hell did ya ever find who was dumb enough t' buy it for two hundred?"

Sherril drove into the growing dusk of Magna and made a right-hand turn. Then he said, "—Me. —I bought it."

After a time Clair said, "—You dumb sonofabitch. You really got gypped."

"Well, hell, nobody ever accused me a' bein' too smart."

Clair touched Sherril's shoulder in the shadows. "You ain't only not too smart, but you're goin' in the wrong direction t' our place."

"Oh, no!" Orlean said. "It's the right direction, now." Unable to hold back at this last moment, she hugged and kissed Clair. "You'll see!"

And just then Sherril pulled up into Louise Avenue, a tiny, curved street off the main dirt road, where there were seven or eight nicely built, slightly separated houses. He stopped at the third house, where there were lights inside and three cars in the small drive-way.

"This is some nice place," Clair said.

"It's *ours!*" Orlean said with another hug. "And it has *two rooms!* —Come and see!"

"Also," Sherril added, "we're havin' a comin' home party for ya. So try an' behave."

Inside, the small front room was filled with people who overflowed into the second room behind it. Vivianne, Evelyn and Margaret were serving small sandwiches and soft drinks, while Guila was quickly rinsing and drying glasses. Miles had set up a small bar on the table in the front room, and was making hard drinks for those who wanted them.

"Say, Clair," Miles said loudly. "What'd the doc say about booze?!"

"He warned me only t' drink with m' right hand."

There were friends from up at the mine, and from town, gathering around and shaking hands, welcoming Clair back. Bull Barstow was there, and even old man Swenson put in an appearance, drinking a strawberry pop and making one of his rare jokes by telling Clair he should have stayed at his grocery store, where there wasn't quite so much danger of locomotives.

Over the next two or three hours, there must have been almost thirty people who came in and out, and then it started to quiet down. There was only family left, when Ken showed up with a skinny, thin-faced girl.

"Jeez, brother," Sherril said. "I'll bet you're late for your own funeral."

"One thing an' another. —Got held up."

"Better late than never," Clair said. He held out his hand. "Sure is good t' see ya, Ken."

Ken shook the offered hand briefly and limply before gesturing vaguely toward the girl. "This here's Lauretta, from over t' Big Sandy."

Orlean stepped toward the other girl, smiling. "I'm Orlean, Lauretta. Can I take your coat?"

"No. We ain't stayin' long."

"Sherril," Ken said. "C'n I talk to ya, outside?"

"Sure."

They went out, and Miles said from his table-bar, "How 'bout a drink, Lauretta?"

"I *never* touch it."

Miles grinned. "—Lips that touch mine, huh?"

She didn't answer him, and a moment later Sherril and Ken came back in. "Well, we gotta go," Ken mumbled to no one in particular.

"Okay, Ken," Clair said. "I'm glad ya got a chance t' stop by, at least."

"Yeah. Well, so long."

They turned and left, and there was a brief silence in the room. Miles shrugged philosophically at their abrupt exit, and made himself another drink.

Clair said quietly, "I sure am glad he got a chance t' come by."

Sherril handed his glass to Miles for a refill and said, "How many times he visit ya in the hospital?"

"—I heard he was kinda,—busy."

Sherril took his refill from Miles and downed a deep drink of it. "Doin' what?"

"—Never got mentioned."

Sherril took another drink from his glass. "Hell, I guess it don't matter. But it sure beats me how a fella c'n have a brother like you, an' Old Wayne here, an' Marvin up in Canada,—an' then luck out with one like him."

"Sherril," Wayne said in a low voice, "Ken did come t' welcome Clair home."

"No." Sherril finished the drink and put it down hard on the table. "He come t' borrow ten bucks is what he come for."

"Maybe," Vivianne said, "it was both."

"—Maybe," Sherril said, pouring himself another drink. "But he sure cut out fast with the tenner."

"Not many people," Vivianne continued softly, "know or feel as much about,—love, and loyalty,—as you do."

"Everybody does." Sherril raised his glass in a slightly wavering, drinking salute. "Everybody,—here gathered, does. Sure as hell the people who live here, Clair an' Orlean, sure goddamn well do." He raised his glass a little higher. "He'd a' ruther been *dead,* than give *her* some kind of a rough time. —And she'd a' ruther been *dead,* than have *him* have some kind of a rough time. —An' that's the beautiful kinda thing I'm about t' drink to!"

Some of them drank with him, and when Sherril put his glass down, Clair lowered his own drink and said, "Orlean an' me gratefully accept all that deadness, an' the other nice things ya said. —But now we're all here alone,—will somebody please tell me, finally, what a flat-broke, outta work guy like me is doin' sittin' here in a two-room house?"

Orlean's eagerness suddenly won out over her normal shyness.

"Can I answer?!"

"Sure," Clair said.

"Sherril and some friends got you an even better job up on the hill!"

"Thirty dollars a week," Sherril said.

"Thirty dollars?!"

Sherril nodded. "You got a supervisory job on Railroad Signal Maintenance. —Guess they figure you're the only livin', bona fide expert on the hazards a' that there tunnel."

"And Clair!" Orlean went on. "Everybody here

helped get things and put this house together! Both
rooms are furnished nice! We've got a stove, and a
sink, and a couch! Just about everything! Even *two*
kerosene lamps, one for each room!"

Clair lowered his head, and it was his sister Evelyn
who said quietly to him, "—The rest of us didn't do too
much. —Orlean almost killed herself doing it, and we
just helped her, a little bit."

Clair looked back up, but just then didn't seem to be
able to say anything, except with his warm eyes.

"Well, hell," Miles said gruffly, "we got a long haul
home."

"Vivianne an' me are only a mile away," Sherril
muttered, "but in my shape, that's a longer haul than
yours."

"Us too," Darrell said quietly. "Gotta get a move on,
or Margaret'll fall asleep where she's sittin' there."

Wayne and Guila were the last to go, and Wayne
turned in the doorway and said to Clair, "—Ken
meant good."

"You bet he did," Clair said. "I'm sure glad he
came."

And then at last, Clair and Orlean were by themselves.

They hugged each other, alone in the front room,
and Clair said, "One last question, very pretty lady
who is a princess of some very special kind." Still
hugging her, he leaned back and said, "What have you
done with our two children? Sold them into slavery?"

She frowned and looked with suspicious eyes from
right to left. "I left them in the care of the Wicked
Witch of Fifth East, who is my evil sister Melva, who
would rather have come to the party, but got stuck with
the kids."

"Then this whole castle is ours, tonight?"

"The whole two rooms."

And then he hugged her so hard that she couldn't
breathe. —But she didn't care at all about breathing,
just then.

13

When You and I Were Seventeen

Once more I hold you to my heart,
As thru' the waltz we sway,
And tho' so long we've been apart,
It seems it was just yesterday.
When you and I were seventeen,
And life and love were new,
The world was just a field of green,
'Neath smiling skies of blue.
That golden spring, when I was king,
And you my wonderful queen,
Do you recall when love was all,
And we were seventeen. . . .

CLAIR NEVER could figure out just how Sherril and his friends had managed to get him this new job. He was a signal dispatcher, and not only was his office job easier and the pay better, but the hours were shorter. He rarely had to work more than a nine-hour day, which gave him more time with Orlean and the children, and also more time to try to improve himself by studying at home.

One night after supper, when Little Clair and Delores were already sleeping, he said to Orlean, "I've decided the field of electricity's not f'r me."

"Oh?"

"Guess I kinda got sucked in t' that because they called me an electrician's helper. But I don't like electricity. —It has a habit of spittin' at ya."

"That's not very nice of it."

"An' I sure don't want t' work up there on the hill forever, like most fellas around here. No matter how high ya go, there's always gonna be a boss over ya. —An' sooner or later, I want t' be my own boss."

She studied him quietly. "Have you decided what to do?"

"Yep. I'm goin' t' be the world's number-one, highest-paid, absolutely best supersalesman."

"Good for you. —Selling what?"

"I was afraid you'd get around t' that detail," he grinned. " 'Cause I ain't got no idea, yet. But it don't really matter. They've got these Spenser mail-order courses, with books and everything. What they do, they just teach ya—plain, basic salesmanship. An' then with

161

a good job like mine, ya can save a little money an' start y'r own business sellin' anything, from—from pencils t',—ocean liners."

"I like the ocean liners best."

"Okay. But maybe we'll start,—with a rowboat, at first."

"Oh, either way," she shrugged, "as long as we get a sea voyage out of it."

Somewhat to Clair's own surprise, the Spenser mail-order course was thorough and tough, and hard to pass. There was a difficult part on Basic English. They even had a section on penmanship, which they called, "The vitally important, written measure and mark of a salesman," and another section on "Sales Psychology," involving different ways of dealing with various clients, and under what circumstances to use a "hard" or a "soft" selling approach.

Four months later, when he received his "Spenser Diploma of Salesmanship," he was proud enough of it to stop by The Smokehouse after work and show it to Sherril. His brother was on the late shift, and he and Vivianne had stopped in here for a drink or two before he went on up the hill to work.

They were at a corner table, and Clair went over to sit down with them.

"Hey!" Sherril said warmly. "What'll ya have?"

"Whatever you're drinkin' suits me."

Sherril waved to the new owner, a small, sullen man whose swarthy face didn't seem to match up at all with his nickname, "Dutch."

Sherril ordered drinks for the three of them, and when Dutch had left, Vivianne said, "Place's sure never been the same since Big Bertha Pearl left."

"Yeah," Sherril agreed. "But at least it's still some kind of a hangout. An' in this old world, ya always gotta try t' be a philosopher." He looked at Clair. "Right, kid brother?"

Clair frowned thoughtfully and said, "I'm not at all sure that you're really equipped t' talk t' me on that kind of a high level."

"Oh?" Sherril nodded faintly. "Pray tell, how the hell come?"

"Because I'd overwhelm ya." Clair handed Sherril the envelope from Spenser's. "This paper proves how smart I am."

"That sure does need *some* kinda proof." Sherril took the diploma out and studied it. "—Goddamn. I wasn't never too sure whether you really could actually read 'r write."

Vivianne said eagerly, "Let me see," and Sherril handed it to her. Then he grinned at Clair. "Soon as ya get rich, will ya do like it says in 'The Big Rock Candy Mountain'?"

"What part?"

"Have a lake, a stew, an' a whiskey too,—for when I come t' visit."

"I'll have 'em installed directly."

"How 'bout if this comin' weekend we all have dinner at our place t' celebrate you not bein' quite so dumb as ya look?"

"You bet. —Can I buy us another?"

"Nope." Sherril stood up. "Duty calls. Car's outside. Will you see Vivianne home?"

"Sure."

Vivianne looked up from the diploma. "This is really great!"

Sherril leaned down and kissed her lightly on the cheek. "Insult the kid as much as ya can. —Good f'r his ego."

She smiled and returned his light kiss. "Now stop being jealous of how smart he is. And hurry home."

Walking through the growing night up the long, steep path to the mill, Sherril found himself whistling a happy, tuneless melody. And he still was whistling a little later, as dark fell and he got to the Electrician's Shop. His young assistant of four years, Joe Wolfson, was already there.

"You're pretty cheerful," Joe said.

"I feel good."

"That's the trouble with you. Ya always feel good. I think you're a nut."

"Anything doin'?"

"Nah." Joe was checking some meters, making notes. "Got a report that the lights dimmed a couple a' times over at Chemical Storage, early on. But they didn't go out, an' the juice seems okay over there now."

"That's funny."

"What's funny?"

"Lights dimmin' in Chemical Storage. That buildin's hooked up on the same circuit as the Ore Crusher. Forty thousand volts. —Should be enough power there t' light all a' Salt Lake."

"Well," Joe shrugged. "It's okay now, anyway."

Sherril went carefully over the daily reports on his desk, and then started to examine Joe's meter readings while Joe went out to make his field spot checks.

Sometime later Joe was back. "Damnit," he said, slightly irritated. "Them lights over in Chemical started actin' up again."

"Yeah? Well, let's go take a look."

They crossed the dark hundred yards or so to the big Chemical Storage building where the lights inside flickered and dimmed, but never quite went out.

Outside the two men who worked there were relaxing, having smokes.

"Rotten electricians we got around here," one joked.

"We're here t' rescue you dumb bastards," Sherril said. "Ya oughta be grateful."

Inside the single, huge room, there were long, high rows of stacked boxes, wooden crates and metal containers. The electric panel and main switch were located on the far side of the building from the entrance, and they had to wind their way between the tall stacks of containers to finally get to it.

They were a few steps from the large electric panel when the lights suddenly went out totally, plunging the building into complete darkness. Much worse, the sudden, hideous smell of furiously smoldering heat and melting rubber came harshly to Sherril's nostrils.

Flicking on his flashlight and leaping toward the electric panel, Sherril yelled, "Get *outta* here Joe! Throw the main switch up at the shop!"

He burned his hand badly, snatching open the already hot metal cover of the panel, and inside there was a small, concentrated hell of flashing, sizzling electricity gone crazy. Still he tried desperately to throw the switch here, but the incredible heat had already seared it in place.

Then, at some point behind him, the swiftly growing electric heat touched off a container of volatile chemical that exploded like a bomb, showering fiercely burning flames over most of the large building. Sherril ran back, twisting and turning between the stacked chemicals and the quickly spreading, searing flames.

Some men were already gathering outside the door as he burst out, his clothes smoking. Glancing at them, he yelled, "Where's Joe?!"

"Nobody but you come out!" someone shouted.

"He's still in there!" another voice called.

A couple of men yelled, "No!" and "You're crazy!" as Sherril spun around and ran back into the swiftly growing inferno.

With the crackling roar of angry flames all around him, the heat almost too intense to see through, Sherril finally found Joe sprawled face down on the floor, the back of his jacket already starting to burn. Sherril picked him up and, struggling with Joe's dead weight, started back for the door as fast as he could make it.

Then, between them and the door, a solid wall of fire suddenly erupted into thundering existence, forcing Sherril into a backward, off-balance step or two. But there was no other way out. And the thought never even occurred to Sherril to drop his friend and spring through the flames by himself. Instead, he took as much of a half-breath as he could, the oven-hot air scorching his lungs, and staggered through the roaring wall of fire with Joe in his arms.

Just outside the door Sherril collapsed and other men, braving the intense heat even here, dragged the two men farther away, frantically beating the flames from their clothing and hair.

"They're still alive," someone said.

"Jesus!" another man muttered, gasping for breath himself, "even their shoes was on fire!"

It was five days later when the doctors finally let two people see Sherril, and then only one at a time.

Vivianne came out in tears, unable to speak, and Clair was the second one to go in.

Almost all of Sherril's body was bandaged, including his entire face except for his lips and his eyes, which were clear and showed faint humor lurking in them. Looking up at Clair, he said, "Well, I spent enough time lookin' down at you. Guess turnabout's fair play."

"Did they tell ya, yet? —You saved Joe's life."

"Yeah, I heard," Sherril said quietly. "An' I sure am glad."

"That,—sure was somethin'," Clair said in an equally quiet voice. "—Goin' back in after 'im."

Sherril forced a tiny grin. "Hell, I didn't have no other choice. —Joe owed me six dollars from a poker game."

Clair shook his head slightly. "That's my brother," he murmured. "Just as money-mad as ever."

"Is Vivianne,—okay? She didn't have much t' say."

"Sure. She's a brick. But she's been goin' half crazy, worryin' about ya."

Sherril was silent for a moment. Then, again, he forced the tiny smile. "Chances are,—I may've lost a little bit of m' beauty."

Clair touched him gently on his thickly gauze-encased arm. "Hell, not much t' lose on that count,—you bein' s' damn homely in the first place."

Again that tiny, irrepressible smile came to Sherril's

lips. "You always did see the bright side a' things." And then, suddenly, he was asleep.

Miles and Evelyn took the still-unspeaking Vivianne to stay with them, and Clair drove Wayne and Guila back to Magna in Sherril's car. Then, after dropping them off, he continued on through the night to his own home.

Orlean had supper waiting for him, but he only wanted coffee. She brought it to him, then sat silently near him at the table.

At last he said, "I saw him. —He's gonna be okay."

"Well, thank God," she murmured. "But then, what's wrong, Clair?"

He took a sip of coffee. "—Vivianne. She can't even talk."

After a moment Orlean said, "She's in shock, Clair. Nothing like this has ever happened in her life."

"No kiddin'?" Clair said in a hard voice, though his eyes looked at Orlean gently. "Then tell me. How many times 've you ever had y'r husband get run over by a goddamned train?"

"Well," she hesitated. "I'm glad to say, only once."

"An' if you couldn't have up an' talked, and talked damn good, I'd be walkin' around here with a four-teen-inch limp."

Orlean said nothing, and Clair took another drink of coffee almost angrily. "Sure he's gonna be scarred up a little, but right now he needs all the help he can get. An' she can't even talk to 'im, or comfort 'im. She's scared t' death before they even take his goddamned bandages off. An' ya know what that means?"

"—No."

"It means the difference b'tween you an' her." He reached over and gripped her hand so hard that it hurt. "You always just worried about me. —She's worried about herself."

"I'm not sure that's fair to her, and—"

"I am." His grip remained fiercely tight. "It's all a

matter of spirit. An' that's what you are, honey. A hundred an' twenty pounds of pure spirit."

Slightly embarrassed by this, and correcting him softly, she said, "A hundred and *fifteen* pounds. —And you're hurting my hand."

"I'm sorry." He released it, then held it again gently.

Very seriously, she said, "He'll be all right."

"Thank you, more than ever just right now, at this minute, for being my girl."

"—You're welcome."

The way it turned out, Sherril was all right. But much of the small world he lived in was not. When he was released from the hospital he was the same gentle person, with the same warm sense of humor and kindness. But his face was scarred, and his body. And in a strange way, perhaps the worst thing of all was that he'd lost all of his hair, and even his eyebrows and eyelashes wouldn't grow back.

Vivianne soon left him, and in his grief some of the wits around The Smokehouse pool table nicknamed him "Cueball."

Sherril took to spending more and more time at Clair and Orlean's home.

One day, playing with the baby Delores, who was just learning to speak, he bounced her on his knee for a long, galloping pony ride. And then, as she was giggling wildly at the exciting ride, he said, "Hey, you! We do have some pretty good old times t'gether, don't we?!"

Still laughing uncontrollably, she beamed up at him and said her first full sentence. "You beaut-ful, Uncle Sherril!"

Very gently and very slowly he put her down, and then walked outside.

That night, after supper, he sat with Clair on the edge of the small front porch and said, "—Think I'm gonna bust outta here f'r a while."

"What for?"

"Just f'r the hell of it."

Orlean had finished the dishes now, and she came out to sit with them, drying her still damp hands on her apron.

In the star-lighted darkness Clair said, "—Sherril's thinkin' a' takin' off."

In the faint, starry light, she managed a half-smile toward them. "I hope it's not because of my cooking."

"No. Your cookin's great, except ya overdo the meat a little."

"If you'll stay," Orlean said, her voice very low and controlled, "I'll just wave it over the stove a couple of times."

"No," Sherril said. "I'm goin'. M' house is about even, so I'll just leave that t' the bank. Car's paid for, an' I'll use that t' move on in." He hesitated. "Just leaves the Indian, an' that cycle's yours anyway, Clair."

"No, it ain't. It's yours."

"You stubborn, pardon me Orlean, bastard. —Then let's give it, t'gether, t' Wayne."

"Done." Clair nodded in the dim starlight. "But where the hell ya gonna go?"

"Read someplace,—that beauty's in the beholder's eye. You two sure as hell are beholders, just like that little girl a' yours, Delores." Sherril stood up from the edge of the porch, and his voice suddenly wasn't quite as strong as he wanted it to be. "—I'm gonna go see if I can find me somebody, somewhere in this world,—who won't see me quite as ugly as I am."

"Sherril?" Orlean stood up and hugged him, and his rough, scarred cheek moved softly against hers in a gentle embrace.

"Take care a' this dumb kid brother a' mine," he said.

"I will."

Clair was now standing near them, and Sherril looked quietly at him before touching his shoulder briefly. "Don't look so goddamned sad. Just consider me an explorer, lookin' for a goddamned beholder.

—There's gotta be one, somewhere." Then he walked quickly to his car and drove away.

It was long, long after the sound of the car had gone that they turned silently in the dim starlight and went back into their home.

About a month later, with early winter upon them, Margaret came into Orlean's house. She came in the front door and patted Little Clair on the head, then tickled Delores on her way to the back room where Orlean was hurrying back and forth between the hot stove and the sink where there were several bottles and two bushels of tomatoes.

"What ya doin'?" she asked.

"Putting up tomatoes, I think!" And then she added, "I *hope!* Nothing's working right!"

"Can I help?"

"Yes! Peel some tomatoes! It looks like it only works if they're peeled!"

Quickly taking a paring knife and starting on the tomatoes, Margaret said, "Hey, d' you know what a stock market crash is?"

Struggling with a heavy pot of steaming water, Orlean said, "No."

"Well, we had one."

"We did?"

"I guess. —Back t' New York City, in a place called Wall Street. —It's like, somehow, everything's gone crazy, an' everybody's broke." Margaret handed her two fresh-peeled tomatoes. "Darrell told me, an' then he went off t' see some friends. —It sounds like it could, maybe be kind a' serious."

Orlean wiped some sweat from her forehead and said, "Clair will know about it when he comes home. We'll see."

Clair came home and said that as far as he knew those big business problems back East couldn't hurt the rest of the country too much. Though it still didn't sound good to him.

And then, a few weeks later, Clair came home again, through the now deep winter snow, and for a time he didn't want to talk.

Finally he sat at the table, and she silently brought coffee for them both. "Orlean," he said, "—I got laid off, t'day."

"What for? You've been doing so good on your job."

"—They laid off half the town. Seniority's all that matters, an' they only could keep on the old-timers. —I guess that's fair."

She nodded quietly. "—What do you think we should do?"

"I don't know. —I sure as hell don't know."

Orlean smiled briefly and said, "You're so darn smart. You said before we got married, that there'd be tough times up ahead."

"Hell, I didn't have no idea they'd be as tough as they're turnin' out t' be." He got up tiredly and went to sit on the sofa. And when she joined him there, putting her arms around him, he said, "—Seems t' me, I sure have let you down."

"You sure have," she agreed. "Here we are, twenty years old, and our whole life behind us."

"Goddamnit, you're makin' fun a' me."

"I am *not.*" She tried to make a fake, imitation sob. "But all that I can think of is how great everything was before, when we were young. And how terrible it is, now that we're old."

"You *are* makin' fun a' me."

"Is that so?" She tickled him a little bit.

"Yes, it *is!*" He tickled her more, until they were both laughing.

And finally, much later, after a warm, quiet silence, he at last said in a low voice, "—Quite a lot's happened, in the last three 'r four years."

"Yes," she whispered. "Quite a lot."

"Are you sorry,—or happy about them?"

"I wouldn't trade any one day of those years for a

whole other lifetime." She hugged him so fiercely that Clair almost lost his breath.

And then, holding each other tightly and closely on the sofa, they became silently and warmly lost in their embrace.

14

Welcome to Hard Times

Welcome to hard times, stranger,
We have a whole lot of fun,
We ain't got a dime, between us all,
An' we ain't got a bean or a bun,
But there's one thing we got plenty of,
And that is time by the ton.
We got time to starve, an' time to freeze,
An' time to stand in line,
For a slice of stale bread, a cup of bad soup,
Or a watermelon rind.
An' we got the bulls to drag us bums in,
For thirty days or a fine.

Payin' the fine would be fine, if we had it,
But there just ain't no choice but the jail.
Maybe if we written to President Hoover,
He'd hurry on down, an' come up with the bail.

ONE SATURDAY night Clair got home from Salt Lake in the darkening evening before Orlean had heard the distant, familiar bell of the Bamburger trolley.

She could see by his face that he hadn't had any luck in finding a job, so she didn't ask. She just helped him off with his ice-speckled jacket and then gave him a hug.

He kissed her and said, "Boy, is it *cold* out there."

"How did you beat the trolley home?"

"Easy." But before explaining, Clair crossed to where Little Clair was toying with the last few of his supper beans. "Have a piece a' candy, kid. But finish y'r supper first." He handed his son a black jawbreaker and the boy grinned up at him with wide-eyed gratitude. Then Clair went to the stove to warm his hands, rubbing them briskly together over it. "*Damn,* it's cold."

"That's why I put Delores to bed early," Orlean said. "Even in the house, it's warmer in bed." She started to dish up some beans from the pot on the stove. "Well then, how did you beat the trolley?"

"Well, I got t' thinkin'. I've been wastin' twenty cents a day on the train, every time I go t' town t' look for a job. So I invented a new thing, called hitch-hikin'."

"In *this* weather?"

"Well, it sure is refreshin'," he shrugged. "An' just now I got home even earlier."

As if to back up his words, there was now the dim, distant sound of the trolley bell. "See," he smiled.

"You've now had the pleasure of about ten extra minutes more of m' company."

Orlean now put Little Clair to bed, as he was happily sucking on his jawbreaker. And then, just before the boy went to sleep, she took it out so that he wouldn't choke on it, stored it by his bedside for the morning, and rejoined Clair in the front room.

"—Do you think that kind of candy is good for Little Clair?"

"Not those jawbreakers," he said as he ate. "Somebody musta figured out some way t' put a sugar taste in a round, solid rock. —But kids go for 'em. An' just the way he grinned at me made it worthwhile."

"I don't like you standing out on the road in this kind of weather."

"—I don't like standin' on the road in *any* kinda weather. But it seems t' work, an' it does save money."

"Your coat had ice on it. You could freeze to death."

"Oh, come on. It ain't all that bad, an' if I hitch in an' outta Salt Lake, we'll be savin' over a dollar a week. An' so that's just plain that, pretty lady."

She could see that there was no possible way to argue with him, so she waited a quiet moment and then said, "Melva and Margaret are coming by with Al and Darrell to visit for a while."

"Good." He finished his beans and smiled at her with his eyes. "Then we can talk about somethin' besides penny jawbreakers an' hitchhikin'. Both a' which, if I judge right, you don't approve of a whole damn lot."

"There are a few things I do approve of." Her eyes smiled back at his. "One of them being that Margaret is pregnant."

"Great."

"That's why they're coming over. Sort of a celebration."

Orlean's two sisters and their husbands came in shuddering with cold and taking off their coats that were lightly covered with newly fallen snow. As Orlean and Clair hugged Margaret, congratulating her, Al snorted, "That dang weather! It's bad enough out there t' freeze a witch's broomstick!"

Orlean served them hot cocoa, except for Clair and Darrell, who elected for drinks out of Clair's last bottle of home brew, and they sat around the small front room, their combined bodies making it warm, even away from the stove.

Darrell had been laid off a couple of weeks after Clair, and now Al sipped his cocoa thoughtfully and said, "Well, I just joined you two fellas in the ranks a' the unemployed. —Axe fell t'day."

"Good hell," Clair said. "You got better'n ten years seniority!"

"Yeah," Al shrugged, "but there's others up there got twenty years an' more,—an' they're even lettin' most a' them go, too."

Melva said, "Al's been hearin' about a thing called the CIO, that he thinks might help us all outta this fix."

"Sure," her husband nodded. "Them CIO organizers say this whole d'pression thing's a big, phony deal t' force the workin' man right down on t' his knees,—so that finally he'll be willin' t' go back t' work f'r anything, even f'r starvation wages. They say that if enough of us stick t'gether, we c'n force the mill an' the mine t' open back up an' hire us all back on at fair wages."

"Don't see how they can open back up," Clair said, "when there ain't nobody around t' buy their copper. —An' there can't be no market f'r copper, 'r nothin' else, till people start workin' again so they c'n afford t' start buyin' things again." He grinned wryly. "It sure as hell is one vicious damn circle."

"I'm tellin' ya!" Al insisted. "It's them big shots that're trickin' us. They're b'hind this whole thing."

"Well, if that's so," Clair said, "they're sure doin' one fine job a' foolin' me. I was in half a dozen job lines in Salt Lake t'day, an' there was ex-big shots standin' b'side me in every line. A doctor, a couple lawyers."

"No!" Al grumbled, "I mean them back-East *business* big shots! Them Rock'fellers, an such! It's all their doin'!"

Not wanting to argue with Al, and seeing that he was deeply upset about losing his job, Clair shrugged and said, "—Maybe you're right."

"Darn well, I am."

"Me, I got a whole other thing in mind, just t'day," Darrell said. "I got this brother that's got himself this ol' dump truck. But he's laid up an' can't drive 'er. So we're goin' in partners, me drivin' his truck an' doin' the work, an' we'll split all we make fifty-fifty."

"Swell," Al grunted. "All ya need t' do now, is find somebody who wants t' hire a dump truck, an' can afford it. —Ya gonna take your truck under y'r arm, from door t' door, like them kids sellin' Liberty magazine?"

The younger man was at a loss to answer Al, and Orlean said in a quiet voice, "Maybe, Darrell, you ought to drive over and talk to Miles. That's in his line and he might have some ideas, or maybe even hire you himself, sometimes."

"Yeah, Orlean," Darrell nodded. "That's a real good idea."

For the first time now, Margaret spoke, her voice small and a little frightened. "—We're all of us down t' a few dollars—or less. —What if none a' this works? Al's CIO, Darrell's truck, Clair's lookin' for a job. What happens, when ya just plain run outta anything t' eat, or if ya just plain run outta coal in bad weather like this?" She looked from one of them to the other. "—What happens then?"

There was a silence. And then Melva looked at her little sister and said, "Honey? —What happens if there's an earthquake tomorrow,—or if the Day of Judgment comes? —No matter what comes to pass in this life, why you just go on, and you do the best you can."

After a moment, Margaret nodded silently.

Melva smiled at her and said gently, "You're carry-in' your first born. An' more often than not, that tends t' make a girl sort of on edge."

But still Margaret couldn't quite let go of her question. "Maybe I am edgy, an' what you said was real good, Melva. But I ain't talkin' about earthquakes 'r Judgment Day. I'm talkin' about,—when everything you've got, or ya need, just plain an' simple runs out." She glanced at Orlean, including her in the question. "How do ya feed your kids, if there ain't nothin' t' eat?"

"We'll always help each other," Orlean said. "And one of us is always bound to have something."

"Sure," Melva agreed. "An' if worse comes t' worst, there's always the relief, too. Maybe the gover'ment might help a little. An' the church's got relief, too."

Darrell made a small face. "That's kinda,—like beggin' f'r help, ain't it?"

"No!" Al said. "Be it Uncle Sam or the Mormons, they both been paid for it up front, either with taxes 'r with church tithin's. T' go on honest relief sure ain't takin' no kinda handout."

"Hey!" Clair said. "This here kinda talk is gettin' us all down." He grinned and shook his head. "Hell, we're sittin' around plannin' a big, fancy funeral b'fore anybody even died! Personally, I got a strong hunch that there 'r all kinds a' good times just up ahead of us! An' furthermore," he raised his glass in a small salute, "there's even one a' them damn good times right *here,* an' right *now!*"

Darrell returned the raised-glass salute. "By golly, I'll drink with ya t' that!"

"Me too!" Al lifted his cup of cocoa.

"As long as you're all drinking to something," Orlean said, "it seems to me you could at least include Margaret's coming baby."

"Darn right!" Darrell agreed. "Here's t' the baby bein' triplets!"

"Triplets?!" Margaret laughed a little now, through a puzzled frown. "Why?"

Very pleased with the joke he had in mind, Darrell forced back his own growing smile. "—Think a' all the work that'd save me, havin' t' make them next two kids with ya."

It took Margaret a brief moment to understand. Then she slapped Darrell on the shoulder and as he leaned away from her, laughing, she said, "Oh,—*you!*"

And when the four of them left a little later, they were all still in a happy mood, their laughter growing dimmer as they walked away on the cold night street.

Now alone with Clair, Orlean turned from the door and gave him a hug, stretching up to kiss him lightly on the cheek. "You sure did good, dear husband."

"Hmm?"

"You know what I mean. You turned tonight from a sad, scared time to a good, happy time."

"Yeah,—maybe so." He ran his fingers gently through her hair, his eyes looking vaguely, thoughtfully somewhere off over her shoulder.

"—You really did," she said in a low voice.

"Thing is,—I don't know how much of what I said I believe."

She hesitated. "You—were just trying to make Margaret feel better?"

He nodded. "And Al, and everybody, maybe even includin' you an' me, honey."

"Well, you sure did do a good job." She hugged him once more, softly. "—Tell me what else there is."

"Couple a' things. One is this." His eyes, still looking somewhere vaguely beyond her, grew hard. "Whatever happens, I ain't just about t' accept 'r t' take no kind of relief from nobody, under no circumstances. —It just ain't a part a' my nature."

"I know," she said. "I understand."

"Second. If times do turn real hard, I ain't about t' let you an' the kids go without."

Reading the strength in his troubled, far-seeing eyes, Orlean felt a moment of great fear. Taking his hand, she sat slowly down on the sofa, her own hand gently coaxing him to sit down beside her. "What are you talking about, Clair?"

His eyes finally met hers and he said firmly, "Real simple. —If I can't get honest work,—then there's lots of—other things."

She squeezed his hand and managed to come up with a very faint smile. "—My husband, the bank robber?"

"If need be." He was deadly serious. "This depression ain't even hardly begun yet. An' however in hell I have t' go about doin' it, I'm gonna damn well see you an' our kids through it."

"That kind of talk,—scares me, Clair."

Now it was he who gripped her small hand firmly, reassuringly. "Don't be scared. If things get s' rough that I have t' go in t' bein' a crook, I'll only go up against big, rich outfits that won't really feel the dent. You know darn well I'd never take one penny from a regular person, or even ever dream a' hurtin' anybody."

"But,—if you ever did try that kind of risky thing,— *you* could be hurt."

He grinned at her, but there was grimness rather than humor within him. "—Tell me, then, about locomotives comin' full speed at ya in tunnels,—'r about chemical fires."

After a moment of silence, she said quietly, "Clair, I love you in all ways. —But this is a way I never saw before."

Trying to make it easier for her, he said lightly, "Still scared half t' death a' the new me?"

"—Well,—of what the new you could do."

He took a long, deep breath and exhaled slowly. "All it boils down to, honey, is that we're down t' four dollars an' twenty-eight cents. An' I'm gonna make damn sure that you an' them two kids get through these times okay, come hell,—'r come high water."

She moved down from the sofa, kneeling before him and resting her arms and her head lightly on his knees. "—I know you mean that."

"You bet your boots I do, honey."

"Then,—I'll pray to God that you can get a job."

He rubbed her hair again, gently. "While y'r at it, tell 'im t' hurry up, an' with all this rotten weather we got, ask 'im for a job in sunny California."

Two days later, hitching another ride, Clair arrived home from Salt Lake in the late afternoon, his face shining from far more than the bitter cold, and with three gaily wrapped packages under his arm.

Knowing that good things must have happened, even before Clair spoke, Orlean left the children playing at the table and moved toward him. "You're just in time to help us draw some more kittens, with crayons."

"Are they good?" He kicked the door shut behind him.

"Considering that most of them are purple and green. —I'm not too sure about Little Clair's sense of color."

Putting his packages down, Clair struggled out of his coat. "Anybody can draw a normal kitten. But f'r a purple 'r green one, ya need a real special artist. Right, kid?"

Little Clair nodded in agreement and called out, "Right, Daddy! —But Delores keeps makin' the ears too big. Her kittens all look like rabbits!"

Still drawing, Delores looked up with an angry frown. "They do *not!*"

Their small disagreement was forgotten now, as Clair brought over the two presents he had for them. "Here, kid. —An' this one's for you, pretty little girl."

Little Clair's quickly unwrapped gift was a wooden, hand-carved pony, a black-and-white pinto that could just barely stand up when the boy placed it carefully on the table. "Don't move," he whispered to no one in particular, "or it c'n fall, an' git itself hurt."

Delores now tore through the wrapping paper covering her present, and opened the box. "A *dolly!*" she cried out. Pulling it from the box, she cradled it loosely in her arms, and when the doll fell into a roughly prone position, its eyes suddenly went closed.

Delighted, Delores almost screamed, "It *sweeps!*"

Orlean gently rearranged the doll more naturally in her daughter's arms. "It 'sleeps,' " she said quietly.

Delores held the doll very closely to her. "That's why I wuv it, Mommy," she explained. "Because it *sweeps!*"

When the two children were finally in bed, Clair handed Orlean the last of the three gift packages. "—Hope ya like it."

She started to unwrap it and then he put his hand out, covering both of her hands, and stopping her. "Listen," he said quietly, "maybe I oughta tell ya somethin', first."

Looking up at him nearly in tears, she tried as much as she could to make her voice sound very tough. "Okay, Legs. Which bank job ya runnin' away from this time?"

"Oh, come on!" He frowned up briefly at the ceiling, and then looked back down at her. "I'm happy t' report t' you that I'm still not up there on the Ten Most Wanted list. What you got, there, is just a natural present."

It was a white wool robe, covered with red flowers. She stood up and held it close against her, feeling its warmth. And then she saw the paper below, in the bottom of the box.

"There's more? That?"

"You bet."

She took it out and just glancing through it she somehow knew instantly that it was a life insurance paper on Clair, and somebody had typed in that he was worth two thousand dollars.

"I don't know how you got this," she said. "But I don't want it. —It's insurance against your life."

"No, it ain't," he said. "It's insurance that makes sure you an' the kids'll wind up bein' okay."

"I don't like it." She let the paper fall back onto the table. "What it says is, that sometime, you'll be dead."

"Goddamnit, honey," he said, "I thought that it was a fair present. —All it means is just that you an' the kids got some kinda security,—with or without me."

"We don't ever want any piece of paper. We want you."

"Okay." Clair picked up the paper she'd dropped. He slowly folded it into three very careful folds, putting it back into an envelope as he spoke. "This was part of my goddamn deal, damn it. —Plus twenty bucks in advance. Your prayers come out half-way, Orlean. I got me a job. Not out in sunny California, but in frozen Omaha, Nebraska."

"How did you get a job?"

"That 'Spenser Diploma' really came in handy t'day. All of a sudden, it seemed t' sound like I graduated from Oxford, over there t' England, 'r somethin'."

"It did?" Orlean poured Clair the last of the home brew, and moved to the stove to make herself a cup of coffee. "Then, are we selling pencils, or rowboats, or ocean liners?"

"Turns out there's no big market for boats a' any kinda size in Nebraska just now," Clair said. "An' the consensus is there ain't enough people there yet who can read 'r write t' make it a real, red-hot pencil market for us."

"Then what?"

"People seem t' still have t' sit down, 'r lay down, 'r have some kind of a place t' talk around. —That's chairs, an' beds, an' tables." He shrugged. "That's why my deal could let me afford them three presents for us, on a twenty-dollar advance. —I'll be sellin' *furniture*."

"I guess furniture,—is something everybody needs."

"You bet they do, honey! Everybody's got t' have some stuff t' *live* with."

She grinned at him faintly. "The more you think about it, the truer it gets."

He touched her shoulder, then held it gently. "The rest a' the deal I made is, they loan me a car that runs, an' twenty-dollars-a-week commission, against what I c'n sell. An' we gotta be in Omaha by next Monday."

She looked at him for a long moment. "Clair," she finally said, "I'm really so very, very proud of you."

He looked down, and then moved his hands in a short, almost apologetic gesture. "—I just went out an' got me a job,—is all."

She went to him and held his face gently in her two hands, looking softly up at him. "What you did, Clair, getting a job like that,—was really something."

"Well." He raised his eyes at last to look warmly down at her. "We'll go an' see how long the world works, and how good it turns out t' be, back there in Omaha."

"It'll be good," she said, putting her head against his chest. "And the world will last, forever."

Hugging her to him, he said, "How c'n a little girl like you claim that the world'll last forever?"

"—Because, it already has." Suddenly exhausted, she looked at him and said, "Can we go to sleep?"

He said quietly, "You bet we can."

15

In My Merry Oldsmobile

Come away with me, Lucille,
In my merry Oldsmobile,
Down the road of life we'll fly,
Automo-bubbling you and I,
All our cares we'll leave behind,
As romance and love we find,
And you'll be the lovely queen,
Of my shiny gas machine.

To the church we soon may steal,
Where sweet wedding bells will peal.—
We can go as far as we like, Lucille,
In my merry Oldsmobile. . . ."

CLAIR AND Orlean divided their furniture and household things between Melva, Margaret and Wayne, for safekeeping. And two days later, on a drizzling, bitter-cold morning, they were ready to go. The car that Clair brought home that morning, on loan from "The Hatfield Furniture Manufacturing Company, Main Headquarters, Omaha, Nebraska," was a 1924 Ford sedan that had seen better days and had a roof that leaked.

"It ain't exactly a fancy Packard, 'r a Cadillac," Clair said. "But it don't leak too bad, and she'll get us where we're goin'."

"—Our first car!" Orlean said, touching the shiny radiator cap almost reverently.

"Well, not yet, exactly. But if the job works out, it will be our first car, in a year 'r so." He grinned at her. "I was thinkin' that, maybe, right at the last minute, you'd be kinda nervous about makin' this trip. —But you're as excited as the kids are."

"You bet I am! —Maybe you can teach me to drive, so I can spell you off sometimes?!"

"We'll see. —But generally, honey, it's just in the magazines an' movies that women drive cars. — B'sides, I honestly happen t' really love drivin'."

They put Little Clair on top of their clothing—piled high in the back seat, where he would have a good view of the passing world, and with Orlean holding Delores in her lap Clair started the car and they were on their way.

Beyond Salt Lake, Orlean finally said, "We're al-

ready farther away from Magna than I've ever been!"
Then she added, "—Aren't we going north?"

"Uh-huh."

"But, I thought Omaha was sort of somewhere back
east."

"It is. But this car'd have t' be part mountain goat t'
make it over the mountains out that way. We gotta go
up north an' then cut back east through the bottom
part a' Wyomin'. An' then head kinda southeast on
down an' over t'ward Omaha."

"—Oh." After a thoughtful, frowning moment she
said, "Maybe it is best if you do the driving, Clair."

The trip took four days. They had three flats, two of
them on the same rear tire. But Clair knew how to
patch them and fill them up again with the hand pump,
so they weren't too much of a bother. And twice the
car started steaming up front, but in both cases it only
needed some more water added to the radiator to make
it stop.

Two of the nights they just pulled off the road and
slept as best they could in blankets in the car. And the
other two nights they splurged, paying the fifty cents it
cost to rent one of the small, single-room cabins in the
trailer courts that lined the road here and there along
the way.

When they were finally driving across the endless
flats of Nebraska on the last day of the trip, Orlean
said quietly, "Clair,—there's something funny."

He glanced at her. "You okay?"

"Yes. I feel fine. It's just,—like being a little bit
dizzy, or off-balance, somehow."

After a moment, he nodded. "Yeah. I kinda feel
that same way, too. —Maybe it's a touch a' that thing
they call car-sickness."

Two or three minutes later she said in sudden astonishment, "Clair! I know what it is!"

Slightly startled, he said, "What?!"

"No *mountains!* There aren't any mountains *anywhere!*"

"Well, I'll be damned," he muttered. "That's it! Ya c'n look off forever, an' still not see nothin'!—An' all this here big emptiness just kinda snuck up on us."

"Well, at least now that we know what it is, we can start trying to get used to it."

"I guess we better," he grinned. "It'd sure as hell be too damn much effort t' go all the way back an' haul us a bunch a' mountains clear over here."

They got to Omaha late that evening, and though it was too dark to see very much, the city managed to give the feeling of being gigantic.

Clair had been given the address of a rooming house, and he at last found the two-story building on the corner of a shadowy, quiet block. Carrying the two sleeping children, they went to the front door.

Mrs. Sheen, a soft-spoken, elderly woman, showed them a large, clean, furnished room on the first floor. "I've roomed to many Hatfield Furniture folks," she smiled. "They've always been very fine tenants."

"This is real nice," Orlean said.

Clair nodded and asked, "How much is the rent, ma'am?"

"Seventy-five cents by the day. Four dollars by the week. By the week you save a dollar twenty-five."

"—We'll take it by the week."

"Good. I'm glad." Mrs. Sheen stepped toward Orlean to take Delores from her tired arms. "You're all four of you exhausted," she said. "So let's see about getting you all settled in comfortably."

They stayed with Mrs. Sheen for nearly six months, and in that time Clair did better and better at Hatfield. His sales territory gradually expanded to include furniture stores in both Lincoln and Beatrice, and often he was gone on the road for as long as two or three days at a time. His weekly commissions were never less than twenty dollars, and sometimes ran as high as thirty dollars, or even more. Mr. Hatfield himself called Clair his "crack salesman," and was so pleased that he at last arranged to get rid of Clair's old Ford and replace it with a shiny and much newer 1929 Oldsmobile.

To celebrate the new car, they drove the children and Mrs. Sheen to Omaha Park on Sunday and had a picnic near the bank of the river. It was a perfect day, except that Little Clair got lost and wandered off in the wrong direction for nearly a mile before a park attendant found him and brought him tearfully back, weeping more out of pained embarrassment than fear.

Their Sunday outings in the car became an almost weekly occasion. And unless Clair was away on the road, they went to one or another park, or to a museum, or simply for a happy, carefree drive out into the country.

Then, near the end of those six months, Clair came home to their room from a sales trip to Lincoln late one night and found Orlean strumming very quietly on her guitar. She put a finger on her lips to ask for silence, so he shut the door slowly behind him.

She crossed the room softly and kissed him. "I was just singing some songs to the children," she whispered. "That always puts them right off to sleep. —But it doesn't say much for my musical talent."

Whispering back, he said, "Think ya got enough talent left over t' make some coffee, without wakin' 'em back up?"

"Being quiet," she smiled, "is my really *big* talent."

As they drank their coffee, she said in a low voice, "—Mrs. Sheen says she wants us to move."

"What?!" he whispered loudly.

She smiled again, making him know that it wasn't a bad thing. "And maybe she's right. You're doing real well, and—she thinks we should have a bigger place, with more room, so that we won't have to whisper like this everytime the children are asleep."

"—Oh. But, wouldn't Mrs. Sheen kinda miss you an' the kids?"

"We'd only be a few minutes away," Orlean said with growing eagerness. "She showed me a big apartment house where for only two dollars a week more we can get *three* nice rooms, and there's even a little balcony!"

"All that f'r only six dollars?"

"Yes. But,—there is a catch." She dropped her eyes for a moment. "They're not furnished rooms. And getting all the things we'd need would be a big expense. Do,—you think we could afford to take on something like that?"

"Hell," he grinned, "furniture's right down my alley. Sure we can!"

"Good!" She gripped his hand in a quick, happy squeeze. "And we'll even be on the third floor! —How's *that* for moving up in the world?!"

"How 'bout that? First time we'll ever 've really gotten off the ground."

They moved into the five-story Belvedere Apartments with only essential furnishings, and then began gradually adding to them, usually buying on time and finally even getting what was advertised as "The Epitome of Elegance," a big Zenith console radio.

But it was during their first few days at the Belvedere that Orlean learned one terrifying disadvantage to living in a third-floor apartment. Little Clair came into the kitchen where she was washing dishes and said, "Mom. —D'lores." He said it so very quietly that Orlean felt an instant, grim foreboding even before she'd stepped quickly into the living room. Out on the balcony, the baby Delores had somehow managed to climb up onto the top of the three-inch-wide balcony railing, and she was standing there on it now, balanced precariously three floors above the cement driveway below.

Turning slightly, she saw her mother and called out happily, "Wook at me!"

Fighting down both her sheer terror and the almost overpowering impulse to rush out swiftly and grab her skittish, capricious little girl, Orlean forced herself to speak casually. "Hi there, are you having fun?"

"Oh, yes!"

"That's nice." Knowing that any quick or unexpected movement on her part could cause her daughter to retreat in quick panic, to lose her balance and go over the edge, Orlean smiled quietly and stepped slowly toward her, picking up a doll from a chair along the way. "Would you like to have your dolly to play with out there?"

"Sure, Mommy!"

"All right, honey. —I'll bring it out to you."

Still smiling, Orlean crossed the balcony in an unhurried way, holding the doll out toward Delores.

And then, at the very last moment, she suddenly grabbed the little girl in her arms with such swift strength that Delores gave a small shriek of startled, breathless shock. Her heart now beginning to pound thunderously within her, Orlean carried her daughter back into the living room on unsteady legs that almost gave way beneath her.

Regaining her breath, Delores said, "Mommy! You *hurt!*"

Finally, Orlean managed to say quietly, "—I'm— sorry, honey."

That night, after they'd eaten supper and put the children to bed, Orlean was still shaken and frightened. "Good Lord, Clair! It—it's just *impossible* for her to have climbed up on that railing! She can't even reach the top of it!"

"Hey, darlin'. She's okay, an' that's what finally matters." He touched her cheek soothingly, then grinned, trying to calm her. "She always has seemed t' be part monkey. —Probably from my side a' the family."

"Oh, Clair, it's just,—" She took a long breath. "If it hadn't been for little Clair coming and telling me,—"

"Listen, I've got a pint in the kitchen. Ya think maybe a stiff drink'd help ya relax?"

"No."

"Then,—I think, maybe, I'll just have m'self one, anyhow."

She managed a very faint shadow of a grin. "You sure are a big phony. —The whole thing scared you almost as much as me." Then she said, "I'll just lock up that door to the balcony, and then I'll nail it shut too, and never open it, ever again."

Pouring a drink and adding some water to it, he said softly, "Now c'mon, little girl, that'd be kinda silly. That's a darn nice balcony, an' also with that door shut, an' no air movin', it gets hotter'n a pistol in here."

"I can't help it, Clair. Since I saw her standing there, the very idea of that balcony scares me to death."

He sipped his drink and they sat down at the kitchen table. "First thing in the mornin', I'll go an' get some stuff over t' the hardware store. An' I'll build us a gate across that door with a lock that only you an' me can open. That way, the kids'll only be able t' play out there when one of us is with 'em." He grinned at her. "Honey, I'll build that gate s' high an' s' strong that neither a full-grown gorilla, or even a two-year-old girl, can climb it 'r bust through it."

Finally she nodded slightly. "—Maybe."

"Damn right." He became quietly serious. "Can't go through our lives nailin' off nice balconies, 'r nailin' off any other good things, just outta worryin' about what might happen. Ya always take sensible care, but ya still enjoy them good things. —Hell, that'd be like turnin' in our Olds, an' givin' up all them fine times we have in it, just b'cause there's a chance a' runnin' into a telephone pole 'r somethin'."

At last she looked at him and said, "Of course the gate's the best idea, Clair. —I guess, for a while there, I was just still too plain scared about Delores to think straight."

He studied her with quiet, thoughtful eyes. "—You tell me about you bein' scared an' not thinkin' straight, after ya first explain t' me how ya got all the way from the kitchen door t' the balcony railin' without spookin'

Delores. Anybody makes a fast move t'ward that kid, an' she's off in the other direction like a scalded cat."

"I sort of—fooled her a little bit, with her doll." She smiled faintly. "—The one that—'sweeps.' "

He nodded. "Thought it was kinda like that." Then he took a long drink from his glass. "—Boy, Orlean, when somethin' really counts, you sure ain't never too far away."

Winter came and brought a rich, warm Christmas with it. Clair gave Orlean a delicate, silver Waltham watch, and she gave him a handsome silver cigarette case, both of the gifts flowerly engraved with each other's first name. Delores was ecstatic over her new doll that not only opened and closed its eyes but actually cried a small baby's cry when it was put down to sleep. And for the boy they got an expensive "Lindbergh Flying Uniform" that included warm gloves and a leather jacket, topped off by a leather flying cap complete not only with ear straps that buckled under his chin, but also with big, impressive goggles that he could pull down over his eyes.

It was a good time, and so were the seasons that then followed, coming and going so quickly that it was hard to keep track of them.

But in the middle of autumn Delores, who was now three, almost gave Orlean another heart failure. Her son and daughter had been out playing with some other children in the field behind the Belvedere, when Little Clair, now six, came into the apartment where Orlean was sewing and said casually, "Mom? Can ya freeze t' death in an old icebox that somebody's thrown away?"

"No."

"Well, it's okay, then. I guess I'll go play some more." He turned to go back out of the apartment.

"Wait a minute." She looked up from her work. "What's okay?"

"Delores won't freeze." He turned again to go.

"Clair?" She put her work quickly aside. "Just what are you talking about?!"

"Nothin', Mom," he shrugged. "Delores just got in t' an old icebox an' pulled the door shut b'hind her."

"What?!" She was on her feet in an instant. *"Where?!"*

Startled by her tone of voice, he said, "In the field!"

"Show me *where! Run!*"

Now genuinely frightened, the boy dashed away down the hall and then down the stairs, Orlean running swiftly after him. Outside, they sped past some playing children and on across the wide field behind the apartment house, finally coming to a deep gully where there was an abandoned icebox leaning partially on its side against the far bank. Orlean raced down the steep slope before her and ran to the icebox to swiftly throw the door open.

Crouched inside, her face beginning to turn faintly bluish, Delores said with great disappointment, "You *found* me!"

"Come out of there!" Panting, Orlean helped the little girl down out of the box and to the ground. "What in the *world* were you *doing?!*"

"Just hide-'n'-seek, Mommy."

Kneeling before her, Orlean rubbed the little girl's wrists briskly, and then her face, bringing color back into it. "Do you feel all right?"

Delores nodded, then made a face. "But the air inside that ol' thing was sure startin' t' taste *awful.*"

That night, after he'd learned what happened, Clair silently took a hammer and a flashlight and went out to the gully where he broke the door off the icebox.

"Thank God you did that," Orlean told him when he came back.

Finally speaking, he said, "One thing I'd a whole lot rather break than that icebox. —That's the neck a' the guy who put it there."

A day or two later, he and a couple of his friends

from the apartment house hauled the icebox away to the nearest junkyard.

Then winter was on them again, filled with drives to the country and fierce, laughing, snowball fights, and a huge, community-built snowman in the front yard of the Belvedere Apartments.

And then, finally, an early spring started taking away the snow and ice with its warm weapons of sunshine and light rains.

On a Monday afternoon, Orlean had taken her two children to a Tom Mix movie. Little Clair had been particularly impressed by a sequence where a ten-year-old boy, grieved by the death of his horse, had lain down on the tracks in front of an onrushing train. Tom Mix had just got there in the nick of time to snatch his young friend from the murderous, oncoming wheels. She wondered if, perhaps, her young son still had memories remaining from his even younger life, of his father's train accident. In any case, he'd been almost deliriously overjoyed, even leaping to his feet, when at the last split second, the train hadn't hurt anyone.

She'd left the two children to play with some of their friends down in front of the Belvedere Apartments and was just starting to peel some potatoes, getting ready to make supper, when Delores and her brother came into the kitchen, both of them looking slightly troubled.

"Why aren't you two playing?" she asked.

"Clair made me stop playin'," Delores muttered, frowning.

"Why?"

"Well," Little Clair said, " 'Cause it seems t' me, we maybe got,—kind of a problem."

"What problem?"

"Well, a big piece a' somethin' burnin' come up outta the chimney."

"Yes?"

"An', it came down an' landed on the roof."

"Still burning?!"

"Yeah, Mom." He shrugged slightly, as though almost embarrassed by bringing her possibly bad news. "The roof's on fire."

"Are you *sure?!*"

"Pretty sure. It was startin' t' go like nobody's business."

Orlean picked Delores up and grabbed her son by his hand as she rushed to the hall and down the stairs. Bursting out of the front door, she ran into the yard to where she could look up at the fifth-floor roof.

A large section of the roof was in flames, and she could already begin to hear from high above the hissing and crackling of the growing fire. Now other people began pouring out of the apartment house, and there were the frantic, screaming sounds of swiftly approaching fire engines.

Everything started happening too fast to really know about, and yet in Orlean's mind it seemed that everything and everyone was moving in a terrifying, slowed-up dream. The fire grew with a roaring, screeching life all of its own, suddenly leaping like a giant, flaming spider spreading huge, burning tentacles down from the roof to the fifth floor, and then the fourth floor. Fire engines and crowding people were suddenly all around them. And now, the third floor would be the next to go.

Orlean knelt beside her children and said, "Stay here. I'll be back."

And then she ran toward the blazing apartment house. Two big firemen tried to stop her, but she shouted something they couldn't hear, wrested free from them and plunged on into the burning building.

Little Clair and Delores saw this, and with tears streaming down his face the boy picked up the garden hose and turned it on full blast to help put out the flames. But the firemen's engines and their big hoses had taken up the entire water pressure, and all that the nozzle in the boy's trembling hands could do toward fighting the raging blaze was to put out a few, helpless drops of water that fell hopelessly at his feet, along with his tears.

The flaming spider of fire now dropped its roaring, red-and-yellow tentacles to the third floor, engulfing it within seconds.

And it was then that Orlean rushed back out of the front door and ran to her two weeping children. "It's all right," she said, hugging them breathlessly. "I didn't mean to scare you, but it's all right."

It was after midnight two days later when Clair, totally exhausted from a trip to both Lincoln and Beatrice, parked his Olds in the dark, a half block away from the Belvedere. Hardly able to stay awake, and mostly staring down at the familiar sidewalk, he turned into the front yard of the Belvedere Apartments and walked almost completely to the front door before he looked up and suddenly realized it wasn't there. All that was before him was a concrete foundation filled with a mass of charred wood.

At first he couldn't believe it, thinking that somehow he'd made a terrible mistake, arriving in the wrong town, or on the wrong block or the wrong street. But then, looking around him with numb, unbelieving eyes, he knew overwhelmingly that this charred wreckage had been his home.

Holding his stunned horror and fear within him as much as possible, he went back to his car and did the only thing he could think of to do. He drove the few blocks to Mrs. Sheen's.

She opened the door in a bathrobe and seeing his face said quickly, "They're all *right,* Clair!"

Then, a few minutes later, he was alone with Orlean in their same old room, and she was bringing him coffee, being careful not to wake the two sleeping children.

"Was—anybody hurt?" he asked quietly, lifting his cup with a slightly trembling hand.

"No. Everybody lost just about everything, but they all got out in time."

He inhaled deeply, and then let his breath out slowly, in a long sigh. "—Sure did scare me, quite a little bit."

"The paper said it was one of the fastest spreading fires on record. —And we tried every way to let you know about it. We left a message with Mr. Hatfield, and even tried a telephone call once, to Beatrice. But you'd already left the store there, and no one knew where you were going next."

He sighed again, still trying to get his emotional balance back. "—Well, we just got all the apartment stuff finally paid off, an' now here we are, right back where we started. —But with you all windin' up okay, nothin' else matters a damn."

She smiled. "—Broke again."

He grinned back at her. "Broke again, flat. —But hell, I got the job, an' the Olds's almost paid for, an' we'll sure as shootin' make 'er all over again."

She touched her cup against his in a small, almost soundless salute. "You bet we will."

They sipped coffee to her words, and then Clair said, "One thing. Mrs. Sheen said she heard ya went runnin' back in t' that big bonfire." His low voice now came out with quiet, rumbling anger. "—What the hell did ya go an' do that for?"

"Are you mad?"

"—It's just that I still kinda remember Sherril doin' somethin' like that. —Why the hell did you do it, too?"

Orlean's eyes fell to the top of the table. "I,—had to go back in,—for just one thing."

"Jesus, honey," he murmured quietly. *"What?"*

She got up and went to the bureau, where she pulled the top drawer out gently. Taking something out, she closed the drawer silently and sat back down at the table, handing Clair a folded piece of paper.

After studying it a moment, Clair frowned up at her and said, "Goddamnit, honey. All this is, is just our goddamned weddin' license."

"Yes. —That's all it is."

Both angry and puzzled, he tried to keep his voice down. "—An' you risked your life f'r *this?!*"

"Well," she said, "I just couldn't stand the idea of it being burned."

Very slowly, he refolded the paper and handed it back to Orlean. "—I am much too tired right now t' even begin t' tell ya what a dumb nut ya are."

"But do you like me?"

He leaned over and kissed her and said, "—A little bit."

Three weeks later, on one of those sunny-cool spring days when nothing can be wrong, Clair came home in the early afternoon with something slightly glazed and wrong in his expression. Orlean was sitting on the floor, playing a new game called "Gas Station" with the children. She had a tiny toy car on the large, cardboard station, and was about to order five gallons of gas from Delores, who was the owner of the station.

"I'll take five gallons and drive to Kansas City," she said, getting up. "You two go ahead, and don't bother your dad and me."

She went into the kitchen with Clair, and he closed the door behind them before saying in a low, tight voice, "I been fired."

"—Why?"

He poured himself a drink and said, "Nothin' t' do with Mr. Hatfield, or with me f'r that matter. Company just up an' went bust, is all."

"You mean, whole big companies can go broke, just out of the clear blue,—like people can?"

"Looks like. —An' if a fella was smart enough, maybe he coulda seen it comin'." He took a small drink and tried to grin at her, though he couldn't manage to bring humor up into his eyes. "Anyhow, Hatfield an' a whole bunch've others've lost everythin' but their shirts in just these last few days 'r so." He paused, frowning down absently at the drink in his hand. "—Nobody seems t' know exactly the why 'r wherefore of it all. —But hell, guys that've been high-up bosses an' even owners, 'r all of a sudden out on the streets lookin' for jobs, an' even them not havin' any luck."

"Oh, Clair," she said in a small voice. "You were trying so hard, and doing so well. —I'm sorry, for both you and Mr. Hatfield."

"Yeah." He took another sip and shook his head slowly. "Poor old sunofagun was damnere cryin' when he told me there was no way I could even have our Olds. He wanted me t' have it, an' there was only seven damn weeks' more payments due on it. But—" he shrugged.

She leaned forward and kissed him lightly.

"Well then, Clair, what do you think is the best thing for us to do?"

"We've got about thirty-six dollars. Fella I know, name of Ralph, is drivin' out t' California, an' we c'n get a ride back t' Utah with him, by payin' f'r the gas. Your two sisters 'r there." He hesitated. "—An' with them around, you an' the kids'll get along, somehow an' whatever."

"What do you mean by that?"

"They're a kind of a last resort. —But nobody's gonna go hungry, an' nobody's not gonna have no place t' live, as long as I'm around t' make things work."

"Who ever said you're *not* going to be around?!"

"I mean just what I said b'fore, honey. I won't never stand by an' let you an' the kids go without." He finished his drink and put it very firmly down on the table, but when he spoke to her, he spoke gently. "Darlin', it's a time when already hard times 'r gettin' harder. An' I ain't never forgot that—that thought a' doin' whatever I have to, if need be, t' make things work out all right f'r the three a' you."

After a moment, Orlean somehow managed to grin slightly and even shake her head a little. "—Every time things start getting bumpy, my husband decides to become the new John Dillinger of the U.S.A."

"That ain't too bad an idea," he nodded, grinning

faintly back at her. "All that fella's got that I ain't, is a Thompson submachine gun."

"There's a little bit more," she said quietly. "And that is that you don't have one mean bone in your whole body, you big,—big dummy. You couldn't hurt a flea!"

He laughed quietly. "Oh, yeah? Well, I just killed one in a boardin' house two nights ago, or at least injured it severely." He paused, and then became serious. "You know I won't do anything wrong in this world, just as long as there's some possible way t' take care of you." And then he became even more serious. "—But if worse comes t' worst in these here harsh an' rugged times, then the devil'll sure have t' take the hindmost. —B'cause it just ain't nowhere in my nature t' let you an' them two kids git hungry, or not have no home, or for you t' be hurtin' in any kind a' way."

"But, as long as you can get a job?" she said.

"As long as it's a survival job."

"—And, if you can't?"

Trying to make a joke of it, he said, "Then that there pussycat Dillinger will have t' start takin' some lessons."

She managed to smile at his half-joke, and tried to gently draw him further out of himself. "You really and surely do sound like a very frightening person."

He smiled back at her, but his troubled eyes stayed strong and level. "—It's just, when it comes t' takin' care of you an' them two, I'll always try t' be as close in there as ten strong tigers."

"You sure are that," she said. "We wouldn't trade you for all ten of them."

"Well," he grinned. "—Let's go an' see what's happenin' back up in them mountains."

"All right," she said. "Let's go and do that."

For both Clair and Orlean, the long drive back to Utah became a slowly moving nightmare of the sadness and shabbiness that they could see on every side. The '26 Pontiac that they and the children were crowded into with Ralph and his fat wife, sputtered and coughed endlessly, yet it somehow kept on going. But there were so many very old and hopelessly overloaded cars along the way, with so many of them either broken down completely right on the roads, or pulled only partly off to the side for repairs, that it was often impossible to go more than a few miles an hour. But what was much worse than the sad cars themselves were the vacant, aimless faces of the tired and beaten people within them, who didn't really seem to know quite where they were going, or why.

Early in the trip, on a wide and deserted Nebraska plain, they passed a scattered group of five stricken cars, the large families from within those cars milling pointlessly back and forth between them.

Orlean asked Clair very quietly, "Isn't there,—some way we can help those people?"

He shook his head silently, then muttered, "There'll be more of 'em around the next bend, an' the next after that. All of 'em busted, an' bad up against it." Then he continued, an anger creeping into his low voice. "There's just too damn many, darlin'. If we split up every penny we got, we could maybe give 'em all about a thousandth of a penny apiece, an' that sure ain't gonna help nobody a real whole lot."

"Then,—there's just nothing we can do for them back there, Clair?"

"Just one thing. —Just hope there's one person,— just one single person among 'em, with some spirit." He closed his eyes hard, clamped his jaw shut even harder, and said no more.

But Ralph, who had somehow heard their conversation over the noise of the sputtering engine, shifted the two-day-old wad of chewing gum in his mouth and said loudly, "By golly, that there's right, Missus, about never stoppin' f'r nobody! They ain't s' bad off! Hear down t' Oklahoma them folks's pushin' wheelbarra's with their goods in front of 'em, no cars 'r livestock 'r nothin' a'tall! Why heck, all us'r sleepin' off the road in blankets ever' night! Like he says, in this here world, man's got t' watch out just for hisself, just ol' number one, an' that's all!"

She said quietly, "That's not what he was talking about."

But Ralph, swerving around to miss another car that was stalled ahead on the road, didn't hear her.

She didn't care, very much, that he hadn't heard.

At this time, the mountain roads had been improved enough for them to drive due west, straight on through Denver and Steamboat Springs, and finally across the top of the Great Divide of the Rocky Mountain Range at Rabbit Ear Pass, so that they could at last, and in early night, come down from those high mountain ranges toward the dim lights in the Great Salt Lake Valley that were spread out in twinkling patterns against the darkness far below, like a million tiny, welcoming candles.

Delores woke up briefly in Orlean's lap, looking out at the vastness of dark stretching forever beneath her, and only seen because of the countless, distant specks of light below. "Mommy," she said sleepily, "—that sure is beautiful."

"It's home," Orlean said. But even as her quiet words were spoken, Delores was asleep again.

16

The Red River Valley

From this valley,
They say you are leaving,
I shall miss your sweet face,
And bright smile,
For you take with you,
All of the sunshine,
That has brightened my life,
For a while.

Come and sit by my side,
'Ere you leave me,
Do not hasten to bid
Me adieu.
And remember,
The Red River Valley,
And the sweetheart,
Who loves you,
So true. . . .

ORLEAN'S LAST, quickly written letter about their returning had arrived from Omaha to Magna, by train,
three days before they themselves got there.

It was a simple and strange coincidence that Melva
and Margaret had found them a small house to rent,
right alongside the tracks of the Bamburger trolley that
had brought them that very letter.

Later that night they were in the front room of the
two-room house by the tracks, with the two children
put to bed in the back room. The furniture they'd left
behind had been put in, so the house was already for
them to move into. Wayne and Al were building a fire
in the front room stove, while Darrell helped Miles
make drinks for the two of them and Clair from a
bottle Miles had brought.

And almost everyone in the small, crowded room
seemed to be talking and listening at once. There was
so much that had happened, and so little that could
really be told in the occasional letters back and
forth.

Melva and Al now had a little girl, Carol, who was
over a year old, and Margaret and Darrell had a son,
Monte, who was a little younger. Miles was holding on
in his gravel business, and Guila was beamingly proud
that Wayne had just managed to get a job in Salt Lake
delivering for a dairy.

Miles raised his glass. "Well, here's to it! Omaha's
loss 's our gain!"

Starting to make cocoa and coffee on the now-
heating stove, Melva suddenly said, "Good golly! We

haven't yet had one minute t' ask if this house is all right!"

"Oh, Melva!" Orlean smiled. "It just couldn't be better! Right, Clair?"

"That's for darn sure."

"We all thought," Margaret said a little shyly, "that if we went ahead an' got this place, an' fixed it up a little, an' moved in the stuff you let us have,—it'd be sort of a little surprise for ya."

Orlean hugged her younger sister and Clair said, "Well, it sure is. We'd kinda wondered just where we was gonna start, at gettin' squared away."

Looking around the room, Orlean said quietly. "We —thank you all."

Al shrugged and snorted. "No need t' thank us f'r nothin', 'Lean. —Ain't no damn work *else* t' do, anyhow."

There was a moment of silence in the room, and then Wayne asked his big brother quietly, "—Is it like this clear across the whole country, Clair?"

"—Yeah. —Everywhere we saw, anyway."

There was another heavy silence, and then Guila smiled slightly. "Well sometimes, if ya try real hard, ya can make things go good. Like Wayne gettin' hired on by the dairy."

"Ah, honey," Wayne said in a low voice, "that was just plain, dumb luck. Bein' at the right place at the right time."

"Sure," Al agreed gruffly. "One lucky chance in a thousan'."

"But still Guila's right," Orlean said softly. "You have to keep on,—even if all you're doing is, mostly just hoping, and trying."

Evelyn nodded. "That's the way Miles feels. Otherwise he could have given up and lost his business a hundred times."

Miles suddenly laughed and said, "Goddamn *right!* It's that very stick-to-itiveness that's made me what I am t'day! I got one stupid employee. That's me! An' I got the toughest bastard of a boss I ever ran into.

That's me, too. I make that dumb worker a' mine slave fourteen hours a day, loadin', haulin' an' unloadin' about a million tons a' gravel an hour just t' barely squeak through." Chuckling to himself, he poured another drink. "An' I *hate* gravel in the first place. So one a' these days I'm gonna up an' punch my boss right in the mouth—an' quit!"

"—It sure is inspirin'," Clair said mildly, "t' hear the personal success story of a big gravel tycoon."

"Sure is," Wayne grinned. "Ol' brother Clair took the words right outta my mouth."

The earlier, brief moments of heavy silence were gone now, giving way to smiles and a warm feeling in the room as Orlean and Melva began to serve cocoa and coffee to those who wanted some.

Even Al finally grinned a little. "—Well, hell, one good thing. At least it sure can't git no worse. I doubt too many people'll starve t' death, 'r nothin'." Taking some hot cocoa from Melva, he shrugged slightly and went on. "There's a few hours' work up t' the mill ever' now an' then. An' we usually git the relief purty regular. Somethin' t' eat an' all." Then he nodded to himself, at some inner thought. "—An' I'll just bet th't that there new fella Roos'velt'll git the mill workin' at full blast again, in no time a'tall." Again he nodded to himself. "I'll just bet that everythin's back t' the way it used t' be inside a' six months, 'r even less!"

"Boy," Melva said lightly, "when my Al starts lookin' on the bright side, there's just no way t' stop 'im."

"I think he's right," Darrell said. "The unions ain't done no good so far, but I'll just bet that Roos'velt c'n pull it off, an' put things around here right back in shape."

"Well," Clair said, "he's sure gonna have t' do it by himself. 'Cause I'll be too busy lookin' for a job t' help 'im."

Miles pulled out his watch and glanced at it. "Speakin' a jobs, we got t' go. I'm puttin' m'self t' work at five in the mornin'."

Miles and Evelyn took Wayne and Guila to drop

them at their home along the way, and as they were leaving Clair said to Wayne, "How's y'r Indian doin'?"

"That's the best ol' cycle there ever was," Wayne told him. "Been usin' it t' get back an' forth from work." He suddenly hesitated, and then continued sincerely, "Ya know, Clair, that Indian's really your cycle, an' always will be. —Ya want it back, t' get around on?"

"Hell, no." Clair squeezed his younger brother's shoulder slightly. "Just wondered if ya'd wrecked it or not, knowin' how clumsy ya tend t' be."

"Nope. And it's yours, anytime."

"It's yours, kid brother, an' no more about that."

"I will admit one thing," Wayne grinned. "I never have got so I c'n drive it as good as you."

They started toward Miles' car in the road, and Miles turned back to say one last thing. "Hey, Clair, there's a fella up t' Logan, might be somebody for ya t' talk to. I'll check 'im out."

They pulled away as the others in the house were putting on their coats to go.

"I'll tell ya," Al said. "I'd give a million bucks t' know how all these things're gonna work 'emselves out."

"Speakin' of high finances," Clair said, "an' just by the way, what's our rent here, and who d' we pay it to?"

"To Mr. Perkins, up the street," Melva said. "And it's—nine dollars a month." She paused. "Sure hope that's okay."

"Hell," Al muttered. "We made the deal f'r nine, but Perkins'll take five, six dollars a month, 'r even less if it comes down to it."

"Sure he would," Darrell agreed. "Anythin's better'n nothin'."

"Nine sounds fair," Clair said. "We'll figure on that."

"You two've been on the move a long time," Melva said. "An' you've both gotta be dead tired." To the others she said, "C'mon, let's let these two world travelers alone so they can get some rest."

A little later, by themselves in the small front room, they hugged each other for a long, tired, warm moment.

"That was so nice of all of them," Orlean finally said. "Getting this place ready for us, and everything."

"It sure was." He hesitated. "Almost too much t' accept. But what the hell, once it's done there's no way not t' go along with it." He paused again, grimly thoughtful. "The way the world is, seems t' be about the same tough times all over, wherever ya go."

"—Things will be all right, Clair," she said, hugging him gently.

Staring beyond her, looking at nothing, his eyes and his jaw hardened into the strong expression of iron determination that she had learned to love, and yet couldn't help but be a little afraid of at the same time. In a very low voice he said, "You're right, honey. You c'n just bet things'll be all right."

"I'm glad to hear that. But I'm so tired." She gave him one more small hug and looked up with wide, exaggeratedly innocent eyes at his hard, grim face. "Could we please get some sleep now,—Mr. Dillinger?"

Long, grinding weeks of looking for a job went by and Clair found absolutely nothing. But then the man Miles knew in Logan, a Mr. Whitehall, made a trip to Salt Lake where Miles managed to have him meet with Clair.

Late that afternoon Clair got home to find Orlean struggling with the little vegetable garden she was trying to start in the small back yard. He took the shovel from her and began to turn over the almost rock-hard, dry earth for her. "You sure are one stubborn lady," he said. "No vegetable in its right mind'll ever grow here."

"Well, it's a sporting gamble at least. All we can lose

is some seeds." She studied him as he hit a rock in the ground and pried it out with the tip of the shovel. "—How did your meeting go?"

"Well, t' be real honest,—I just ain't too sure."

"You mean, there's a chance?"

"What I mean is, if I want it, I got me a job."

"Good!" But she could see by his expression that something was wrong. "—Or is it?"

He finished the spading and said, "Let's sit down an' talk."

There was an old wooden bench behind the house, and they sat near each other on it, facing the sun now lowering behind the mountains to the west. "This job ain't no guaranteed bed a' roses," he told her quietly.

"But there's more to it than just that."

"Yeah," he nodded. "If I d'cided t' take it, honey,— it'd mean that you an' me'd, have t' be kinda split up, f'r maybe quite a while."

"—Oh," she murmured.

"This Whitehall owns the Diamond Furniture Store up t' Logan. New an' used. He's kinda old, an' needs somebody who knows furniture, an' who he c'n trust, t' help him."

"Well,—couldn't we just move up there? It's only a hundred miles or so."

He shook his head slowly. "That's the first thing that came up. But old Whitehall's as tight as a nail in a plank. All he'll go for is a place for me t' sleep in the back, an' no salary. Not even any draw against commissions. Just a flat three percent of what I personally sell." He lighted his last cigarette, and slowly crumpled the pack of Luckies. "Be a seven-day week, with one weekend a month off, t' come see you an' the kids."

"Well," she said, almost in a whisper, "what if things went good? I mean *real* good. Wouldn't we be able to move up there with you in two, or maybe three months?"

"Bein' practical, honey, more likely six months, 'r even a year."

"—Oh." She looked down toward the ground.

"You don't much want me t' go."

"I sure *don't*."

"Neither do I." He paused, and then said, "But ya want t' know a funny thing about why I *am* gonna go, honey, an' what wins the whole argument, finally?"

"What?"

"This damned cigarette."

"—How?"

"It's m' last one, an' I dearly love a good smoke." He took a final puff, dropped the butt and ground it out in the dirt. Then he forced a small grin and put his arm around Orlean. "An' until some money starts comin' in that I can send down to ya from Logan, I ain't just about t' throw away a dime on another pack."

Somehow forcing herself to smile, she said, "—I just hope those girls up in Logan aren't too pretty."

"Oh, they're real lookers, an' speedy, too. They call Logan the Hollywood a' the Hills."

The "Diamond New & Used Furniture Company" turned out to be mostly "used." It was a dilapidated, run-down store on the corner of a little-used street, and in his first weeks there Clair spent more time cleaning and straightening the place up than he did with the occasional customers who wandered in. Yet each week he managed to send a few dollars home by letter, and the letters between him and Orlean became the high points of their lives, second only to their brief monthly visits together.

On the second of those visits, Clair gave the children a small sack of penny candy he'd brought for them, and they ran happily outside to begin the lengthy and very serious business of dividing it up between them.

When they were gone, Clair hugged Orlean and kissed her, and then said, "All right, now it's turn f'r your present."

"Me, too?!" she asked, smiling and happy. "What is it?!"

"Well,—" He hesitated. "It's somethin', like nothin' I ever bought b'fore."

"Yes?"

"But, well, this here fella come in t' the store. An' what he had, seemed like somethin' a girl might like." He paused again. "But it's somethin' I don't know nothin' about. —An' it's kinda,—embarrassin'."

"Come *on* now," she laughed. "What is it?"

Almost reluctantly he went to the open front door and got a large package that he'd left just outside.

As she began to eagerly open it, he grinned faintly and said, "Guess he was a better salesman than me. —I couldn't sell him one damn thing."

Orlean unwrapped a large, highly polished wooden box and opened the lid. The inside of the top of the box was a mirror, and neatly arranged within the box was every conceivable kind of makeup, from a wide selection of lipsticks to rouge and face powder, and even several shades of fingernail polish, plus emery boards, files and a pink buffer.

Orlean was so surprised that for a stunned moment she couldn't find anything to say.

Clair said uncertainly, "Like I said, I don't know,—much. —But is it okay?"

"It's,—it's just *beautiful!*"

"Thank God," he sighed, relieved.

"But Clair," she said, her eyes beginning to dampen. "To spend so *much—!*"

"Only $4.95."

"*Only?*"

"Well, hell, honey," he said with a mischievous grin, "Bein' surrounded by s' many gorgeous gals up in Logan, I just wanted you t' have a fair chance t' outshine 'em all."

She smiled and kissed him, her tears softly wetting his cheek. And then after a moment, still hugging him, her own mischief began to show through the dampness in her eyes. "—I just hope that all of those gorgeous girls surrounding you up in Logan don't have the same news for you that I do."

"Hmmm?"

"Because I'm going to have a baby."

His own sudden surprise slowly changed to a smile, and then a low laugh. "Well, I'll be damned! —You sure do seem t' have a terrific knack f'r goin' a fella one better."

Their third child was a little girl, and they named her Nancy. Clair managed to get a few extra days off to be home when she was born, but Mr. Whitehall wasn't too happy about it.

Orlean cut up an old, worn-out pair of Clair's homespun pants to make a warm, comfortable robe for the baby. During those days there was a woodpecker that tapped vigorously on the front of the house every morning, and Clair explained to Little Clair and Delores that the woodpecker was a Rocky Mountain stork.

Back in Logan, probably because of the aging owner's growing forgetfulness and surliness, business at the store began to get worse and worse. Despite doing the best he could, Clair's letters home included very little money, and sometimes none at all. But Orlean's letters to him were always cheerful ones, filled with news of their children and friends.

Then, toward the end of that year's light winter, there was a full week with no letter from Orlean at all. This had never happened before, and was enough to concern Clair, but his concern gradually became deep worry and finally bordered on genuine panic when the second long week came and went without one piece of mail.

On the fifteenth day, a Friday, he went to the small, cluttered office and said, "Mr. Whitehall, I want a couple of days off."

The old man looked up at him over the rims of his glasses balanced on the end of his nose. "Y'r two days off come at the end a' the month."

"I haven't heard from my family. I'm worried about them."

"—Need ya here."

"Is that final?"

"—Sure is." Whitehall looked back down at a paper on the desk."

"Then I quit."

The eyes came up again in frowning, angry surprise. "You don't know how good ya got it, young fella! Ain't no jobs growin' on no trees!"

"You owe me seven dollars and thirty cents."

"You're crazy! You an' that fam'ly a' yours'll *starve!*"

"If we do, we'll do it t'gether."

The old man made a few penciled scribbles on a pad. "I only figure seven dollars and *ten* cents."

Clair's jaw tightened. "Then pay me that. I'm in a hurry."

Clair hitchhiked to Magna, his last lift dropping him off on Main Street at about ten o'clock that night. Walking so swiftly that it was almost a run, he got to the small house by the railroad tracks and burst into the darkly shadowed front room calling "Honey?!"

"Clair?" Orlean said in sleepy surprise, sitting up in bed.

"You all right?!"

"Yes."

"The kids too?!"

"Sure they are."

"Well, thank God!"

Now more awake, she said, "Can you see to light the lamp?" Then, as he struck a match and touched it to the wick, she added, "—What are you doing here?"

Clair's built-up tension was now dissolving into relieved anger. As light filled the room he said gruffly, "Well, I'll tell ya. I just come by t' pick up m' goddamned mail!"

"—Ohhhh." She strung the word out, nodding with sudden understanding. "But darling, I *couldn't* write."

"Why the hell *not?!*"

"Now come on, don't look so mad. Sit down here, and try to calm down, and I'll tell you." When he sat beside her she took his hand in hers and said, "About two weeks ago, I somehow got down to where I only had three cents."

"That's *all?*"

She nodded. "And I knew you wouldn't want me to ask anyone for money, even if they had it."

"Well,—yeah."

"And we didn't have hardly anything left in the house to eat. So, honey, I had to decide whether to spend those three cents for a stamp to send you a letter, or to spend them for a cake of yeast to make some bread. —I thought you'd agree with the yeast."

"Damn!" he muttered. "I didn't know you'd got down that short."

"I even thought of sending you a penny postcard," she said quietly. "—But that would still leave only two cents, and a cake of yeast is three."

Clair's grip tightened warmly on her hand, and then his stored-up emotions suddenly broke loose in a small, continuing laugh that he found it hard to stop.

"—What's so funny?"

Finally controlling his laughter a little, Clair said, "What I *did* is funny. —I just up an' quit m' job over a loaf a' bread!"

"You quit?"

"I sure did."

"Oh, I'm *glad!*" She gave him a brief, fierce hug. "I just couldn't have *stood* you being away much longer!"

"Well, I'm glad about it too, right at this minute. —An' we'll see about t'morrow when it gets here."

Putting her head against his chest, she whispered with quiet delight, "That's just *wonderful*."

"What?"

"Quitting a job over a loaf of bread."

Smiling, he said, "Well, I never did lay claim t' bein' too bright."

"But it wasn't just one loaf. I baked four of them."

"Oh?" He shrugged. "Hell, in that case then, I guess it was more'n worth it."

For the next short while Orlean's concern grew at about the same rate that their small amount of money diminished. Clair hitched rides into Salt Lake early each morning, and back late each night, but the best he could do was to very rarely get a one-day job on the spot. Once, when a few men had been hired for a single day, Clair paid one of them fifty cents so that he could work in his place all day for one dollar. And Clair's normally smiling, easy face was sometimes so grim and hard at night, that Orlean couldn't help but worry about what he was thinking, or what he might do out of simple, final desperation.

But then one spring day he came home earlier than usual and tossed little Nancy into the air, catching her gently and making her laugh with delight. "Believe it or not, I got a *job!* With the WPA!"

"What's that?" Orlean asked excitedly, drying her hands on her apron.

"The initials f'r a big federal thing called the Works Project Administration." He put Nancy back down in her crib. "They're hirin' lots of fellas, all over the country, t' do all kinds a' things."

Orlean's face dropped. "—How far will you have to go for the job?"

"Right up here in our own mountains! I c'n *walk* t' work!" He now picked her up and swung her around, laughing. "An', the pay's nine dollars a week, f'r only five days a week!"

"Good grief!" she laughed too, as he put her down. "We'll be able to get to know each other again!"

"Oh, I already know you by face," he said, hugging her, "it's just your name I have trouble rememberin'."

"I thought you knew," she pouted. "It's Kathleen."

"Okay. Then will ya sing that song about Orlean, t'night?"

The WPA crew Clair worked with had the job of building half a dozen rock dams in nearby mountain canyons where there were often flash floods that had to be stemmed and checked. It was hard, healthy, outdoor work with a pick and shovel. And generally working stripped to the waist, he was soon deeply tanned and his muscular body was as flat and hard as an anvil.

The nine dollars a week wage was just about exactly what Clair had had in mind as a "survival" job. There was never a lot, but usually enough. And only once in a while was there almost nothing at all. One of those times came in the middle of the summer, just before payday. Little Clair, who was eight and growing like a weed, and who loved to hike, was going to take a lunch the five miles up to the WPA work site to share with his father.

Orlean made sandwiches and put them into a brown paper sack that she handed the boy. "——Will you,——tell your dad that that's all we have,——today?"

Eager to be off, the boy said, "Okay, Mom," took the sack and hurried out.

When he was gone, Orlean's eyes became miserably sad, and she sat at the table, resting her face in her hands.

"What's the matter, Mommy?" Delores asked.

"Oh. ——That's just a *heck* of a thing to make for your dad and brother. ——Plain onion sandwiches!"

After a moment Delores reached out and touched her mother's hand. "That's okay, Mommy," she said quietly. "——We all like anything, if you make it."

In the evenings Orlean would play the guitar quietly and sing songs to them. Or they'd turn the kerosene lamp off, and sitting around with only the thin cracks of light from the stove to dimly see by, Clair would tell ghost stories, making them up as he went along. The children were always delightfully petrified by his imaginary phantoms and ghosts and witches, but sometimes

Clair's stories got so frightening that even Orlean found herself glancing around her shoulder at the dark shadows in the room behind her.

Often, later on, when the children were asleep, friends or Melva and Margaret and their husbands would come by for a few games of cards, or just to sit around and talk.

And the summer slowly gave way to a cold, early autumn.

One Saturday night Miles and Evelyn and Wayne and Guila had made the drive to Magna for a visit, and after they'd gone Orlean said, "What Miles was saying is true, I guess, about this being the worst depression the country has ever had. —But broke or not, there sure are some good, fine times."

"That's true, honey."

"Like just visiting tonight. But mostly it's you."

"Me?"

"Just being with you, the way it's been since you quit up at Logan. Now you take that spooky story you told us the other night, about the haunted house with the head floating around in it. —Brrrr!" She shuddered slightly and then went on. "I wouldn't trade that one story, sitting around the stove with the children, for every program we ever heard on that big Zenith radio in Omaha."

"Frankly, honey, neither would I." He grinned, "But that *was* one hell of a story I made up. Especially when the head found its own body in the basement an' was goin' crazy tryin' t' get the two t'gether."

"Let's not ever get in that sad fix."

"We'll never be in no sad fix, honey. Hell, with all the diggin' I'm doin' up in them mountains, it's just a matter a' time before I find us a gold mine."

"I mean, let's always stay put together in the first place, with or without a gold mine."

"That's sure okay with me, if it's okay with the WPA. But those dams up there're almost finished."

"Work slower."

"Most a' the fellas are. They say the only way ya c'n tell a WPA worker is by how he sleeps."

"—How does he?"

"Leanin' on his shovel."

The next Thursday, Clair was late getting home from work. Orlean fed the children at the regular hour, and put her and Clair's supper in the oven to keep it warm. With deep, growing worry as dark night fell, she finally put the children to bed, telling them that their dad would be home soon and would come in to kiss them goodnight.

It was nearly eleven, and her worry had turned to numb, heartbreaking fear, when he opened the door and came into the dimly lighted room.

"Clair?" She stood up. "Where have you been?"

"—T' Salt Lake."

"Salt Lake?!" Without meaning to, her words sounded angry.

Then, as he moved closer in the room, she now saw his face, that was hollow and empty, and lined with grief. "Oh, *Clair*." She went to him quickly. "What is it?"

"—Wayne's dead."

Saying nothing, except with her eyes, she put her arms around him. And finally he managed to speak again. "—He was killed, honey,—drivin' t' work,—on the Indian."

17

Jolly Old Saint Nicolas

Jolly Old Saint Nicolas,
Lean your ear this way,
Don't you tell a single soul,
What I'm going to say.
Jennie wants a drawing book,
Susie wants a dolly,
Jimmy wants a pair of skates,
He thinks dolls are folly.
As for me, my little brain,
Isn't very bright,
Bring for me dear Santa Claus,
What you think is right. . . .

THE MORNING they buried Wayne there was a bitterly cold, drizzling rain, one of the first signs of an oncoming winter that was to be filled with enormous blizzards and so savagely cold that even the birds would die.

Standing near Clair in the now muddy, tumbleweed-covered cemetery on the low foothill above Magna, Orlean only vaguely heard the bishop's droning words as they lowered the plain wooden casket. Somewhere beyond her tearless grief, she was remembering a sunny day that now seemed an eternity ago, when Clair and Wayne had first driven up to her house on the motorcycle. Both of them so young and handsome and carefree. Both so filled with the joy of life. And from there her memory moved, almost with a numb will of its own, to the shattered fence, the mean, spotted cow that had fainted, and then even on to the precious, long-gone, red geraniums.

Clair's own stricken thoughts were also torn equally between the stark reality of the rain-swept grave before him, and the good, happy memories of Wayne in the past. He remembered fleetingly, and with bittersweet pain, the day he'd taught Wayne to drive the Indian, out in the alley and in the empty field behind Swenson's grocery story. Wayne had taken two or three small, laughing spills before he'd finally got the hang of it. *Goddamnit,* he thought, his eyes damp with both rain and tears. How could all those good times over all those years, wind up in one split second like this? That big truck had hit Wayne so hard that it hadn't been an easy job for them to separate his body from what was left of the mangled Indian. And poor Guila. It was almost as though the truck had somehow hit her too. She could hardly stand on her feet, so Clair was supporting her gently on one side, his hand on her elbow. And on her other side Sherril, who had just showed up an hour before the funeral, was helping to hold her from falling.

Then, when it was over, the large, rain-drenched crowd began to silently break up and move away in small groups, some to cars on the muddy cemetery road, and others walking down the mile-long slope toward Magna.

Helping Guila, Clair and Orlean got into Sherril's car and he drove them down the wet and slippery dirt road toward town.

Like almost everyone else, they stopped at Frank and Enzy's house to give the parents their final, after the funeral, sympathies. It was the first time Clair and Orlean had been in the house since that sad, unforgettable night many years ago when they'd brought over their newborn son. In the crowded but quiet front room, Clair and Orlean joined the line of people moving by Frank and Enzy to murmur their condolences. Enzy was sitting in an overstuffed parlor chair, still wearing the black veil she'd worn at the services, and Frank was standing near her.

When it was their turn in line, Clair said in a husky, low voice, "—We both sure are sorry,—Mom an' Dad."

Frank muttered woodenly the same thing he'd been saying to everyone else. "We'll miss 'im, an' we do appreciate your kind thoughts." Enzy said nothing from behind her veil, but she nodded her head once, briefly.

A moment later Sherril came over to them and whispered, "Let's get outta here."

"Guila?" Orlean asked.

"She couldn't stand bein' here no more. —Miles an' Evelyn took 'er with them."

A few minutes later Orlean was making coffee for the three of them in her own, small front room.

"—My God," Sherril finally said, "it still just don't seem possible. He was just,—still a kid."

Orlean poured coffee into the three cups on the table. With a faintly trembling hand Sherril took out a flask and poured whiskey into his and Clair's cups. He looked at Orlean, but she shook her head silently.

"—Damn," Sherril went on. "We shouldn't *never* a' give 'im that cycle. —Or at least, why couldn't it a' happened t' a worthless bastard like me, instead?"

"—C'mon," Clair said quietly, touching Sherril on the shoulder. "You're hurtin' bad enough already, without lettin' yourself get in t' that kind a' thinkin'."

"—You already had them thoughts, y'rself."

"Anybody who ever loved anybody has. —But ya gotta put 'em down."

After a long, silent moment, Sherril at last poured more whiskey for himself and Clair. "—What's little Guila gonna do?"

"She's got family down south," Clair said. "She's goin' down an' stay with them. —Try t' pull the pieces back t'gether."

There was another long silence, and then Orlean spoke softly to Sherril. "—We were all of us, Wayne and everyone, just talking about you, last week. Here in this very room. —Wondering how you were."

Moved, Sherril said, "That's nice t' know." Then he shrugged faintly. "Hell, I been okay. Workin' here an' there, different places. Even clear t' California, once." He paused thoughtfully. "—Ain't had much luck at findin' any a' them b'holders I was talkin' about. Mostly, there's just the two a' you—an' that Evelyn an' her Miles sure are champions, too."

"There's one more," Clair said in a low, husky voice. "—But we just lost 'im."

Now, in his own turn, it was Sherril who reached out and touched Clair's shoulder gently. "Looks more an' more like, around here, it's gonna be up t' you, ol' kid brother, t' keep the fam'ly flag flyin'."

Through his sorrow, Clair managed a shadow of a puzzled grin. "What the hell do ya mean by that?"

"I dunno. But whatever it is,—I mean it."

The Saturday after next, in an early afternoon flurry of snow, there was a knock at the front door. Clair was just coming in from the back with a bucket of coal, and he put it down quickly near the stove before going on to open the door.

"Marvin!" he yelled, and he and the man in the doorway grabbed each other in a huge bear-hug.

It was the first time Orlean had met this older brother of Clair's, and she liked him instantly. He was a little shorter than Clair, with husky, broad shoulders and kind, quiet eyes.

Being suddenly together after nearly ten years, their meeting was a strange, touching mixture of the giant grief they both shared over Wayne's death, and the lesser but good feeling of finally seeing each other again.

When the news of the tragedy had reached him in the far north area of Twin Falls, Canada, Marvin had left for Magna immediately, but it had taken him all this time to get here.

Their talking quietly together, and their being reunited at this sad time, became so filled with quiet, underplayed emotion that Orlean, after making them a fresh pot of coffee, said, "—I think I'll take the children and go over to visit Melva for a while."

"Okay, honey," Clair said.

"But Marvin?" she asked. "When I come back, will you, please, stay for supper?"

"I'd like nothin' better, Orlean," he said in his warm, low voice.

While she was at Melva's, Orlean took a few minutes to walk downtown and buy twenty-three cents' worth of fresh meat so that they could have a particularly good supper for Marvin.

And later that night, after the children were in bed

and she'd finished the dishes, Orlean finally sat back down at the table with Clair and Marvin.

"That sure was a fine meal, young lady," Marvin said.

"I'm glad you liked it," she smiled.

He smiled back, but his voice became serious. "And now I'm gonna have a small argument with your husband. I hope you'll be on my side."

Clair frowned in faint surprise, and Orlean put her hand in his on the table. "Oh, I always take a strong stand against this brother of yours."

"I c'n see that you two are like my Janice and me," he grinned. "—At each other's throats every minute." Then, once more very serious, he went on. "What are your plans, Clair?"

Still puzzled, Clair said, "Well, right now, Marvin, my plans are just t' make it through this comin' winter somehow."

"It's shapin' up t' be a killer."

"Yeah, I know. —But we'll make it."

"What I mean, Clair, is if you had a bigger choice."

Clair glanced at Orlean, and then said, "Well, hell, ever since I took a Spenser Salesman's course a few years ago, it's been in the back a' my mind t' get a few dollars t'gether an' start up m' own business, sooner 'r later."

"What kind?"

"Well, with my background that we talked about t'day, an' my experience so far,—a furniture store."

Marvin nodded. "Dad's been tryin' somethin' like that, but it's never worked too good. Would you be willin' to take him in as a partner?"

His puzzled frown deepening, Clair said, "—Well, a' *course* I would."

"What would it take, minimum, t' start somethin' like that?"

"Oh,—maybe five hundred dollars."

"Would you take some help?"

"—Goes against m' nature."

Marvin turned to Orlean. "Here's where you come in. —You know how damned hardheaded he is."

"Yes, I know how he is," she said. "—I guess that's why I'm proud to be with him."

"You're not bein' a whole lot of help to me so far." Marvin got up and paced a little in the small room. "When we were kids in school, Orlean, and sometimes it worked out that he didn't have any lunch, he wouldn't even let me share a sandwich with him." He paused. "—Now I'm not rich, but I've put a little money aside, and—"

"Hey, Marvin," Clair interrupted quietly, "I love ya for what you're gettin' at,—but no."

"Now you *listen,*" Marvin said firmly. "I've talked t' people t'day, and I see how things are." Again he hesitated. "—Wayne was our little brother, an' we all wanted the best for him. Over a time, I been puttin' a few dollars aside especially for him, in case he wanted t' go on farther in his schoolin', or somethin' like that."

Clair said in a low voice, "—That was a real good thought, Marvin."

The older brother came to the table and put his hands down on it, leaning slightly toward Clair. "Will ya, please, for the first time in your stubborn life, let somebody give ya somethin'? Will ya take the five hundred? Not just for me. —But as a hell of a big favor both t' me *and* t' the memory of Wayne."

Clair was silent, and Marvin said, "—Orlean?"

"—Whatever he says."

Marvin looked at Clair again. "Well then? —Will ya?"

Finally Clair stood up, facing Marvin. He slowly raised his hands and put them on his brother's wide shoulders. Then finally, and very quietly, he said, "—Yeah. —I will."

Orlean had seen Clair work hard before, but never so hard as he did now. He was out of the house before daylight, and often didn't come home until midnight, or

even later. He met with his father several times before
Marvin went back to Canada, and they decided to take
over a large, old brick building at the end of Main
Street as their store. Clair's father had leased that
building before, with the financial backing of a partner
from Salt Lake, but it hadn't worked out well. This
time, though, Clair was doggedly determined that it
would work.

In getting the old place ready for business, he became a painter, carpenter, bricklayer, plumber and
replacer of broken windows. Luckily, he was already
an electrician and he was able to fix the slipshod, even
dangerous, wiring throughout the building.

Finally, late one bitterly cold night when the children were in bed and Orlean was dozing in a chair by
the stove, she was awakened by the sound of a car
pulling up in front of the house. A moment later, Clair
came in, smiling and rubbing his cold hands together
briskly. "Boy, is it chilly out there!"

"Warm yourself up, honey. I've got our dinner waiting in the oven."

"Hold on just a minute. —Listen, sweetheart, would
it be okay t' leave the kids alone for just a little
while?"

"Well,—if it's not too long."

"Good," he grinned. "It'll just take a few minutes.
Put your coat on. I've got two surprises for you!"

As they went outside he said proudly, "This is the
first one! Our first delivery truck!"

Parked hub-deep in the snow in front of the house
was a small, old Model A coupe with a small platform
rigged where the back would normally be.

"This,—is a delivery truck?" Orlean said.

"I took out the rumble seat and fixed the back up
like that so it'll carry furniture."

"But it's so—little, Clair."

"You can put almost anything in it. Even a sofa, if
ya stand it on end."

"Well, it is nice."

"Got it f'r only twenty-five bucks." He opened the door. "Get in, f'r surprise number two."

The front, and only, seat of the coupe was more warm and comfortable than Orlean would have ever imagined. And within one or two minutes Clair pulled to a stop in front of the big, dark old building that he'd been working on so hard. "C'mon!" he said eagerly.

He unlocked the front door, and as they stepped inside he flicked on a light switch.

Orlean was dazzled as the large showroom in front of her was suddenly filled with the bright glow of ten big, round light-fixtures hanging in two rows of five each from the high ceiling. The large, nearly empty room was clean and bright, and there was still the faint smell of fresh paint in the air. At the far back corner there was a waist-high counter and a swinging door leading into a spacious office enclosure.

"Oh, Clair!" she murmured. "You've made it into a whole different place! —It looks just *wonderful!*"

"And look!" He pointed toward several large cardboard boxes stacked near the far wall. "The very first shipment of furniture from Salt Lake!"

In a hushed voice, Orlean said, "—Even *furniture?*"

He hugged her and laughed. "Well, bein' real astute, it did occur t' me that one of the key things about havin' a successful furniture store might be t' maybe have some furniture in it."

She managed a very small smile. "—Darn good thinking."

Seeing her uncertainty he said, "Hey, honey, what's the matter?"

"Well, being almost all set to go, and everything,—I just can't help wondering,—if anybody will *ever* come in and actually *buy* something."

He hugged her once again, laughing even more this time. "*Sure* they will." Then he added in a low, confidential voice, "If worse comes t' worst, I'll burn down a couple a' church Wards in town, an' they'll *have* t' get all new furniture."

Her smile became wider. "I wouldn't *hear* of you doing anything like that,—except in an emergency."

He grinned and said with growing excitement, "Right here where we're standin' there'll be sofas an' easy chairs an' livin' room sets. An' over there, tables an' chairs f'r kitchens. Then linoleum an' carpets. Past that, stoves, an' then bedroom sets, dresser drawers an' mattresses an' all. That wall'll be t' display mirrors. —And maybe even some nice paintings when times get a little better so that people c'n afford fine extras in their home, like that."

"All that on five hundred dollars?"

"What little's left of it, plus things on consignment, plus buildin' up good credit, plus blind faith an' a lot a' luck. Hell, honey, it'll all work great!"

Clair's confidence was impossible to resist, and Orlean now said through teeth that were almost beginning to chatter with the cold, "—I think over there on that side—would be a good place for some of those fancy new refrigerators."

"Haven't ordered any a' them, yet."

"No?"

"Forgive me f'r puttin' it just this way," Clair grinned, "—but in this cold kinda weather, right now, stoves're gonna be a lot hotter item."

Orlean closed her eyes as though in brief pain. Then she said, "I'll forgive you if you'll take me back home. I'm starting to freeze."

A few minutes later, after driving through a heavy, growing snowfall, they were finishing their warmed-over bacon and beans in the small front room.

Quiet and thoughtful, Orlean finally said, "That little bit of talking about the bad weather made me think of the dream I was having when I was half asleep, here before, and waiting for you."

"What was the dream?" Clair asked.

"It was cold,—terribly cold. And in my dream we were on two white horses, riding through an awful, blinding blizzard." She hesitated. "I don't know where we were coming from, or where we were going. We were just there, with snow all around us, and piling down over us, and everywhere."

Clair silently poured more coffee into their two cups, and then said softly, "—Yeah?"

"I was carrying the baby, little Nancy, in front of me. We were both dressed fairly warmly, her in that robe I made out of your old pair of pants. But the main thing, the real important thing about the dream, was you. You were riding there beside me, but just a little bit ahead. —You'd taken off your jacket and put it around Little Clair. He was riding behind you, holding on with his arms around your waist. And you were carrying Delores in your arms. You'd taken off your shirt to wrap it around her, and keep her warm." She paused for another long moment. "So you were naked from the waist up in that awful, freezing blizzard. —And yet you just kept riding along with the two of them, so quiet and strong, and never complaining. —Somehow, Clair, you seemed to know where we were going." Once more she hesitated. "—And even half frozen, and nearly dead from all that icy cold,—you were quietly bound and determined to make sure that we got there all right."

There was a silence, and then Clair grinned a little. "—Hell, did we make it?"

After a moment Orlean smiled and looked quietly up at him. "Darned if I know. You and our new delivery truck woke me up just then."

Orlean poured the last of the coffee for them, and then Clair finally said, "Damned shame. I'd a' kinda liked to 've known how it turned out." He took a sip of the hot coffee. "But I guess we'd all like t' know how everything's gonna turn out,—an' that's kind of an impossible thing."

"After going down there with you tonight," Orlean said, "I think I know how the furniture store will turn out."

"—Ya do?"

She nodded. "It will be slow and hard for a while, but then it will work. —You'll make it work."

"Well, I c'n guarantee I'll give 'er one hell of a try, anyhow."

"Funny thing, though." She looked at him with quiet, loving eyes. "I don't know which will be the best part of our lives. These mostly lean times, up front"—she grinned a little—"or the plush, fancy times later on, when you get to be a great big success."

"—How 'bout both bein' the best?"

"Both?"

He nodded. "There's an old sayin' that kinda fits what I mean. 'If a man cuts his own firewood, it warms 'im twice.' "

After a moment, she said softly, "Yes."

He took her hand in his, holding it warmly, "Honey,—I sure do, somehow, like that dream ya had."

That shatteringly hard winter not only caused most of the birds to die, but very nearly killed Clair's furniture business too, almost before it had really even gotten started. People were hopelessly snowed in as often as not, and when they did venture out with the little money they had to spend, it was spent on groceries and coal.

Early one mid-January morning, Clair built a small fire in the stove to take the icy chill from the dark front room before the others got up. Then he opened the front door and found himself not looking at heavy snows, but simply staring at a solid wall of snow before him.

Now up herself, Orlean came to stand beside him in sleepy, blinking astonishment. "—My *God*, Clair!" she whispered. "What will we *do*?!"

"Well, f'r one thing, we c'n be grateful this damn door opens inwards an' not outwards."

She quickly went to the two windows in the midnight-dark room, and then hurried into the rear room. She came back with wide, frightened eyes. "Clair! We're *surrounded*! The whole house is snowed under!"

"—Sure as hell is."

"Not being able to see anything,—that snow around us could be a *mile deep!*"

He put a reassuring arm around her waist. "I doubt it's quite *that* high, honey. —Maybe half a mile."

"This is scary!" A sudden memory of Delores locked in the icebox in Omaha flashed through Orlean's mind and she said, "Clair?! Will there be enough air in the house for us to breathe?"

"Oh, sure," he told her in an easy voice. But he didn't know either, and it was a frightening thought. "Uhh,—snowflakes, an' snow, carry their own air with 'em. That's how come the Eskimos get along s' fine up at the North Pole in them igloos a' theirs."

Little Clair and Delores now came in from the back room, both of them making a beeline for the warming stove. Then the boy looked at the solid wall of snow filling the doorway. "Dad?! Is all a' that *snow?!*"

"Sure is." Clair laughed and pulled some of it from the doorway to firm up a snowball in his hands. "Remember we told ya that Santa Claus might bring us a few more things b'fore winter was over? Well, he's just brought us all the snow in the whole world t' play with."

"I don't like it," Delores frowned. "It's too much. —How can we go out an' play?"

"We'll start playin' even b'fore goin' out," Clair said. "It's a game called diggin'-a-tunnel. Want t' get me the shovel in the corner of the back room, son?"

"Okay!" the boy said. "C'n I shovel some, too?"

"Sure ya can."

Clair dug out and up at an angle, piling snow behind him in the front room. Finally resting and catching his breath, letting his son dig for a short time, he looked at the stove and suddenly said, *"Honey*, the top a' that stovepipe's got t' be stickin' up outta the snow, or the smoke from our fire couldn't get out!"

"Of *course*." She took a long breath. "Wow, that's a relief! —I never was too convinced, before, about that igloo story of yours."

"Well, it is true that I ain't talked t' too many Eskimos about their housin' conditions, lately."

Working on the rising, dark tunnel, finally crouching down on his knees to dig, Clair at last burst out into the light of a clear, blue day, the final, upper level of snow cascading down on him.

"We made it!" he called back down.

Standing up now, blinking against the dazzling bright, snow-reflected light around him, he saw that only about a foot of the black stovepipe was sticking up out of the snow that formed huge, billowing drifts as far as he could see. Other stovepipes dotted the white expanse here and there, and where the drifts weren't quite so deep there were white, triangular outlines of the roofs of the houses below.

The sound of Nancy crying, voicing disappointment about something, came up to him through the tunnel, and then Little Clair and Delores came scrambling up in quickly thrown-on coats and boots, both of them delighted and overwhelmed at the sea of snow around them.

"Honey!" Clair called back down through the tunnel. "We'll be back in a while!"

"What are we gonna do, Dad?" his son asked.

Clair stood up on top of the gigantic drift, sinking knee-deep into it. "We're gonna go around an' play find-the-top-a'-the-chimney. —Any we c'n find that're covered by snow, we'll uncover 'em."

"That sounds like fun, Daddy!" Delores said. "We never been high enough up like this, t' play that game before!"

Orlean had read somewhere that spring meant the new beginning of life, and as the murderous, hard-fought winter began to finally and gradually release its icy tentacles on the still-frozen land, this "new beginning" seemed to touch Clair's furniture store as well as the few green, growing things that put their tiny sprouts timidly up in a hopeful search for the sun.

Word began to get around that there actually was

such a thing as the "Huffaker Furniture Store," and that it wasn't necessary to go clear into Salt Lake to buy whatever was needed for the house. And it also became increasingly known that Clair was a fair and understanding man who personally backed up anything he sold with an almost fierce pride. On top of that, with money still in a crucifyingly short supply, the downpayment on most of what he sold was a simple handshake. He trusted everyone, and it was a natural thing that his outgoing trust almost always came back to him in full, grateful measure.

Clair's father, Frank, was a quiet, good-natured shadow to his son in the business, though Clair would never admit that, always taking the point of view that whatever success the business had was due to his dad, and to his brother Marvin.

On one of those very few Sundays when Clair got home in the evening at a normal time, Melva and Margaret had stopped off on their way from church with Al and Darrell, and an older, fortyish friend of theirs, Tom Hancock.

"By golly," Al said, "looks like y'r doin' purty good in that store a' yours down there t' Main Street."

Exhausted, Clair sighed and shook his head. "Ya know, Al, we had thirty-three customers yesterday. A couple of 'em from as far away as Weber Valley. Things are lookin' real lucky."

"Lucky, my eye," Darrell said in his own, quiet way. "You been killin' yourself, much as eighteen hours a day, t' make a go of it."

"Yeah, well,—it's a lot a' work, but dad keeps on top a' everything, from the office."

"Bull," Old Tom said. "He just sits there in the office, lookin' over a bunch a' papers he ain't never read in the first place."

"That's not really true, Tom," Clair frowned.

"An' you do all the sellin'," Darrell went on. "Plus ya deliver all them things. Husky as you are, still how the devil do ya deliver a five-hundred-pound stove all by y'rself?"

Clair shrugged. "Best ya c'n do is t' get madder'n hell at it. An' then swear under y'r breath a lot, an' move it one corner at a time." He grinned. "But t' be perfectly honest, I sure do prefer deliverin' ironin' boards an' lampshades."

Later, in mid-summer, the Utah Copper Company started up again on a cautious, part-time basis, and the employees began to average about three or four working days a week, which helped all the businesses on Magna's Main Street.

Even though most of the growing profit the furniture store made went back into the store, and to repay Marvin for his loan, Clair's take-home pay at last started to run between fifteen and twenty dollars a week. So that by August he felt the time was right to go ahead with a surprise for Orlean.

Over a very early breakfast of coffee, bacon and eggs, while the children were still asleep, he said, "Hey, honey. —I was thinkin' about it all last night, an' it's time we pulled an Omaha."

"Pulled an Omaha? —What's that?"

"That's a thing you invented back in that city a' the same name." His eyes smiling, he said, "It's where things're finally goin' good enough t' move to a bigger, nicer place."

"Can we?!" she asked excitedly.

"You bet we can. An' I even found a house, makin' a delivery yesterday, that might be okay with you."

"Where?!"

"That big old place next t' the Russells', up on Fifth East."

"I *know* the house! It's really nice!"

"I'm glad ya like it. We c'n rent it for eighteen dollars a month. An' it's got four rooms."

"Wow!" she said, and then added suddenly, "Hasn't it even got a *garage* for the delivery truck?!"

"Yeah," he grinned. "That's kinda like, even our car c'n afford its own house."

"When can we move?!"

"Right away. An' one more kind of important, good thing, honey."

"What?"

"That house will be the very first house we ever had,—that has *electricity* in it."

"Good grief!" she smiled. "We may have to start wearing tuxedos and long, sequined evening gowns!"

"No doubt about it. Hell, all things equal, I'm beginnin' t' feel like the man who broke the bank at Monte Carlo."

Since Fifth East was only seven blocks away, Little Clair and Delores had the joyful job of helping out with many of the small things to be moved. Delores had a play baby-carriage, and her brother had a red wagon, both of which could hold a limited amount of towels or clothes, or pots and pans. In five days they made nearly twenty trips back and forth, enjoying every minute of it except one. On the fifth day Delores pushed her baby buggy at a bad angle down a ditch to be crossed, and it overturned with a rather heavy load of cups and plates, and knives and forks and spoons. A moment later, pulling a wagon-load of canned goods, the boy came along and found her sitting on the side of the ditch near the wreckage, weeping.

"Stop cryin'," he said brusquely. "Boy, can't you never do nothin' right?"

"I *did* everything right! Until just now!"

He got down in the ditch to examine the overturned baby buggy and its spoiled contents. "Well," he said finally, "Ya only broke seven plates an' four cups. Nobody'll be too mad about that."

"I know nobody'll be mad, you big dumbbell!" she said through her tears. "But Mom'll be *sad!* She trusted me with all this stuff, an' I *broke* some of it! An' you know how Mom loves her dishes!"

Placing the overturned baby buggy upright, and putting the spilled but unbroken things back in it, he pushed it up onto the top of the far bank. "We'll tell 'em we was racin', t' see who could get there fastest. An' that way it'll kinda be both of us who done it."

"Good!" Delores said.

But it turned out that when they were all moved in, Clair and Darrell and Al moving the heavier things, there was never any need for an explanation. In one of the first days in the big, new house, with everything clean and put in its own, proper place, Orlean made lunch for the three children and said, "I'm really proud of you, Clair and Delores, for all the help you've been."

"But Mommy,—" Delores muttered, tears gathering in her eyes.

"And the *best* thing that's happened," Orlean said, putting her arm around her daughter, "is that we somehow lost some plates and cups. So Daddy's promised to get us a whole new set of kitchenware! It'll be real pretty, with red and yellow flowers on it!"

This year, the winter coming upon them was a gentle one, a winter that gave soft, almost warming snowfalls and allowed the sun to be in the sky almost every day.

That was the winter when Clair threw rocks up to the stars. At night, out on the front porch with his chilly-warm family, he'd go down to the front yard, pick up a pebble, and throw it as high into the sky as he could. And no one would ever hear the sound of it coming back down.

The first time that happened, Delores finally screamed, "Daddy! You threw it clear into the sky!"

"Oh, sure," he shrugged. "I can do that every time."

"Dad?" Little Clair said. "Did it land someplace off in the soft snow, where ya couldn't hear it?"

"Well, son, it seems t' me that your kid sister's right, an' that it did go clear up t' the stars. —But I guess that's somethin' we all have t' figure out for ourselves."

And that Christmas was some kind of a Christmas.

The Christmas tree was nine feet tall, which brought

it right up to the ceiling of the big living room. Just judging by eye, Clair went up into the far mountains to cut it down. And with the sparkle-paper star on top of it, the big tree was an exact fit, from floor to ceiling.

On Christmas morning, the children woke up to find plates of nuts and popcorn around the warmly glowing, electric-lighted tree, and bowls of gaily colored ribbon candy twisting happily back and forth within itself, and dishes of chocolates and marshmallows on every hand.

But the crucially important and overwhelming things were those lovingly wrapped and beautifully mysterious packages tempting them brightly from under the tree.

Little Clair hit the jackpot with both a Red-Flyer sleigh and a pair of white, long-haired Angora cowboy chaps. There were even two cap-shooting six-guns in holsters on the engraved leather belt that held up the chaps.

Delores did great by getting not only a doll, or a doll that slept or cried or closed its eyes, but a doll that did all of those things and also came in its own big doll house, so that she could lift the roof off and rearrange everything in the house just the way she wanted for her new dolly.

And Nancy was soon so surrounded with pretty clothes and fascinating toys that she couldn't quite make up her mind which of her presents to pay attention to, or play with.

But the crowning glory of that happy, gently sparkling, Christmas-tree morning, with all its glowing, ribbon-candied warmth, was the big package in the back, that Clair had brought home for Orlean.

It was so heavy that he had to help her bring it from behind the tree and open it.

"Oh, *Clair!*" she said, seeing it.

Her gift was a big, console Philco radio with a sweeping armband on it that could reach clear to Europe, and around the rest of the world.

"You ain't had a radio," he said, "since that Zenith, in Omaha."

"I just love it," she murmured. "But can I still sing and play the guitar sometimes,—and will you still tell your stories?"

"If it interferes with them things, we'll sure as hell send it back."

"That's fair," she said, hugging him. "But isn't it funny, Clair? —As the world goes on, with all its ups and downs, half of the joy of life just seems to be holding on to all the good things you started off with back in the first place."

"Are we back at that place right now?" he whispered.

"We never left that place."

He smiled and kissed her. "Then Merry eleventh Christmas together, pretty lady."

"Eleven? —Hmm," she mused. "Would you like to try for twelve?"

"Would it be a fair answer, just to tell you that I love you?"

She kissed him back. "Yes, it would."

"Okay," he grinned. "—I sure do."

She hugged him as hard as she could and said softly, "Merry Christmas, Clair. For now and for always."

18

When I Have Sung My Songs

When I have sung my songs to you,
I'll sing no more.
It would be a sacrilege,
To sing at another door.
We've worked so hard, to hold our dreams,
Just you and I,
That they could not be shared again,
I'd rather die.
There's just the thought,
We've loved so well and true,
That I could never sing again,
—Except to you.—

"When I Have Sung My Songs," by Ernest Charles, © 1941 by G. Schirmer, Inc.

IN THEIR second year on Fifth East, another child was born to them. If it had been a boy, they were going to name him Wayne. But it was a girl, and they had decided in that case on the name of Gerolyn.

Sitting beside Orlean and holding her hand a short time after the baby's birth, Clair grinned and said, "You sure are gettin' consistent. —Three girls in a row."

She touched the sleeping child's tiny chin gently, then gave Clair a small, weak smile. "Were you sort of planning on it being a boy,—just to maybe, kind of, even things up in our family?"

His grin widened and he said, "Hell no, honey. If the gals you have turn out anything like you, ya oughta do the world a favor, an' have about a hundred more, right away."

"—And Little Clair?"

"Soon as he found out, he went out in the yard t' start shootin' marbles with a couple friends. He didn't care at all whether it was a little brother 'r sister, just so it was somethin'." Clair now touched the baby's cheek lightly. "—An' this little gal sure *is* somethin'."

"—Yes."

"B'sides, this whole thing'll work out real good for Clair, in the long run."

Sensing an underlying mischief in his voice, she said cautiously, "—It will?"

"You bet." Clair grinned again. "With that kinda girl's name a' mine we gave him,—an' now plus three kid sisters t' look after an' protect, he'll sure as hell

249

have t' get pretty damn strong, just t' barely manage t' survive his childhood."

She shook her head with faint amusement. "Now that's a fine thing. You sound like you *want* our son to be a roughneck."

"Maybe—just a little," he said innocently. "But after all, it was you who told me a long time ago, 'I asked God f'r strength, an' he gave me problems.' An' right now that statement sure seems t' fit Little Clair. An' then after all, too, it was you who named him Clair, an' who had the three girls in a row, honey."

Smiling up at him she said, "If you think *Little* Clair's got problems, just you wait till I get back on my feet, Big Clair!"

"You sure indeed can be terrifyin'." He squeezed her hand gently. "Do ya think, maybe, we c'n have that fearful showdown over on Third East?"

"—All right," she agreed, responding softly to the pressure of his fingers with her own. "But why over there?"

"Well, honey, our family's expandin', an' there's a nice, new place on Third that's got one more, extra room, an' space for a two-car garage."

"—Clair?" she said quietly. "The big house just down from the Deluccas'?"

"—That's the one I had in mind."

"But, can we afford it?"

"We're sure as hell gonna find out. —'Cause we ain't just rentin' it, honey. I d'cided we're buyin' it."

"But Clair?" She turned her head, raising up slightly to look at him. "Can we do that?"

"Damned if I know f'r really sure, an' it is kinda expensive. But you said, once, that I could do anything I had a mind to." He touched her cheek once more, very gently making her lie back down. "So, actin' on your good advice, I'm doin' what I got a mind t' do."

Very tiredly she said, "It just seems like that house is so much for us. —But if you think it's all right, then it is."

"Over there on Third," he told her, "we won't only

just have electricity like we do here. But we'll have our own, complete inside plumbing, outhouse an' all. An' darlin', we'll even be able t' put in a new telephone, hooked up t' right in the house! Along with that new gas heatin', an' all."

He finally stopped speaking. And then, after a long, quiet moment, he realized that what he'd said had been wasted. Orlean was sound asleep, and the baby, Gerolyn, was sleeping even more soundly, wrapped in her mother's warm, encircling arms.

The house they moved to on Third East was, to both Clair and Orlean, the home they finally both loved the best as their own, and the home in which their whole world seemed to grow up.

The telephone, that happy, magic speaking instrument, was the first thing to finally bring them bad news in that house. Clair woke up and answered it in the dark, late one night. "—Yeah? —Yes! —I'll be right there."

He got up and dressed quickly in the flickering light from the stove in the living room.

"—Clair?" Orlean murmured sleepily. "—What?"

"Nothin', honey. I'll be right back."

She waited all that sleepless night through, and even into the growing morning, before he returned.

And then with the beginning sunlight, he came in, quiet and drawn, and he still wouldn't, or couldn't, speak.

She poured him some very hot, long-heated coffee at the kitchen table, where he sat speechless and silent. Then, finally he raised the cup and took a drink of the scalding liquid, as unfeeling and numbly as though it hadn't touched his lips.

"Then?" she asked. "—What is it?"

"M' brother,—Ken," he managed to say. "—He killed a woman t'night, in Salt Lake."

Orlean, her mind frozen, couldn't think of any more questions to ask of him, and after a while Clair went on, almost aimlessly. "It wasn't his drivin' fault, honey. Not at all. —She was just a poor, alone lady walkin' down a dark road in some dark clothes. An' he just couldn't see too good, an' accidentally hit 'er,—an' that car-hit killed her."

"—Neither of us have seen or heard from Ken in such a long time. —Where is he now? Is he all right?"

"Right now he's headed back up t' some flophouse in Ogden, t' try t' forget the whole thing ever happened. —He's in real bad shape."

After a very long time, Orlean asked quietly, "—Is there anything we can do, either for the people who knew that lady, or for Ken?"

He looked tiredly around at the growing light of the yellow morning sun now beginning to beam brightly into the kitchen. "Nothin' I c'n do for that poor lady. An' she was all alone in the world. —But maybe I c'n do somethin' for Ken, honey." He paused thoughtfully. "Ya see, darlin', it's even more'n that terrible accident last night. —Seems like Ken's been kinda bouncin' around from pillar t' post for quite a while. An' I guess drinkin' a little more'n he ought to." He lighted a cigarette and sighed as he slowly exhaled the first puff of smoke. "He's really, kinda out of it. —An' now, especially with the accident t' haunt 'im, he could go clean under, an' wind up an out-an'-out bum."

Orlean said quietly, "I remember when we took our first walk downtown, for ice cream."

He gave her a tired, wan grin. "About ten million years ago."

"You said, then, that Ken was sort of going in circles, but that he'd straighten himself out."

"—Well, he sure ain't got around t' doin' too much of a job of it, yet."

"From what little bit I've seen of him,—he sure isn't very much like Wayne was, or Sherril or Marvin."

Clair nodded. "He's m' brother, an' I love 'im. But he is a different kind of a fella, with some pretty funny ideas." He shook his head slightly. "D' you know, honey, he's against libraries?"

"Libraries?"

"Yep. Had a long argument with 'im one time on that. He says they're nothin' but a waste a' time an' money, an' oughta be done away with. Hell," he shrugged, "I never was the best-read fella around, but I damn well know that one good library is—sorta like a thousand quiet schools f'r anybody who wants t' learn anything. —Maybe, even, the most important thing any civilized bunch a' people ever invented."

Orlean could see that there was much more on Clair's mind. "—You were saying before, about helping him in some way."

"Yeah. I wanted t' talk t' you first about it. An' I'd have t' get Dad t' agree." He hesitated, before going on quietly. "I'm thinkin' a' drivin' up t' Ogden, an' findin' Ken, wherever it is he's hangin' out. —An offerin' him an outright partnership with Dad an' me, in the store, f'r nothin'."

After a long moment, Orlean said in a small voice, "—Boy, Clair, when you feel like helping someone, you sure don't do it halfway."

"Are you against the idea, honey?"

"—No," she said quietly. "I'm for whatever you want to do, Clair."

Studying her, he said, "—But you're not crazy about the idea."

"I just—hope it'll be a good thing, for everyone."

Deep in thought, he said, "It sure is true that Ken never has exactly overburdened us with any signs of friendship. —But he's m' brother, honey, an' right now he sure needs a helpin' hand."

Orlean touched Clair's hand softly. "Well, there's no better one around than this one. —When do you think you'll go to Ogden?"

When Ken became a partner in the store it was, as Clair had thought it would be, a turning point in his life. He got to work on time and cut down on his drinking, finally stopping altogether. But nothing else about him changed. During the first several weeks that he was back in Magna, both Clair and Orlean often invited him to dinner, or just to drop by the house, but there was always some vague reason for him not to be able to make it. So as time wore on, there was finally nothing for them to do but give up. Orlean was not surprised, but she was saddened, not for herself but because she knew Clair was both puzzled and genuinely hurt by his brother's strange, vague and cold behavior.

Coming home very late one night, Clair kissed Orlean on the cheek and sank wearily into a chair at the kitchen table.

"Drink, or coffee?" she asked.

"Both."

"Coming right up."

"*—Jeez,*" he said with tired, quiet emphasis. "D' you know, honey? I had t' explain t' Ken f'r nearly three hours why it's a good idea t' take out a six-dollar advertisement in the paper about a big clearance sale we're gonna have."

She put his drink before him and went to the stove to get coffee for them both. "If I promise never to bring it up again, can I make a small speech?"

"Sure."

Putting their coffee on the table, she sat down near him. "First, I finally figured out the one and only reason why a man would be against libraries."

"Why?"

"Because he's *plain, damn stupid.*"

"Honey," he said, surprised, "are you mad?"

"I'm *damn* mad! Because I love you, and I know that you get hurt easier than anyone else has ever guessed."

"Hell, I'm tough as a nail, an'—"

"Let me finish my speech, darn it! You're tall, handsome, smart and generous!"

"You're prejudiced," he grinned.

"And by no stretch of the wildest imagination is Ken any one of those things! I guess somewhere in the back of his mind he sort of suspects what a giant difference there is between the two of you."

"Hey, now, that's not fair t'—"

"On top of that, you just saved his dumb neck! And

that's a real hard thing for a petty man to ever forgive." She paused briefly. "You did what you wanted to do, what you *had* to do, being you. And I love you. And I love you even more, if that's possible, for helping Ken the way you did. —But all I'm saying is, please Clair, don't keep on hurting yourself by expecting or hoping for him to be a real brother, like your others."

There was a long silence, and finally Orlean said quietly, "—Are you mad?"

Clair shook his head. "Hell no, honey. You were mad enough f'r both of us." And then he said, "You'll see, though. Given time, old Ken'll snap outta his—kinda funny ways."

"Maybe you're right, Clair. I hope so."

In the next few months, so many good things happened that there was only room in the Third East home for laughter and for happy, warm thoughts. With Al's help, they built a spectacular garage in the back yard. What made it so grand and unusual was that it was a *two-car* garage, and there was even space in the back of it for Little Clair to have his own tiny but gloriously independent room, which consisted mainly of an old potbellied stove, a bunk and a bookshelf. And since they were buying this house instead of renting it, Orlean now became a delightfully free-spirited interior decorator. Aside from getting the back porch enclosed so that it was a warm, livable, additional room in the house, she wall-papered four other rooms with the very dubious help of Little Clair and Delores, and painted one back bedroom three times before the subtly changed color finally satisfied her critical eye. And there was always and always the laughter that echoed through the home, even when Little Clair stretched as high up as he could to hand Orlean a long, unwieldly piece of wetly pasted wallpaper, and under its own weight it caved back down through his hands so that he wound up wallpapering most of himself in a bright yellow, floral design.

One morning, Clair answered the phone just before going to work, and spoke on it briefly. Then hanging up slowly, he said to Orlean, "Well, I'll be damned."

"What happened?"

"Ken got married over the weekend."

"—Well, I'll be a sonofagun," Orlean smiled. "That's just wonderful!"

"Yeah," he said, still in a mild state of shock. "It sure is, I guess."

"Of course it is," she laughed. "A good woman can work wonders with a man. Just look at all the terrific improvements I've made on you. And I was starting out with practically nothing."

Late that evening he came home and gave her a tired, warm hug. "Honey," he finally said, "he brought 'er by the store, an' I met 'er."

"Good. I hope you invited them over for dinner, or a visit."

"Yeah, I did. But I wouldn't count too much on 'em comin'."

"—Why?"

"Because, darlin'." He hugged her again. "You know I want t' be fair. But honest, she's got such a real hard, sharp look, that I swear t' God ya could go out an' chop down a tree with it."

"Maybe, she was just nervous."

"No," he said quietly, holding Orlean in his gentle, strong arms. "F'r whatever reasons, Ken's gone out an' found himself the closest kind of a lady he could to our mother."

"Oh,—Clair," Orlean whispered brokenly. "There must—"

"Hey, you," he said, hugging her harder. "—Thanks."

"For what?"

He kissed her on the forehead. "F'r puttin' up wallpaper with pretty flowers on it."

During the next summer, at Clair's insistence, the "Huffaker Furniture Company" bought its first real delivery truck. It was a one-and-a-half-ton flatbed Ford that was shiny black, only two years old, and big enough to haul a fairly large load of furniture all at once. When the company sign and the phone number, "Gar. 25 W.," were painted in white on each door of the truck's cab, Clair drove home on a late but still sunny afternoon to show it to Orlean and the children.

"Boy!" Little Clair yelled from where he was playing in the front yard as his father stopped in the driveway. "She's a *beaut,* Dad!"

Clair got out, honking the horn to let Orlean know he was there, and a moment later Orlean came onto the front porch with Melva and Margaret, who'd stopped by to visit.

"Wow," Orlean said, "you could just about put that other little truck in the back of this one!"

Soon the children and a gathering swarm of their neighborhood playmates were scrambling eagerly and excitedly all over the truck, and Clair stepped up onto the porch with Orlean and her sisters. "Ya like it okay?"

"Oh, yes!" Orlean said.

"It's real nice," Margaret agreed, and Melva added, "Sure is a long way from that beat-up old bike with the wire cage hooked on behind, that ya used t' use f'r deliverin' groceries on."

"Yes," Orlean nodded, her eyes glowing, "—it is a long way."

"I didn't really get the truck f'r haulin' furniture," Clair said with a faint grin.

Orlean gave him a small, quizzical look. "Of course not. That might scratch it."

"Right. —But I've been talkin' to the store owners along Main Street, an' we're all gonna get behind it an' make this year's comin' Fourth of July parade the best one Magna ever had." He gestured toward the truck. "That's the real reason I got that handsome vehicle standin' there. My plan is t' make it into the fanciest an' best float in the whole parade, an' win first prize f'r the store."

"Good!" Margaret said.

Melva nodded. "That's not a bad idea."

"Well, honey," Clair asked. "What d' you think?"

"—I'm just wondering how we could decorate it."

"That's the part I thought I'd leave up t' you, 'cause I ain't got the least idea in the world. You c'n do anything ya want with the truck,—except wallpaper it."

"Oh, shoot," she told him. "That was the first thought that entered my mind."

"The Fourth is less'n two weeks off," Melva reminded them. "Not too much time."

"Orlean'll come up with something really good!" Margaret said. "She's always shined at that sort of thing!"

The next afternoon the phone rang in the store and Clair picked it up. "Huffaker Furniture."

"Honey?!" Orlean's voice was filled with excitement. "I *got* it! The idea for the *float!*"

"Great! What is it?!"

"I won't *tell* you!" She paused. "I mean, I don't *want* to tell you, I'd rather surprise you!"

"Oh? Even me?"

"Especially you!"

"Well,—okay." He grinned slightly at the phone. "—I'm presumin' it won't totally destroy the truck."

"Not a scratch! Those wooden sides on the back of the truck come off, don't they?"

"Yeah."

"Good!"

"But,—can't ya at least give me a hint?"

"Well, all right, but just a little one. It has to do with both the store and the Fourth of July!"

He scratched his head. "That sure does give the whole thing away."

"And I'll only have to have the truck in our garage on the night before the Fourth. You can have it all the rest of the time."

"That's nice."

"—Ohhh." Her voice suddenly took on a tone of distress. "There's one thing I forgot. It'll cost eight, or maybe nine, dollars. Is that too much?"

"Hell, no," he frowned. "But I don't even see what ya c'n do with s' little money. Mr. Parks over at the hardware store says he's spendin' damn near a hundred bucks on his float."

"Mr. Parks can't sew."

"Well, ya got me there."

"Goodbye. *Love* you! I've got to go think up a real good slogan now!"

Orlean worked with great secrecy, so Clair really didn't know what she was planning or doing. All he knew was that more often than not when he came home, the sewing machine had been used so recently that it was still on the living room table, uncovered. And one night at supper, Delores looked up at him with an impulsive smile and said, "Daddy, *I* stand up in *New York!*"

"What?" he frowned, but Little Clair had already reached over and clamped a hand firmly over her mouth. "Shut up, dopey!" the boy told her, and she nodded silently from behind the hand.

"Now, now," Orlean said. "I don't think Delores gave our secret away."

"Not exactly," Clair muttered thoughtfully. "Sherlock Holmes couldn't figure anything out from her sayin',—she—'*stands up in New York?*'"

On the night before the Fourth, Clair parked the truck in the large garage, backing it in at Orlean's request.

Very early the next morning Melva and Margaret arrived to help Orlean and the two oldest children in their mysterious work.

"Okay, honey," Orlean said. "Out on the front porch with you."

"I can't even sit in my own kitchen? Not even on Independence Day?"

"Now, scoot!"

Taking a cup of coffee and his cigarettes, Clair went out the front door and sat in the rocker on the porch. After some time little Bobby Tenney came out onto his front porch across the street, his mother following him.

Clair heard her voice faintly as she said to the five-year-old boy, "Now *stay clean.*"

Bobby nodded and crossed the street toward where Clair was sitting. He was in a jacket and a sparkling white shirt, and was even wearing a little boy's tie. Clair had never before seen him so well dressed and spotlessly clean.

"Hi, Mr. Huffaker," he said as he came into the yard.

"Mornin', Bobby."

"I gotta go out t' your garage. I'm ridin' in the parade."

"Yeah? —Tell me, Bobby. —Just what do ya do in the parade?"

"Sit."

"An' Delores,—stands?"

"Yep."

Clair shook his head slowly. "Well, thanks a lot f'r the information."

"Y'r welcome, Mr. Huffaker." The boy continued on around the corner of the house.

Another, even longer, time went by before Orlean at last came from the back smiling happily and approached Clair on the porch. "It's ready for you to see now!" Then, briefly, her smile faded a little. "—I,—I sure do hope you like it."

He stepped off the porch and gave her a small, one-handed hug. "I got it all figured out," he said wryly.

"You do?"

"Sure." They started back toward the garage. "It's the history a' the invention a' the chair, pointin' out the advantage a' sittin' over standin'."

"You're *right,*" she smiled.

The garage doors were closed, and Clair now swung them open wide to finally see what Orlean had done. After a long, silent moment, he at last said in a low voice, "—Holy *smoke!*"

The entire cab of the truck was almost completely hidden by a mass of long, gaily twisted ribbons of red, white and blue. And the flat truck-bed was covered in the same, ribboned colors. A toy kitchen set, a table and four chairs big enough for the children, had been placed on the back of the truck, and Bobby Tenney was sitting at the table facing Nancy across a carefully arranged, toy table-setting of plates, cups and saucers. And Nancy was as well-dressed and scrubbed as Bobby, with a pink ribbon in her hair and a pink, prettily ruffled dress.

Little Clair and Delores were standing just behind the cab of the truck, facing forward over it. Delores had on a long, white, flowing gown. She held a golden, candle lit torch up in her right hand, and on her head there was a golden, spiked crown. The Statue of Liberty, Clair suddenly realized, who "stands up in New York."

And Little Clair was outfitted as Uncle Sam to the very last detail, from his red-and-white striped pants to the tall top hat with stars and stripes on it. He even had a cotton beard glued to his chin. In his right hand he was carrying an eight-foot pole with a large American flag.

Clair looked at Orlean standing near her sisters and spoke again. "—It's—just *terrific!*"

"But did you read the slogan I made up yet?" Orlean asked anxiously. "Come over here a little."

Stepping more to the side of the truck, Clair now saw the words written in large letters on a wide, white sheet that hung from the bed of the truck down nearly to the ground. Quietly and slowly, he read the words aloud, " 'Make your home like your country. —A grand place in which to live.' "

After a moment Orlean said, "—Is it, all right?"

"It's all right," he answered in a low voice. "—It sure is all right."

"Good," she said softly. "—I'm glad."

A little later that morning, their float was creeping along in its place in the parade, just behind the blaring Cyprus High School Band. Clair had the truck in low gear, able to see enough through the spaces between the ribbons before him to drive. Beside him, Orlean sat facing back through the rear window to make sure Bobby and Nancy stayed safely in their chairs.

The only small problem was that Delores got a cramp in her right arm and had to finish the last part of the parade as a left-handed Statue of Liberty.

In the afternoon, everyone went down to the small ball park on the flats to have picnics and watch the different contests that would take place until it got dark, and there would then be the big, final fireworks display.

At two o'clock, in between the tug-a'-war and the nail-driving competition, they announced the three winning floats in the parade. Puck's Ice-Cream Parlor got third, and after checking their notes the judges gave second place to Parks Hardware.

Then, as Clair held Orlean's hand in the crowd, the main judge called out, "And the blue-ribbon winner, the final choice for first place is,—Huffaker Furniture!"

Clair wouldn't let go of Orlean's hand, but pulled her along with him through the yelling, well-wishing people up to the judge's box. The judge was about to pin the blue-ribbon on Clair's shirt, but smiling and shaking his head, Clair took the ribbon and pinned it instead on Orlean's blouse, then kissed her quickly on the forehead as the crowd applauded happily.

Later that night as the high above fireworks, whistlers and screamers, bombs and soaring skyrockets were exploding over them in huge, swiftly expanding, spider-web-bursts of briefly glowing color, Orlean put one arm around Clair, snuggling warmly against him. "Darling. —I somehow, feel kind of like one of those skyrockets, right now."

He grinned. "I'm glad y'r a little more durable."

"You know what I mean."

"Yeah." Hugging her even closer, he said, "—I do know."

And then, soon, there was that first summer when they were able to afford something they'd never even really thought seriously about before.

Clair came home earlier than usual to find Orlean feeding little Gerolyn in the kitchen. The other three children were still out playing in the long-lingering summer daylight.

"How would you like it, pretty lady," he said, "if we all just up an' took ourselves a vacation?"

"A *vacation?*" Orlean's hand stopped for a moment in midair, and the baby reached out with chubby, impatient hands for the feeding-spoon.

"Say, like, nine whole days."

"Well," she finally said with a small shake of her head, continuing to feed Gerolyn, "—that really *would* be something."

"That's just what we're gonna do. Leavin' Friday after next, an' we'll be free as birds through all that whole week, an' the next weekend."

"That's just great! But,—how did this all happen?"

"I been figurin', an' the store won't be hurt any, as long as there's two of us on hand there. Dad went f'r the idea right off." Clair grinned slightly. "—An even ol' Ken come around, soon as he got it through his head that he'd have exactly the same kind of a vacation, too."

Getting over her first, delighted surprise now, Orlean smiled in a quiet, faintly teasing way. "It sure is nice being part of the leisure class. Have you figured out where to take the family this year? Paris, London?"

He shook his head, frowning. "Not again this year, honey. —You know how overcrowded them fancy, foreign towns c'n get t' be, 'specially durin' the season."

She nodded thoughtfully as she wiped Gerolyn's chin. "—You're right about that, of course. But I will miss buying my usual Paris gowns."

Making himself a small drink, he said, "I thought maybe we might sacrifice all that swanky stuff this year. Maybe do somethin' real simple f'r a change,— sort a' git back t' nature, right here in our own Rocky Mountains."

He sat at the table, and she said with growing eagerness, "Well, come on. *Tell* me!"

"I think it'd be a real nice thing, t' just pile what we need in the back a' the truck an' go campin', way up on the Weber River. —Does that sound as good as Paris?"

"I *love* it!" she smiled. "—And frankly, darling, I was getting tired of all those endless trips to Paris anyway."

By the time they were ready to leave on Friday, it was past four o'clock in the afternoon, and the back of the truck was loaded with food and camping gear. Little Clair and Delores were also in the back, which was their favorite place to ride.

In the cab, Nancy was sitting between her parents, and Orlean was holding Gerolyn in her lap.

As they pulled away, Orlean said, "There isn't very much light left, Clair, and it's a long way. —Do you think, maybe, we ought to wait and get an early start in the morning?"

"No, honey, it's okay," he said. "Weber's not all that far from Park City, an' I know those mountains like the back a' m' hand, from when I was a kid." He shifted gears smoothly. "We'll get there with plenty a' light left t' set up camp."

Heading east to the bottom edge of Salt Lake City, and then south, they made good time past the Cottonwood Canyon turnoff. But then, as they continued, Clair began to realize that much of the foothill country here was no longer as he remembered it. The first time he had to double back on a narrow dirt road, he said, "Boy, they really changed some a' this, since I was a kid."

"—There's not a whole lot more daylight left, Clair."

"There's still enough. —All I need's the right canyon road startin' up t' the high mountains." After a little while he said, "There! That's the way. I remember those two kinda matchin' cliffs on each side a' the canyon entrance."

Two or three miles up the winding canyon road, daylight turned abruptly to deep shadow. And then, very swiftly, it became so dark that Clair had to turn on his headlights to see.

"This is a damn nuisance," Clair muttered. "But at least we know right where we're goin'."

With Nancy sound asleep against her side and Gerolyn sleeping in her arms, Orlean said, "—We sure can be grateful for that."

And then, in the surrounding, ink-black darkness, the dimly probing headlights showed a fork in the narrow dirt path ahead. "Damnit!" Clair said, slowing to a stop. "There was *never* a fork in this road b'fore!"

Leaving the lights on and the motor running, he got out and studied the two, very slightly differing routes ahead. Then he got back into the truck and said, "It's gotta be the left branch. That one's bein' used a lot more."

Driving carefully in the now pitch-black night, Clair took the left fork, and drove on a wildly curving, frighteningly narrow road for over a mile before his headlights suddenly showed absolutely nothing ahead, and he came to a quick stop.

"Don't move outta here, honey," he said quietly. And then he stepped from the cab very carefully, again leaving the lights and the motor still on.

Orlean only had one or two glimpses of him in that blinding blackness of terrifying night, when he appeared briefly in front of the truck's headlights. Twice, she thought she felt the truck shifting very slightly. And then, moving as softly and carefully as a cat, he stepped very gently on the running board near her and soundlessly opened the door.

"—Clair?" she whispered.

"Darlin'," he said, so softly that she hardly heard him, and yet somehow understood there was danger. "—I want you to get out. But don't move quickly."

"I won't."

He took Gerolyn from her arms, and was then almost instantly back beside her, out of the blind, black night. "—Now, carefully, pick up Nancy."

Orlean cautiously drew Nancy up into her lap, vaguely aware of Clair putting his left hand protectively around her back so that both she and Nancy were ready to be held, if necessary, in his arms. And then, with both of them, he backed away from the truck, and quickly put them down with their backs against a nearby, almost invisible high embankment that felt like sandy clay.

"Now listen," Clair said quietly, leaning down near her in the dark. "I got Little Clair an' Delores out, an' they're b'side ya."

"I'm right here, Mom," the boy whispered. And then she felt his hand taking hers in the dark.

"What is it?" Orlean said.

"I made a bad mistake," Clair told her. "This fork's heavy-traveled, because it's a new-buildin' road. In the dark, we came t' where the dynamiters 're just gettin' to. There's no road in front, a straight-up wall b'hind ya, an' a cliff droppin' off t' the valley on our left."

"There's a light down there, Mom," Little Clair muttered tightly. "It's a long way down."

Clair said, "This whole path's about ready t' cave in. So you take the kids an' get back outta here fast, holdin' close in t' the high, goin' up wall on y'r left."

"What are you going to do?"

"I'm gonna back the goddamned truck out."

"In the dark?!"

"Yeah."

"I'll get a flashlight and stay to help you."

"The hell you will! I'll back up with the door open, so I can jump out if I have to! Now get these kids *outta* here, b'fore *everything* goes!"

They moved off, not too quickly, into the dark. And Clair then got into the truck, starting to back it up very slowly, sensing every dangerous inch of the dark way. Several times he could feel his left rear wheel sagging slightly down, partly losing whatever small grip it had on the dark, sandy road. Now and then, he'd feel the right rear end of his truck butting briefly and reassuringly against the wall on the safe side of that narrow path. Once, his left rear wheel dislodged a large rock, so that the back of his truck fell swiftly four or five sickening inches toward the invisible abyss below. But the truck held, and moments later he heard the distant, very faint crashing of that falling rock hitting against other boulders far below.

And then, suddenly, there were some feeble lights behind him. Lights that dimly showed the few inches between his left rear wheel and the deadly, dark void beyond the edge of the path.

With the help of the lights he came at last to a place in the dark road where bulldozers had carved out enough room for a car to safely turn around. There he found out that Little Clair had taken two flashlights from the back of the truck as Orlean led the three little girls back to safety, and then the two of them had come back to help him.

"—Well," Clair finally said. "I think we should've, probably, taken the right turn at that fork back there, instead a' the left."

A few hours later, when the first light of day was beginning to grow, they arrived at Weber Lake, a very faintly blue, pure body of water so crystal clear that it was almost invisible, surrounded by distant, high, snow-capped mountain peaks, and enclosed much more closely by vast stands of pine and fir trees that stretched and reached almost impossibly, and with vibrant greenness, from those far-above, jagged snow peaks down to the very edge of the calm water below.

All alone in this remote, beautiful spot, Clair pulled the truck into a grove of trees near the lake and parked it.

Everyone was exhausted, and the two youngest girls were in a deep sleep. Orlean laid them down in blankets in the shade of a nearby tree, and then went back to help Clair, Little Clair and Delores unload the truck and set up camp.

When almost everything was unloaded, they began to put up a small tent they'd borrowed from Miles and Evelyn, but there wasn't enough room for it between the nearby trees and the side of the truck.

"No problem," Clair said. "I'll just pull the truck out." He climbed up into the cab and quickly backed the truck about three feet, which was just enough for his right rear wheel to run heavily over the cardboard box which contained all of the good dishes that Orlean had packed.

Everyone heard the loud, crunching and crashing sound, and Clair quickly stopped the truck to walk back around it and see what had happened.

"My God," he muttered, "—who's the damn idiot who put that box a' dishes right b'hind the rear wheel?"

Kneeling beside her shattered box of treasures, Orlean looked up in sudden, flaring anger. *"I* am! —But who's the idiot who said he was going to *pull out,* and then *backed out?!"*

"Pullin' out works *either* way!"

Searching through the hopeless debris in the box, Orlean half sobbed, *"Everything's* busted!"

"It ain't *me* who done it!"

"No?!" She stood up holding one small, pathetic shard of a yellow-and-red-flowered plate in her hand. "Then will you get in your car and go catch that damn hit-run driver that just came barreling through this canyon so damn fast I couldn't even *see* him?!"

"I'll do better'n *that!"* He gave the box of already broken plates such a hard kick that it hurt his foot. "I'll *walk* down the canyon t' catch him."

He turned and started down the dirt road that wound around the lake, limping very slightly. And soon he was lost to sight in the thick canyon trees.

Little Clair and Delores looked at each other with the bewildered anguish that only children can feel when, for unknown reasons, their world is falling apart.

"Mom," Little Clair said. "He was limpin'! —That old hurt a' his!"

"He was limping on the wrong foot," she told him in a strangely quiet tone of voice. "—That limp of his was from kicking my broken dishes."

The two children looked at each other again, and then in sudden, silent agreement, Delores went racing down the dirt road, disappearing on the way toward where her father had gone. And Little Clair stayed with his mother. "—Hey, Mom. We still got them tin plates. —An' I'll go get some firewood,—f'r a fire."

"—All right."

It was coming close to sundown when Clair, the sun lowering and beaming behind him, came walking slowly back up the road with Delores' tiny hand held in his own.

Orlean and Little Clair were sitting with the two younger girls around a small, sweet-smelling wood fire as they approached.

When Clair and Delores came up to the fire, Clair said quietly, "—I,—uhh, I been out all day lookin' f'r a hit-run driver, who seems to 've run over some very valuable dishes."

Orlean was afraid that her legs couldn't hold her, so she took a long moment to stand up. "That must have been an awfully tiring day. Much more important than any dishes. —And I'd guess you must be hungry, sir."

"Oh, not really," he said, sitting down near the fire. "—I've only walked about three thousand miles."

"We sure are glad that you happened by here." With great effort, she held within her all the joyful things she wanted to say, to cry out at his return. Instead, she quietly said, "—It's just pure luck that we happen to have a three-thousand-mile Mulligan stew that might be about right for you, in your condition."

Later that night, when only Little Clair was still with them around the coals of the campfire, Clair said to his son, "—You stayed by your mother's side, t'day."

"—Yeah, Dad."

"An' ya stayed right by me with a flashlight on that rough road last night."

The boy looked at him over the glowing campfire coals and simply nodded, not answering.

"—You don't do too bad. An' y'r all of a sudden gettin' too damn tall t' call 'Little Clair' anymore." He paused. "What name, of your own choosin', would ya like, son?"

"—Oh," the boy shrugged, gazing into the low fire. "—I dunno. —Up t' you, Dad."

"How 'bout, 'Young Clair'?"

"—Okay, Dad." He stood up, ready to go to bed in his sleeping bag. "—Dad?"

"Yeah?"

"Well,—just b'tween you an' me. If I grow t' be ten-foot tall,—you'll always be 'Big' Clair."

And then he was gone, and Clair and Orlean were left alone, sitting quietly together by the faintly glowing coals of the fire.

Orlean picked up her guitar and very, very softly strummed a few notes.

"—Ya know, honey," Clair finally said. "—I was thinkin' that after the way I yelled at ya t'day,—ya might just up an' leave."

She stopped her gentle strumming on the guitar. "—It was you, darling, who left."

"Well, yeah," he nodded in the flickering coals. "—But I came back."

She reached over to put her hand on his. "And I never went away—in the first place."

He turned his hand so that it was now holding hers. "—I guess, f'r now, an' f'r all time, we're just stuck with each other, honey."

Very softly she said, "—I guess so, Clair." After a very long time, still holding her hand, he whispered into the dying fire, "—Life goes too fast."

"No."

"No?"

"It lasts always. It's always there,—if you think that way."

Bye Bye Blackbird

Pack up all my cares and woe,
Here I go,
Singin' low,
Bye bye, blackbird . . .

Make my bed,
And light the light,
I'll be home,
Late, tonight,
Blackbird, bye bye. . . .

AND THEN, seeming to happen so swiftly and unexpectedly, the frightening and terrible horror called World War II was suddenly upon them, and was engulfing everyone's lives.

Clair could dimly remember some of the maimed veterans and the hideousness of World War I from his childhood, but he was still one of the first to volunteer for this new war.

"They won't take you," Orlean said in a small voice, though her words were much more hopeful than confident. "You're thirty-four years old and you've got a family. —And whether you admit it or not, you've got a bad leg."

He smiled at this last reason, kissed her and left the house to drive to the main recruiting office in Salt Lake.

When he came back later that afternoon, he frowned slightly at her and shook his head slowly. "You didn't, by any chance, put in a personal call t' the commandin' general up at Fort Douglas?"

"—No."

He grinned very faintly to hide his disappointment. "Well, they turned me down on *exactly* the three counts you said. —F'r a minute, there, I thought that big, tough recruitin' sergeant was you in disguise."

"—No," she said quietly, trying not to show her overwhelming relief. "—Wasn't me."

But as soon as he was seventeen, Young Clair had better luck in volunteering, at least from his own eager point of view. This time though, since it was now their

273

son going instead of himself, Orlean knew that Clair felt the same worry and fear that she did.

Yet when it came time to see him off at the bus depot in Salt Lake, they both acted as though he was simply on his way to another Boy Scout jamboree, or going to visit a friend somewhere.

When Young Clair leaned down to kiss her goodbye on the cheek, it came as a faint, sudden surprise to Orlean that her boy was so big, and that he had to lean so far down to kiss her. Just at that moment, those bitter tears that flowed backward within her, sometimes, came very close to flowing forward, and showing in her eyes.

But then Clair and Young Clair were shaking hands with hard-gripping warmth.

And a moment after that, the boy was on the bus and it was pulling away.

A few months later, Clair came home to find Orlean seated at the kitchen table reading a letter. She looked up at him, smiling, and her eyes were damp with tears. Sitting near her, he took her hand in his and grinned. "—You gotta be the only lady in history who ever gave good news away by cryin'."

"It's from Young Clair."

"Well, what's it say?"

"They picked him to go to college, to get a degree and become an officer. They're sending him to a school back East, called Princeton."

"Princeton?!" Clair whistled, then very slowly and very deliberately lighted a cigarette. "—Then he's not about t' be under direct fire, unless somebody d'cides t' bomb Princeton, which ain't a likely prime target. An'— if he ain't careful, he may even learn somethin'."

The war years began to move so swiftly that it was often possible for both Clair and Orlean to think back on them as one long, blurred, bittersweet memory filled about equally with sorrow and happiness. And linked among those memories was the passing away of Clair's father, who died quietly and peacefully one night in his sleep. Clair talked to Marvin, and they agreed that between them they'd see to it that their mother, Enzy, was well taken care of, and would have no money problems for the rest of her life. Later, after he and Marvin had told their mother what they were going to do, Clair came home and poured himself a drink.

"Well," Orlean asked quietly. "How did it go?"

"Okay, I guess," he said equally quietly. "We told her we'd opened an account in her name an' that we'd put in enough every month t' more'n cover whatever she needs. Ken may chip in. —An' probably Evelyn an' Miles."

"Yes," Orlean nodded. "Evelyn will want to, for sure."

"So, anyway, Mother'll be all right."

"Maybe, honey, all of this will help bring the two of you a little closer."

"No, that won't happen. She was as far away from me t'day as the coast of Africa." He shook his head and took a sip of his drink. "—When I was sent t' stay at Grandma Brown's one time, she told me, 'An Enzy is an Enzy,' almost as if she was talkin' about a make of car 'r something, 'and there's no way on earth of understandin', explainin' or changin' one.' " He shrugged. "But hell, all of that doesn't matter. I'm just glad we c'n help her."

"Hey, mister," Orlean smiled. "—I sure am proud of you."

He smiled back at her. "I guess, by the same token, an Orlean's an Orlean. —An' that's just about the niftiest model on the market."

And though Clair was right about Enzy not changing, most of his and Orlean's world did change, and with incredible swiftness. Not only during that hectic period of war, but through the times that followed, the years seemed to almost play leapfrog with each other in their pell-mell, headlong rush to come and to go.

Incredibly, and seemingly overnight, their entire family was suddenly grown up. Young Clair, having survived World War II with nothing more serious than a bloody nose from a college boxing match, had gone to study for three years on the French Riviera, and had then come back to New York to work as a magazine editor.

Delores had won half-a-dozen teen-age beauty contests before marrying a husky young war-hero who was now working as a fireman in the town of Tooele, about forty miles west of Magna. And soon they'd had a little girl, making Clair and Orlean grandparents for the first time.

Then, again very suddenly, even their two babies, Nancy and Gerolyn, were somehow grown-up young ladies, each with a strong, good young man for a husband.

During these swiftly moving times, Clair was constantly building and improving on the store. Until finally, at a given point, there were three delivery trucks and several men working for the company.

And also in these years, the two of them were able to travel as far as Canada, New York and California, and one time even down into Mexico.

Without quite realizing it, or trying to make it so, Clair somehow became the spearhead of everything good that happened to Magna. Working with the Lion's Club and other civic groups, he finally even managed an impossible victory over the gigantic Utah Copper Company, making them at last pump their mine's poisonous, arsenic-laden smoke far away and up into some barren mountains to the west. Then, with those ugly, killing fumes gone, flowers and grass and trees began to gradually come forth, and even flourish in that greening and growing town. When, upon occasion, letters arrived addressed to "The Mayor of Magna," a township with no mayor, the postmaster just naturally took those letters to Clair. And Main Street had never looked as good as it did now, with well-kept sidewalks, handsome display windows in the stores, and a constant flow of cheerful, smiling people.

With more time and freedom on her hands than she'd ever had, Orlean became more and more active in the church, where her great love was teaching songs and poetry to the very young children in the primary classes.

One warm summer evening they drove into Salt Lake in Clair's new Lincoln for a formal dinner party being given at the Hotel Utah by the state Lion's Club, of which Clair was an officer. Orlean wore a white gown, with a yellow ribbon at the throat, that was remarkably similar to the first formal dress she'd ever worn, when Clair had taken her to The Salt Palace Pavillion long ago.

The dinner party was on the roof of the hotel, the Starlit Gardens, and there was a dance floor and an orchestra playing. They were seated at a table with a pleasant, elderly couple, Mr. and Mrs. Blaine who lived in Sugartown. And when they'd introduced themselves, Mrs. Blaine said, "Orlean Huffaker. I've heard of you!"

"You have?"

"Why of course. —You're the primary teacher who was at the state conference last year, in the Tabernacle." She turned to her husband. "John, I wish you'd been there to see and hear it. She was leading a chorus of two hundred children, and every one of them just singing their little hearts out for her! She's a wonderful music teacher!"

Orlean could feel herself beginning to blush, while Clair was beaming with proud delight.

"As a matter of fact," Mrs. Blaine went on, "one of my little granddaughters was in that Tabernacle group of yours, and she told me,—" the older woman frowned in thought, "—'We don't sing because Mrs. Huffaker makes us sing—we sing because she *wants* us to sing.'"

"—Well, that's really nice," Orlean murmured.

"And what's that wonderful thing that you worked out, that they're teaching in all the Wards now?"

Orlean hesitated. "Something about,—The Story Book Ball?"

"No, it's a little poem, that you sing."

"Oh, sure!" Clair said suddenly. "You mean her traffic-safety jingle. The Sheriff's Department had copies of it made an' sent them all over, to schools an' everything."

"How does the poem go?" Mr. Blaine asked.

Orlean laughed a little. "It's not really quite up to William Shakespeare."

"But somehow it works," Clair said. "An' kids never, ever seem t' forget it. C'mon, honey, do it."

Smiling shyly, and taking a small breath, Orlean sang, "—Always remember, before crossing the street, —look both ways, and *stamp* your *feet!*"

They all laughed now, and Mr. Blaine said, "That's a great way to teach kids something. And I don't think *I'll* ever forget it, either!"

Later that evening, Clair spent some time talking to a few of the other club officers, and when he found Orlean she was standing quietly near the edge of the Starlit Gardens, looking out over the softly lighted Mormon Temple and Tabernacle of Temple Square, just across the street that lay far below them.

"Well, there you are, famous teacher of children," he smiled.

She returned his smile and said. "That was nice of Mrs. Blaine to say those things."

"She was right. If you had a flute, you could be a lady Pied Piper a' Hamelin. All the kids'd follow you, includin' kids in their late forties, like me."

"Funny," she said quietly, putting her arm around his waist and looking back out over Temple Square. "When you were a young boy, you were already a man. And now that you're a man, there's still a little boy within you. I think that combination is the,—best thing in the world."

Equally quiet and thoughtful, he said, "I'll tell you a big secret, Orlean. —That same kinda thing works with a girl, who's growin' up t' be a woman, too."

Then, after a time, while they were still standing there, the orchestra started to play, "I'll Take You Home Again, Kathleen."

They looked at each other, and there was no need for either of them to speak. Making their way to the dance floor, they began to waltz in each other's arms. And even when the music was finished, there had still been no word spoken, or needed, between them.

Later that night, on the drive home, Clair looked at Orlean seated near him and said, "Seemed t' me, you sure had somethin' on y'r mind, when ya were lookin' at Temple Square back there."

"—Yes."

"What?"

After a moment, she said, "Clair, what do you think of the Mormon Church?"

"—Oh, I c'n take it 'r leave it. —I guess mostly the latter."

"But you've been sort of active lately, gone to some meetings and all."

"Well, some a' the things they get into, sometimes, are kinda generally good f'r everybody." He shrugged. "But that don't hardly mean I'm about t' sit down an' memorize the whole Book of Mormon, honey." He looked at her with a faint grin. "What're you gettin' at?"

Very quietly and seriously she said, "We're married. —Right?"

"Yeah."

"But only for this life," she murmured, her voice almost choking.

Clair glanced at her quickly, frowning. "—Go on, darlin'."

Composing herself, she said in a low voice, "I know this may sound silly to you. And it would take some hard work at being a good Mormon on your part. But,—I'd like us to be Sealed in the Temple."

"What?"

"It's a religious marriage. And we'd have to be able to get a Bishop's Recommend before we could have the ceremony performed in the Temple. But if we did it," she continued, her low and husky voice almost impossible to hear, "—we'd be bound and sealed together, you and I, not just for this life, Clair, but forever and for all eternity,—together beyond death, and beyond time."

Clair realized that in listening to her quiet words, he'd slowed down nearly to a stop, and he now nudged the Lincoln's gas pedal with his foot, bringing the car finally back up to a more normal speed. "—Do you believe that?"

"Yes," she whispered.

He drove ahead quietly for a long moment. And then he said very softly, "Well, I don't. —I don't think we need anybody sprinklin' us with holy water, 'r whatever, t' guarantee us bein' t'gether through eternity." After another silence, he continued his thoughts. "But if you feel so strong about what ya said, then we'll go ahead an' do it."

"We will?"

He nodded. "It's a fair gamble, considerin' eternity, an' all."

"—I sure do love you."

"Well, who knows about all that stuff?" He made a turn on the dark street. "But I'd sure as hell be embarrassed if it turned out I was all wrong, an' was on my way up t' heaven t' see you, an' got stopped along the way by a bunch a' irate Mormons."

That fall, in a brief ceremony within the inner confines of the Temple, Clair and Orlean were Sealed together by the Mormon marriage that was supposed to last until the end of time, and beyond life and death.

Afterwards, he told her, "Honey, I feel just exactly the same way right now, that I did b'fore."

"What you don't know," she said with her faint, teasing smile, "—is that I've *really* got you, now."

For a short time, after their children were grown and married, Clair and Orlean's home seemed vaguely empty. But then, subtly at first, it began to be more and more crowded than ever.

"What it is," Clair grinned. "—is we didn't lose four children. We seem to 've gained roughly five thousand grandchildren. All of a sudden, all them little kids seem t' be comin' outta the woodwork."

"You're right," Orlean said. "But I guess we can always pitch a tent in the back yard to take care of the overflow."

"You know who the overflow'll wind up bein'."

"Who?"

"You an' me."

"Right again," she smiled.

"So I got a better idea. Let's do that thing we've thought about a lot, an' never gotten around to. —Let's d'sign an' build our own new place, exactly like we want it, an' make it big enough f'r whomever, 'r whatever."

"—Could we do that?"

"You bet, honey, I been lookin' at a real nice piece a' land up a little on the rise above town, not far from the old Shield's Addition, where you used t' live when you was a kid."

"—Could we do the house in brick?"

"Hell," he laughed. "If you d'cide the grandkids might go for it, we c'n do it in gingerbread."

"I think brick's more practical." She hugged him tightly. "But you know, honey. After all the times we've talked about someday building our own home, and all the dreams I've had about it for so long, I could darn near draw the plans up in my sleep!"

"Okay then, draw them up right now, an' tell me."

"Well, let me think just a minute, Clair." She hesitated. "—When you first enter, through the main front door, there'll be a big, comfortable living room on your right, with almost a whole wall that's made into a warm, stone fireplace. And on the left of the entrance, there'll be a nice, spacious dining room, with the kitchen just past that."

"So far, so good."

"And in front of you, across the entrance, there'll be not one, but *two* staircases, one going up, and the other going down."

"Holy smoke," Clair said. *"Two* of 'em?"

"It will be on three levels," she told him. "—If that's all right with you. One staircase will go up, to the bedrooms and all. And the other will go down, to where your big, private den will be, with ceiling-to-floor windows looking away off, down the slope and across the valley. And there will be a fireplace in there, too."

"Okay. I like your whole idea, especially about that den a' mine, with its own fireplace an' the big windows. —Have ya considered puttin' a pool-table in there?"

"Well, I hadn't thought about it, exactly."

"Want t' make a deal?"

"Sure."

"Then you work out the final details on the whole rest a' the house. An' I'll work out the details a' my den. How's that f'r a bargain?"

"All right," she smiled. "But I'll want you to double-check everything I do."

"There's nothin' you could possibly do that I wouldn't love," he grinned, "—except t' maybe not make my den big enough f'r a pool table."

It was about a year and a half later that they moved into their big, new brick home on the gentle rise above town.

They had a house-warming party to make everyone welcome, and even though nearly a hundred people came, it still wasn't crowded. Evelyn and Miles came out from Murray. And Melva and Al, and Margaret and her Darrell were there. Even Marvin, who'd moved down from Canada to Salt Lake, came along with his pretty and petite wife, Janice. Everyone from the Lion's Club was there, plus most of the people from nearby church Wards.

It was unanimously agreed that their new home was far and away the finest house in Magna. And the entire party was perfect,—except for one thing.

Shortly after midnight, when most of the guests had left, Orlean heard strange rasping sounds from downstairs in Clair's den. She went down to find Clair and Marvin playing a game of pool. But Clair, instead of taking his turn at shooting, was frowning as he made those faint rasping sounds by sawing off a foot or so of a cue stick.

Looking up at her, he struggled to maintain his frown, though a tiny grin was tugging at the corners of his mouth. "This is an absolutely perfect house we built," he muttered. "Except that some dummy miscalculated the width a' this room an' the size a' this pool table, an' there's a point where ya can't make a decent, close bank shot on this fireplace side, with a regular-length cue stick."

"That's a darn shame, Clair."

"What makes it even worse," he said, his grin finally winning out, "—is that the dummy just happens t' be me."

"Some dummy," Marvin shrugged. "The sonofagun's still four dollars ahead of me."

Not knowing the game, Orlean asked, "Will you have to saw off all of those sticks?"

"No," Clair said. "Just one, in case anybody else gets stuck in this tight spot."

Marvin smiled at Orlean. "I kind a' hate t' say it, but I think trying to make this impossible shot is kind of appealing to your crazy husband."

"Well," Orlean smiled back, "he's your crazy brother."

"Enough of this loose talk," Clair said, finally cutting through the wooden handle. "Anybody c'n make an easy, normal shot. But startin' off with your back up against the wall, an' a sawed-off cue stick t' work with—that's a real challenge, in this here world." He got into position with the shortened pool cue and said, "Nine ball in the far corner pocket."

And he made it.

Much of Orlean's time in their big, new home was spent with the laughter and happy shouts of their grandchildren, mixed with the occasional, brief outbursts of furious anger and terrible anguish that are a natural part of all young lives.

But "Grandma's" was the place to be as often as possible, and it was even better when "Grandpa" was home from work, too.

There came a time, however, when silence slowly began to be an important thing in the house that had sounded so long with joy, and the grandchildren were quick to sense this need of quiet.

Orlean though, of course, was the first.

Clair was not feeling well.

At first he made excuses of simply being tired, or having worked too hard. But they both knew that it was something more than that. After a time, as he grew weaker and weaker, Orlean insisted that he go to a doctor to be examined.

"Hell," he grumbled, "I'm not sick. Only thing that ever did slow me down so far, honey, is a fifty-ton locomotive."

"Well, it won't hurt to find out."

"That's exactly what I'm worried about," he grinned. "—It might hurt."

The doctors, even after an exploratory abdominal operation, found nothing wrong with him, yet he continued to weaken, finally getting to a point where it was either difficult, or impossible, for him to go to work at the store. He was rapidly losing weight as well as energy. And then hideous pain, sometimes blinding and often deafening pain, started shrieking at him from somewhere deep within.

He never cried out, or even whispered, but Orlean could both hear and feel his silent agony, as though it were her own.

So finally, when he'd passed out twice in one day from that recurring pain, she took him to St. Mark's Emergency, and they operated on him.

While Clair was still unconscious, and in recovery, Orlean went to speak to the very young and terribly distressed surgeon, Dr. Sloane, who was trying as hard as he could and with all his will, to be objective and, if possible, reassuring in the face of death.

And somehow she knew this, when she looked at him.

"—Mrs. Huffaker," he began in a grief-stricken, shaking voice, "—I have to tell you—"

"It's all right," she said very quietly. "You don't have to tell me anything. —You already have."

After a moment he said helplessly, "—Cancer didn't even show a sign of itself before. —And now it's all *through* him."

"—Do you have any idea—how long?"

In the face of her courage, he struggled to compose himself. "—A week,—two or three months."

"Can he go home?"

"Yes."

"—I'm glad. —That's where he'll want to be."

"The only thing is,—" the doctor hesitated again. "He'll need some powerful morphine tablets, to keep the pain away, until—"

"—I understand."

Sometime later, Clair came partly awake and realized vaguely that he was lying on a cot in his living room. As his eyes focused a little more clearly, he saw that Young Clair was sitting at the side of the cot, looking down at him.

"What the hell's goin' on?" he muttered weakly. "I'm supposed t' be in the hospital, with a beautiful nurse. —An' you sure are a terrific letdown, kid."

Young Clair grinned and faded away, and a moment later he was replaced by Orlean's smiling face. "Well, it's about time."

"—Time f'r what?"

"Time for you, you big, lazy lug, to start getting up and getting better. I guess you can see that they finally threw you out of the hospital."

"That was a dirty trick," he murmured. "I wasn't really feelin' all that great."

"Well," she smiled, "they say as long as you take

two or three of these yellow tablets every day, you'll be up and around, and as grouchy as ever, in no time."

"Okay," he said, fading away again, "I guess I'll take 'em then. —If only t' please them dumb doctors."

She gave him one then, with a small sip of water, just before he went back to sleep.

During the next, unknown time, he moved in and out of his fitful sleeplessness, dimly aware of taking the yellow tablets, and of many, many shadowy friends who came quietly and almost wordlessly by to wish him well.

Then came a time during one day when Clair awakened and felt good enough to be propped up by pillows. Orlean and Young Clair and Delores were there in the living room with him. "Boy," he said weakly, "I think I'm finally startin' t' get better."

There was a light knock at the door, and Orlean and Young Clair both left the room to answer it.

Orlean opened the door, and Ken was standing there.

"I'm *glad* you finally came," Orlean said. But then she saw the legal sheafs of papers clutched in Ken's nervous hand.

Making no attempt to come in, he said in a low, strained voice, "—Well, uhh, I heard he's gettin' real bad. —An', him an' me bein' equal partners in the business we built up an' all,—uhh, I figured he oughta sign these here papers, b'fore,—well, b'fore,—it might be too late, ya know?"

"I don't think you understand," Orlean said very quietly. "Clair can't lift his hand."

"—Well,—not even f'r just a couple a' signatures?"

"Ken," Young Clair said in a low, rumbling voice, looming up beside his mother in the doorway. "—Go away from here. —Now."

A little later, as the two of them came back into the living room, Clair said, "Who was that?"

"Nobody, Dad," Young Clair said. "Just a delivery man, with the wrong address."

"Well, as long as it wasn't important, I guess I c'n tell ya about m' dream." Clair grinned and shrugged very faintly, using all the strength left in his shoulders as he looked at Orlean. "F'r once, it was me instead a' you, darlin', who had a dream about horses."

"What was it?" Delores said.

"Not much, I guess." He hesitated, frowning slightly. "—But in my dream there were these three, beautiful horses, racin' almost straight up in t' the sky, their manes an' tails wavin' an flyin' out in that rushing wind, so damn pretty as they went up an' up, an' then finally out a' sight."

In a very quiet voice, Orlean asked him, "—What color were they?"

"I guess I'll have t' bow to the expert on horse dreams," Clair grinned. "They were pure white. All three of 'em, immaculate white horses."

"—Immaculate?" she repeated, her voice both soft and puzzled.

"Yeah. —An' that's right," he finally said in answer to her unspoken question. "—I never used that word b'fore in my whole life. —But that's sure the color they were, and that's exactly the word. —'Immaculate' white, honey."

He went to sleep again then, and when he at last woke up it was sometime later at night, and Young Clair was sitting beside him.

"What the hell 're you doin' here, an' still up?" he asked in a slightly choking voice. "I don't hardly need a permanent baby-sitter."

"—Yeah."

With very great effort, Clair stretched out his hand, and his son took it in his own, holding it warmly.

Clair said, "I know you quit y'r job, t' come here an' hold my damn hand."

"—Wasn't all that much of a job."

"An' another thing I know. —I'm dyin'—an' sure don't want to."

"The hell you are, Dad."

"Oh, c'mon. Even that thing t'day with you an' your mom, an' Ken. —We all of us know, son, that it's final."

"Well," Young Clair's voice started to break, and his grip grew fiercely tight, "—Mom an' all of us, sure did try t' keep it from ya."

Clair grinned very weakly and faintly. "She sure does good, that lady. —But I guess we both knew, and we were both tryin' t' ignore it all an' maybe help the other one feel a little bit better, about the whole damn thing."

"—Guess that's right, Dad."

Clair's breathing was starting to come in brief, sharp and faintly whistling intakes of air now. Raising himself, he said, "Go upstairs an' get your mom, an' call y'r kid sisters. There's not a whole lotta time.—" He gasped for breath. "If I don't last long enough, tell 'em,—"

And then his voice choked and failed, and he fell back. Young Clair called out "Mom," in a low voice, and an instant later Orlean rushed downstairs and was at Clair's side, cradling him in her arms.

He awakened one last time, and looked at her with both distance and love in his dimming eyes. "Up,— up,—up," he murmured then, as if watching those horses he'd dreamed of, racing through the sky.

Then Clair leaned into Orlean's arms, as if he were very tired.

And, then, his life was gone.

20

I'll Take You Home Again, Kathleen

I'll take you home again, Kathleen,
Across the ocean wild and wide,
To where your heart has ever been,
Since first you were my lovely bride.
I know you love me, Kathleen dear,
Your heart was ever fond and true,
I always feel, when you are near,
That life holds nothing else but you.

Oh, I'll take you home again, Kathleen,
To where your heart will feel no pain,
And when the fields are fresh and green,
I will take you home again, Kathleen. . . .

FROM THAT time forward, Orlean thought only in terms of first making certain that the people she loved were all right, and then of going on to join Clair.

She remembered very clearly that long-ago morning when Clair was hovering between life and death after his train accident, and she'd promised God that if He'd let Claire live, then they'd both come to Him later.

For the little time on earth she felt she had left, she continued teaching poetry and music, and she paid special attention to her very young grandchildren. Her own three daughters and son were all fine, healthy and strong, and as well prepared for life and the world as she and Clair could make them.

They all spent as much time with their mother as they could, so that while there was always a loneliness deep within her, she was very rarely alone to dwell upon it. And the other people she loved were constantly coming by for a few words, a cup of coffee, or dinner if they were able to stay. Evelyn and Miles, and Marvin and Janice drove out to her home often, and Melva and Margaret were always close at hand, as well as Al and Darrell. So that, particularly with her own warmth and strength, Orlean's home was always a good and welcome place to be.

And strangely enough, most of the very difficult moments were those caused by happiness. Nancy had come over one afternoon with her two small daughters, who were playing in the living room. Nancy helped Orlean put some loaves of bread in the oven to bake, and then they sat down in the kitchen to talk and visit.

After a few minutes, the two little girls came into the kitchen, very quietly and very seriously.

"—Grandma?" the older girl, now five years old, asked.

"What, dear?"

The two children looked at each other briefly, then silently came closer to where Orlean was sitting. "—Well," the older girl said with hesitant shyness. "We been wonderin' about something,—for a long time. —An' we d'cided, that you're the only one who really knows."

"—Yes?"

Both little girls looked up at her with wide, silently thoughtful eyes, and the older sister finally said in a low voice, "—Grandma?—is Grandpa,—an angel now?"

After a moment, Orlean managed to murmur, "—Yes." She reached down with both arms and hugged the two children close to her. "Yes,—he is."

And it was Nancy, sitting at the other side of the table, who burst into silent tears.

Then, in a very short time, a strange and sad thing began to happen. It was first noticeable in the furniture store itself. Though Orlean never went into it, she passed it often, and in the beginning it simply seemed that the store front badly needed a new coat of paint. But soon the big sign that Clair had put up in front of it stopped working properly. Some of the lights in it burned out and were never replaced. Next, one of the large showroom windows was cracked, and it was never fixed. Before very long there was such a sad, gloomy feeling of shabbiness and decay about the entire store that Orlean didn't even want to look at it anymore. And then, as though it were a mysterious disease of some sort, the same drabness and ugliness began to spread all along Main Street. Stores began to fail, and more and more windows were either cracked, or boarded up with plywood, like giant, blank patches over vacant, unseeing eyes.

The realization finally came to Orlean, and to others in Magna, that with Clair gone, the town itself was slowly dying.

Thinking far back, Orlean remembered the grim trip they'd made from Omaha back to the Rocky Mountains, at the height of The Depression. And she remembered particularly that one group of poverty-stricken people near their broken-down cars at the side of the road. Clair had been so saddened, and so hurt by the fact that there was no way on earth for him to help them. He'd told her then, his voice quiet and husky, "—Just hope, honey, that there's one person,—just one person among 'em, who has some spirit."

On the bleak Main Street of Magna, with its growing number of wind-tossed old papers and tumbleweeds, there was no longer any spirit. And Orlean realized that a whole town, just like a person, cannot survive without the spirit that Clair spoke of,—and had.

Ever since she was a young girl, and her own mother had followed after her father so quickly, Orlean had believed firmly that what people called "heartbreak" was a very real, and even natural thing, between two people who loved each other.

So it was neither surprising nor frightening to her when, after a given time, her own heart suddenly began to develop serious problems.

After her second attack, and at the almost tearful pleading of her daughters, she finally agreed to an operation that the doctors insisted she had to have.

The day before the morning of the operation, Nancy was the first one to come visit her in the hospital. Coming to the side of the bed, she took Orlean's hand in hers and said, "How ya doing, mom?"

"I'm kind of,—dopey," Orlean smiled, speaking in a faintly thick voice. "They've—stuck me with more needles,—"

Nancy smiled back down at her. "Well, needles or

not, you sure are lookin' real good." Still holding her hand, she said, "Delores and Gerolyn will be here pretty soon."

Orlean managed a small grin. "—Sounds like,—a regular party."

"Oh, you're a pretty popular lady. —An' there's a flight due in at three o'clock with big brother Clair."

Perhaps it was the mention of that name, Orlean realized numbly, or possibly it was all the drugs they'd given her, but she suddenly saw, just as clearly as she could see Nancy, her own Clair standing at the foot of the bed. It wasn't a ghostly, or vague image. He was even more real and natural than everything else in the room. He was dressed in a very soft, rich material, yet it was casually designed, almost like a flowing, comfortable jumpsuit in a strange, unfamiliar color that seemed to be warm, pinkish beige. He looked handsome and healthy, and somehow agelessly youthful, and he was smiling at her. Putting his hand out toward her, he said quietly and gently, still smiling, "—Come on, honey. —Come on with me."

And then he was gone.

Even in her numbed and bewildered mind, Orlean at last became aware that Nancy was still holding her hand, but that Nancy's grip had become almost fiercely tight.

And then, after a long moment, Nancy finally spoke in a hushed, unbelieving whisper. "—Mother. I saw him,—and heard him,—too."

But by then, Orlean was fading quickly under the influence of the drugs.

When Delores and Gerolyn, and then Young Clair arrived, Orlean managed to force her eyes open very briefly and smile at them. But then the powerful drugs took over again, and she slept. And a little later, a nurse asked them to please go to the waiting room for their long vigil.

Somehow, impossibly weak and drugged as she was, Orlean willed herself the final strength to wake up that night, long enough to write one, last letter.

It was a lengthy letter, written in a beautifully flowing hand, and it began, "To My Darlings: — Just in case! —I want you to know how very, very dearly I love *each* and *every one* of you."

Then, in the same clear hand, and with an incredible, exact awareness of all things, the letter went on to become a flawlessly written last will and testament. It included a complete list of properties and bank accounts, and the stocks and bonds that she and Clair had made small investments in. She left very special and meaningful things to each grandchild, and then with infinite clarity and wisdom, she divided her modest estate evenly and fairly among her four children.

And then, finally, she came to the end of her last letter.

"—These are all my worldly possessions. —But, *oh,*—how I wish I could give you what I have in my heart.

"But these are things you must each find for yourselves. And if you seek, you will find them. —And when you find them, you will have happiness you never dreamed possible. —I love you all, so much.

"—Good night, my darlings."

And, as it was in the beginning, so was it too, in the end.

First, there was the earth.

And then,—there was music.

LOOK FOR THESE GREAT POCKET 📖 BOOK BESTSELLERS AT YOUR FAVORITE BOOKSTORE

THE PIRATE • Harold Robbins

YOU CAN SAY THAT AGAIN, SAM! • Sam Levenson

THE BEST • Peter Passell & Leonard Ross

CROCKERY COOKING • Paula Franklin

SHARP PRACTICE • John Farris

JUDY GARLAND • Anne Edwards

SPY STORY • Len Deighton

HARLEQUIN • Morris West

THE SILVER BEARS • Paul E. Erdman

**FORBIDDEN FLOWERS:
More Women's Sexual Fantasies** • Nancy Friday

MURDER ON THE ORIENT EXPRESS • Agatha Christie

THE JOY OF SEX • Alex Comfort

RETURN JOURNEY • R. F. Delderfield

THE TEACHINGS OF DON JUAN • Carlos Castaneda

JOURNEY TO IXTLAN • Carlos Castaneda

A SEPARATE REALITY • Carlos Castaneda

TEN LITTLE INDIANS • Agatha Christie

BABY AND CHILD CARE • Dr. Benjamin Spock

BODY LANGUAGE • Julius Fast

THE MERRIAM-WEBSTER DICTIONARY
(Newly Revised)